NOAH

Other Titles by Melody Anne

Billionaire Aviators

Turbulent Intentions
Turbulent Desires
Turbulent Waters
Turbulent Intrigue

Billionaire Bachelors

The Billionaire Wins the Game
The Billionaire's Dance
The Billionaire Falls
The Billionaire's Marriage Proposal
Blackmailing the Billionaire
Runaway Heiress
The Billionaire's Final Stand
Unexpected Treasure
Hidden Treasure
Holiday Treasure
Priceless Treasure
The Ultimate Treasure

Undercover Billionaires

Kian
Arden
Owen
Declan

NOAH

AN
ANDERSON
BILLIONAIRES
NOVEL

MELODY ANNE

 Montlake

Published by Montlake, Seattle

www.apub.com

Amazon, the Amazon logo, and Montlake are trademarks of Amazon.com, Inc., or its affiliates.

ISBN-13: 9781542016759
ISBN-10: 1542016754

Cover design by Letitia Hasser

Cover photography by Wander Aguiar Photography

Printed in the United States of America

NOAH

PROLOGUE

Lights flashed in Sarah's eyes as unintelligible words floated around her.

There was so much darkness—too much. The world was full of a myriad of colors, so when you saw it in black and white, you knew something was wrong—very, very wrong.

"Let's go code three."

"Stay with us, Sarah," she heard someone say. They sounded so far away. There was a face above her, but she couldn't seem to focus on it. There were no eyes, no mouth, no nose. It was just a black-and-white blur above her with a halo of light behind it.

"Can you tell me your full name?"

She tried to answer, but she couldn't seem to find her voice.

"Sarah, when is your birthday?"

Again she couldn't answer.

"We have a twenty-six-year-old female who was the restrained passenger of an SUV traveling at approximately sixty-five miles per hour. Their car was hit on the passenger side at high speed, and airbags deployed. She had to be extricated from the vehicle. She has a distended abdomen, labored breathing, and decreased level of consciousness. Her blood pressure is eighty-three over forty-two with a pulse of one hundred and thirty; O2 sats are ninety-three percent and dropping. Possible internal bleeding."

Sarah wanted to know who they were talking about, but she couldn't find her voice. She heard a moan but wasn't sure where it came from. Nothing felt real at the moment. Nothing felt right.

A bright light shone in her eyes, and she tried turning away, but she couldn't move her head. Where was she? She tried to focus. There were sirens, but they sounded distant. She couldn't move her body. Panic was beginning to set in. Where was Noah? She'd been driving with Noah. Suddenly he'd yelled, and then everything had gone dark.

"Do you know what month it is, Sarah?"

Why were they asking these questions?

"Can you tell us what happened?"

If she *could* speak, she'd tell him to give her a second to answer one question before he spouted off another, but there wasn't a point, anyway. She couldn't find her voice.

"Her pupils are equal and reactive," the voice said. "Let's get two IVs started wide open."

Oh no. She hated needles. Those had better not be going into her.

"Stay with us, Sarah. Let's keep those eyes open," the voice said. She was growing more and more irritated. She needed a nap. She'd been working hard. It wasn't a crime to take a little nap. She was in a dream right now, after all, so shutting her eyes was exactly what she needed to do.

"Her blood pressure is now seventy-eight over forty. Heart rate is still in the one hundred thirties. Oxygen has dropped to eighty-four percent, and her breathing is more labored. We are going to need to intubate en route. We're ten minutes out."

Where were they ten minutes out from? That face above her was growing blurrier by the second, and she didn't want to keep her eyes open anymore. They shut, and she felt darkness enveloping her.

"We're losing her."

Sarah wasn't sure what that meant, but it didn't matter. The darkness that had been slowly seeping in washed over her like a cool breeze and took away all her confusion. She sighed as the voices faded away into nothingness.

Noah looked in at the black-and-blue body of Sarah, and for the first time in at least ten years, he felt a stinging in his eyes. *He'd* been the one driving. No, he knew he wasn't responsible for the drunk driver who had smashed into them, but he felt responsible for not reacting faster. He'd walked away from the crash with a few bruises, and Sarah had nearly lost her life.

For months she'd been telling him they weren't right for each other. Maybe she was correct. Maybe he was too dangerous. Maybe his need for excitement and adventure would eventually kill her.

He'd never been so scared as when she'd been loaded into that ambulance. And now the evidence of his recklessness was right there in front of him. She was unconscious in the bed after a long surgery.

He needed to let her go—it was what she wanted. He knew it would be better for her. He just wasn't sure he'd be able to do that.

"Sir, you're not supposed to be back here," a woman said softly as she gently placed a hand on his arm.

"I know. Please, just give me a minute. I won't go in. I won't disturb her," he pleaded. He couldn't remember the last time he'd begged for anything from anyone.

"I'm going to grab some charts. I'll be walking past here again in about two minutes, and I know this doorway will be empty," she said with a sympathetic smile.

He nodded, too choked up to say anything more. The nurse walked away, and his eyes caressed Sarah's battered body. He stood there for another minute and fifty-five seconds; then he silently turned and walked away.

He was as clueless then as he had been from the moment he'd met this beautiful, frustrating, stubborn, amazing woman. He knew what should be done—he'd just never been good at taking the easiest or right path.

CHAPTER ONE

If a smile could break your face, then Sarah was sure hers was going to crack at any minute. The smile wasn't real, but she could sell it—was great at selling it. She'd learned early on in life that you faked it till you made it. Those who said that method didn't work weren't trying hard enough.

She was going to pull out of this project. Joseph Anderson had spoken to her about being a part of this massive veterans center a few months ago, but no contracts had been signed, and she wasn't sure what he'd been thinking, anyway. She'd only graduated school a few months earlier, and yes, she had faith in herself, but getting a project like this one was huge—it was for people like Noah.

She didn't want to work with Noah any longer. She'd been confused from the beginning with this man, and she'd tried her hardest to make it work. But sometimes it took a stronger person to know when to quit versus trying to stick it out. She was smart enough to walk away. She'd nearly lost her life a few months earlier. The accident had caused complications, and she'd been truly scared for probably the first time in her life. That had woken her up. She'd been too carefree in life, had been taking too many chances. Now it was time to get her priorities straight.

She was walking into the huge Anderson Corporation. Her head was held high, and that smile that was killing her to maintain was firmly in place. She was going to be professional . . . and firm. The best thing for the center was for her to walk away.

It felt like an hour in the elevator to the top of the building. Joseph's oldest son, Lucas, now ran the massive Anderson empire, but Sarah was very aware of who the head of the family truly was. Joseph's idea of retiring just meant he didn't sit in the offices for ten hours a day. He now had much more time to mess with people's lives—his current obsession. She just had no idea what he saw in her.

She entered the huge lobby on the top floor, and her stomach tightened as she looked around at the beautiful sitting areas and the plants that reached the three-story-tall ceilings. She couldn't even imagine how much it cost to maintain this place. She didn't want to think about it. She wondered how many people actually told Joseph no. She'd bet all she had it didn't happen often.

"Hello, Ms. Jennings," a perky brunette said from behind a desk the size of most people's kitchen counters. "Mr. Anderson is waiting. You can go on back." The smile the woman wore was just about as big as Sarah's, but hers looked genuine. Of course it was. She worked in a pretty great position for the best company in Seattle.

"Thank you," Sarah said. She didn't need to ask which way. The massive hallway was a good indication of where she needed to go.

"Can I bring you something other than coffee?" the woman, whose nameplate read Jennifer, asked.

"No, thank you," Sarah said. Her smile was beginning to falter.

She moved down the hallway, hearing Joseph long before she neared the door. He said something, then laughed loudly. Her smile turned up, but this time it was real. She wondered how a person could feel that much joy all the time. Joseph was an enigma, certainly a person she'd love to know more about. Maybe she should've majored in journalism instead of design.

She stepped up to the door, not sure if she was supposed to knock. It was wide open, but no one was looking her way. She stood there feeling even more unsure than she had when she'd been outside the building trying to decide if she should enter.

As if he could sense her—or she'd made a sound, which she was sure she hadn't—Noah turned, his gaze boring into hers. Damn! She hadn't seen him in over a month, and the impact of his eyes still had the power to make her legs tremble.

"Hello, Sarah. You look well," Noah said. His voice was a soft purr that contrasted so much with Joseph's deep baritone. Of course Noah could get just as loud as Joseph when he let down his guard. But most of the time he had a purr that would make any woman want to curl up on his lap.

"Hi, Noah," she said, turning away quickly. She couldn't face him too long. She'd rather look at Joseph, even though the man intimidated the crud out of her. "I'm sorry if I'm late, Mr. Anderson." She wasn't late, but since she was the last one in the room, she felt the need to apologize.

"Nonsense, young lady. We were just having a chat while we waited for you to arrive," Joseph told her. "Sometimes it's a real pain to navigate your way through this city."

"It most certainly is," Sarah agreed as she moved forward. "Which is why I live in Cranston and not the city."

"Yes, I've grown quite fond of the small town of Cranston."

"I would think so, with the massive project you're doing there," she said, feeling tense all over again. She needed to spit out the words that had to be said and then walk from the office with her head held high and her dignity intact. She felt utterly tongue tied, though, which was nothing unusual around this beast of a man.

"I'm not the one doing the project," Joseph said before looking at her for a long moment, as if he knew what she wanted to say. It made her even more nervous. He finally looked away to pull out a folder. "I have your contract, which should've been signed a while ago. With the accident and all, we're a little behind schedule, but we can fix that right now."

She felt her throat tighten. Again she wondered how many people told this man no or refused something he asked of them. The answer had to be zilch to none.

"Sir . . ." The look he gave her made her stop what she'd been about to say.

"You know I hate being called *sir*," he said with a slight frown. She shifted in front of the large desk he was occupying. Sarah wondered where Lucas was. It would be so much easier to tell Joseph's son she didn't want the job than to tell the man himself.

"I'm sorry to interrupt, Joseph, but Sarah and I have spoken about this project at length, and she's told me she doesn't want to be on it," Noah said. He was looking at Joseph rather than her, and there were frown lines etched in his forehead. He hadn't been happy with her when she'd told him she was quitting. His mood obviously hadn't improved.

Joseph's knowing gaze centered in on her, and she felt like a grade school student about to be scolded by the principal. She wanted to remain strong, but it was difficult to do with two alpha men who were obviously unhappy with her staring her down. Well, that was just too bad for both of them.

"Why do you want to step down?" Joseph asked. Of all the scenarios she'd played out in her head, she hadn't once considered he might ask her that question. She wasn't sure why not. She didn't know how to answer. "Is it something I've done?" He now looked concerned, instantly making her feel bad.

"No, of course not . . . Joseph. It's just that with the accident we're already behind schedule, and I think Noah will move much more quickly without my help," she said, feeling brilliant for coming up with that on the spot. There was no way she was telling Noah's uncle she didn't want to do the project because she wanted to jump his nephew every second they were together. She also wasn't going to mention how much the project meant to her.

"I'd take it as a personal insult if you were to walk away," Joseph said. "I take time when considering who I want to work for this company, and I personally handpicked you."

Sarah was speechless again. Her friends would find that quite amusing, as she always seemed to have something to say. Sometimes she talked just because she didn't want to have nothing but silence surrounding her.

But to get back to what Joseph had asked—it was fairly simple. She was afraid to work with Noah for many reasons. The strongest was her attraction to the man, but also her pride was in there. Noah's name was the big one on this project, and she didn't want to be jealous about that, but she had no doubt she'd be living in his shadow. She had a lot of pride herself and didn't like to be considered second best. She wasn't sure what she should do.

She found herself unable to answer Joseph. His eyes twinkled. The man knew he was nearly impossible to refuse. She wanted to do just that out of principle. But still she stood there silently. What had happened to her entire pep talk to herself? She was failing miserably.

"Sign this form, and we're right back on track," Joseph said as he pushed a pile of papers toward her. She had no choice but to step a little closer to the desk and therefore closer to Noah as well.

Though in her opinion she felt Noah would rather she walk away, he didn't seem to be thrilled about the idea. She just wasn't sure what was going to make any of them happiest. She decided not to speak as she picked up the papers and began to read through them. For once Joseph was silent. Noah hadn't been saying much at all since she'd stepped into the room. She was used to that. He seemed to be a man who thought a whole lot.

She read the contract. It was more than fair to her. She'd already been doing the job for quite a while, and she was being paid more than she could've ever hoped to be paid for a newly graduated architect. She should just sign the papers and do her job. Still, she hesitated.

When she looked up again, she found both Joseph and Noah staring at her. Joseph was holding out a pen that probably cost more than her rent the last month. She felt like a deer in headlights.

What was she going to do?

Her eyes connected with Noah's, and she lost her breath. There was a challenge in his gaze. Her shoulders stiffened. Tick tock. Time was running out.

CHAPTER TWO

Three days passed, and Sarah spent most of that time pacing in her apartment. She'd always been perfectly content in it . . . until recently. Now it felt almost like a prison. She didn't understand how anyone could break the law knowing they'd have to live out the rest of their days in a six-by-twelve-foot space. Some cells might vary a little in size, but that was the average. Her apartment was slightly bigger than that, but it felt even smaller at the moment.

The contract she'd managed to get out of the office without signing was like a beacon flashing at her from her small counter. It seemed to scream at her every time she passed by it. *Sign me . . . sign me . . . sign me . . .*

Ugh! She needed to just rip it up, wait until three in the morning, and leave a message on Joseph's phone like the chicken she'd become lately. But no matter how many times she'd picked it up with the intention of doing just that, she hadn't been able to do it. She'd simply set it back down, then tossed and turned all night. So the dang contract was not only tormenting her but giving her dark circles beneath her eyes on top of it all.

She passed the counter again for the hundredth time that day when her doorbell rang. She wasn't expecting anyone, but it wasn't unusual for one or both of her besties to stop by. She walked to the door, not bothering to smile as she opened it.

She froze at the sight of Katherine Anderson standing there, looking regal and beautiful . . . and utterly out of place at her tiny apartment complex. Sarah didn't know what she was supposed to say.

"Hello, Sarah. I hope you don't mind me dropping by. I know I should've called, but I was visiting the veterans center and decided to swing in last minute," Katherine told her.

Sarah looked past Katherine at the sparkling Jaguar sitting in her parking lot. It was pristine and expensive, and the neighbors were undoubtedly wondering what in the world a car like that was doing there.

"Of course it's okay," Sarah said. She desperately wanted to look behind her and make sure her place wasn't an utter wreck. She was a pretty tidy person, but when someone like Katherine Anderson stopped in, you wanted perfection. Heck, you didn't want a person like her to ever stop in at your place. She was made to be in only the finest locations.

"Can I come in?" Katherine asked with a chuckle.

"I'm so sorry," Sarah said as her cheeks heated up, letting her know they were flushed. She opened the door wider and took a breath as she turned around, giving her place a once-over. She could spot everything wrong, though it was honestly pretty dang clean. She wasn't a knick-knack kind of person at all, so there wasn't clutter. Her laundry was put away, and the dishes were done. Not that she used a lot of dishes. She was a hot-dog-at-the-convenience-store kind of girl when her friends weren't cooking for her. There were so many more important things to do than to waste her time over a hot stove. She'd never found a love in cooking.

"There's no need to apologize. I'm the one who dropped in out of the blue," Katherine said. She stepped inside and smiled as she looked around. "You have a darling place here."

The way she said the words sounded like she really meant them. Sarah was awed by this amazing woman. Sarah didn't know a lot of

Katherine's story, but she knew she'd come from some pretty humble roots. Though the woman could have had anything in the world she wanted, Sarah had never seen Katherine act superior to anyone else. She was a beautiful person inside and out.

"Would you like something to drink? I have iced tea and soda," Sarah said. She also had coffee, but it was the afternoon and pretty warm out. But she was second-guessing just about everything she was saying right now, so maybe she should've offered that as well.

"I would love a glass of iced tea with a teaspoon of sugar, please," Katherine said.

"You can have a seat on the couch while I get that," Sarah offered.

"Thank you." Katherine walked over and sat, and Sarah took a second to take a few breaths as she poured them each a tall glass of iced tea. She noticed her fingers were slightly shaking as she moved in her small kitchen. She walked the few feet into the living room area and handed Katherine her glass before sitting on the other end of the sofa and looking expectantly at her.

"I'll get right to the point," Katherine said after taking a sip. "This is delicious, by the way."

"Thank you. I don't cook, but I do love to play with different drinks," Sarah said. She'd live on liquids if her body would allow it.

"I've had many struggles in my life. I was born in a time when there wasn't a lot expected out of women except to be a good wife and mother. For those who want to do just that, I say it's honorable and the hardest job they'll ever have. But for those who want more, I say the sky's the limit. I see such talent and drive in you, and my heart hurts for the struggle you're going through. I want to see you sign that contract and finish the project you started. I know it's not any of my business, and I hate to meddle in people's lives, but I have a soft spot for you, and I truly want to see your name on those buildings that are so dear to me."

Sarah sat there as Katherine spoke, and she felt tears well up in her eyes. For such a powerful woman to say the things she was saying to her—it was humbling and motivating at the same time.

"I'm not really needed," Sarah said, not realizing she was going to voice that concern until the words came out.

Katherine reached over and took her hand, not allowing Sarah to turn away. She gave her the most sincere and kind smile Sarah had ever received as she squeezed Sarah's fingers.

"You are more needed than you can possibly imagine. Don't run away because you're afraid. Take your dreams into your hands, and show those men how it's done. I'm proud of the work you've done so far, and I know this project won't be the same without you. I'm not telling you to stay if you truly can't stand it. I'm just saying don't quit because you're afraid, and don't stop because you think you aren't important. If you hate it after another couple of months, then you can resign. But I don't think that'll happen. I think you're going to find yourself valued more than you ever have before by the time it's finished."

Sarah couldn't stop the tear from falling this time. She was a bit mortified as she wiped it away, trying to control her emotions.

"I'm sorry," she whispered.

Katherine squeezed her fingers again. "Please don't apologize for feeling something real. Time goes so quickly, Sarah, much faster than any of us are ready to accept." She looked away as if she was lost in her thoughts. Sarah wasn't sure if she should say something or not, so she waited. Katherine turned back and smiled.

"Live your dreams, and don't give up. I promise you you'll regret it if you do," she finally said.

"Did you give up your dreams?" Sarah asked.

Katherine's smile grew. "No. I've been blessed over and over again in life. From the moment I met Joseph Anderson, my world has been a giant roller-coaster ride that I wouldn't change for a minute. But time isn't always our friend. We need to live life to the fullest and store every single memory and enjoy every moment—even the ones we might think of as bad at the time they happen. Everything does happen for a reason, whether it's to build our character, make us stronger, or teach us that without the bad, we can't truly know how good things are. I can guarantee you won't regret doing this project, but you will always question yourself if you walk away."

Sarah was left speechless, something that seemed to happen quite a bit around the Anderson family.

"Thank you, Katherine," she finally said. She was too choked up to say anything more than that. Katherine let go of her fingers, and Sarah stood up and moved over to the contract. She grabbed a pen and signed. Then she returned to the couch.

"Would you mind giving this to your husband?" she asked.

The smile Katherine gave her left Sarah knowing she'd made the right choice. They chatted for another hour, and Sarah was left feeling at peace—at least for a little while. She was going to live her dreams—she just wished she knew more of what they were.

Chapter Three

Six months later

Travel!

Really, the word should be *trvl* so she could then call it a four-letter word, because anytime Sarah Jennings had to go somewhere, she found her normally pleasant demeanor shattered like a frail windowpane next to a pack of middle school boys with rocks in their grubby hands.

She despised everything to do with traveling, from the packing at the beginning and inevitably forgetting something, to the long lines at the airports and getting felt up like a teen in the back of some boy's car at the TSA station, to the cramped airplane. Then when she arrived at her destination, something had to go wrong at least once, whether it was losing her reservation, her baggage, her purse, or her sanity.

But the moment she arrived back home and took a deep breath, she was fine once more. At least that's how it normally went. Today wasn't that day. She was struggling to hold on to her loaded bag, oversize purse, and apartment keys. She was so tired she felt as if she could fall asleep standing up, and her bladder was uncomfortably full.

After a long struggle she finally managed to get her key in the apartment lock and kicked the door open with her sore foot. She inhaled but didn't find the relief she normally felt when stepping back inside her place after a long trip.

"The peace is coming," she assured herself out loud, not at all worried to be talking like a crazy person to the walls. No one was around to hear her, anyway. She was perfectly fine.

She stepped forward, getting ready to toss her bag aside, when her foot caught on the entry area rug. She knew she was going down, but there was absolutely nothing she could do to stop it. Not right now, not with her arms loaded with a bunch of stuff she hadn't even really needed on her trip.

She hit her knees first before sprawling forward, landing very ungracefully on her chest. Thankfully her purse cushioned some of the fall. Maybe it was seconds or possibly even minutes. Sarah wasn't fully sure. She just stayed exactly where she was, fighting the urge to cry.

Exhaustion and frustration were making her far more moody than she normally was. The weak, pathetic emotions were making her more and more angry with herself.

"Pull it together," she said between clenched teeth. "This is absolutely ridiculous."

Before she could continue lecturing herself, her phone began screaming at her from inside her purse. She really didn't care who was calling. The last thing she needed to do was talk to another human being. So she let it go to voice mail.

When the phone immediately began ringing again, she let out a sigh as she flipped to her side and tugged open her purse. It took a few seconds of digging around before she found her huge iPhone and pulled it out, ready to bite the head off of whoever was calling her twice in a row this late on a Friday night.

Her anger immediately drained, though, when she saw one of her two best friends smiling at her from her screen. Of course it wasn't the most flattering pic of her bestie, but that just made it even better. The evil woman had a picture of her lying in a hospital bed as her profile pic on her phone. Sarah vowed to take an even worse one of Brooke the second she had a chance.

"Hello, Brooke. What's so urgent you're calling me over and over?" Sarah asked.

"If you'd answer the phone the first time, I wouldn't have to call over and over," Brooke pointed out.

"You knew I was traveling all day. What if I was still in the plane?" Sarah asked. She pushed her purse behind her and rolled to her back, using the bag as a pillow. She might just fall asleep right where she was. It *had* been a long flight from London.

"I tracked your flight and knew you'd be home by now," Brooke said, making Sarah laugh.

"Of course you did. You've only been a mom for a month now, and you're already overprotective," Sarah said with another chuckle.

"You're my best friend. Of course I'm overprotective. Well, I worry equally about you and Chloe."

"As I do the two of you," Sarah said.

"I want to hear all about the trip," Brooke said, as if she had all night.

"Don't you need sleep? It's nearly midnight," Sarah pointed out.

"I need sleep, but your nieces are perfectly content to nurse for an hour and then take another hour burping, so I have all the time in the world," Brooke said, sounding way too happy for a sleepless new mother of twins.

"Ah, they are totally worth giving up sleep for," Sarah said, feeling her grumpiness vanish at the mention of her nieces. They really were the cutest little girls in the universe. Of course, they had parents who could grace the cover of *Vogue* magazine, so the chances of them not being adorable were zero to none.

"Yeah, I'm pretty in love with them," Brooke said, sounding happier than she ever had in her life.

There had been a time Sarah had worried Brooke would never find happiness again, especially after the loss of her brother. But then her best friend had met Finn Anderson, and her world had been flipped upside down. Brooke had fought her feelings toward the man, but in the end love had won, and now it was like they'd been together forever; they were so in sync with one another. It gave Sarah the tiniest pang of jealousy.

Sarah didn't stick with guys very long. She loved to flirt and loved to date, but she inevitably was disappointed in the opposite sex. They might hold her attention for a day or a week but never for a full month. Well, that was until she'd met Noah Anderson.

Her smile fell away as she thought about the man she was working on the huge Anderson veterans project with. He drove her absolutely crazy, and not in a good way, she told herself. He made her feel things she had no business feeling, and she wanted to get as far away from him as humanly possible. But since they were the architects for the veterans project, she'd had to work with the man nearly daily.

That's why she hadn't complained too much about jaunting off to London for another personal project she was working on. It was bad timing for work but much needed for her sanity.

"Hey!" Brooke's voice came through loud and clear, making Sarah jump.

"Why are you yelling?" Sarah asked.

"I've been talking for at least two minutes, and you just disappeared. You went into your own head again, didn't you?" Brooke said with a laugh.

There was no use denying it. "Yep. Sorry about that."

"And what were you thinking about?"

"Nothing worth mentioning," Sarah muttered.

"Ah, then probably Noah," Brooke said, laughing hard enough this time that Sarah heard a whimper from whichever niece Brooke was nursing.

"Better calm down, or you're going to have an overly excited baby on your hands, and you won't get any sleep tonight," Sarah said.

"I think it's too late for that," Brooke said. Sarah's eyes were growing heavier by the second, but the floor wasn't comfortable in the least; otherwise she'd probably fall asleep with Brooke still talking. "Get some rest. At least one of us can," Brooke added with a weak laugh.

"Thank you," Sarah said. She barely had the energy to whisper those words.

Sarah hung up the phone to the sound of Brooke's laughter; then she staggered to her feet, leaving her purse and bags right where they were, scattered contents and all. For a clean freak this showed how tired she truly was. She somehow managed to check her lock to make sure it was bolted; then she made her way the short distance to her bedroom.

Her clothes were stripped off in seconds, and then thankfully she fell into her super-comfortable bed. Sarah was out within seconds. Tomorrow was a brand-new day, and she'd definitely have a brand-new attitude to go along with it.

CHAPTER FOUR

Noah walked into Joseph Anderson's ridiculously large-size den and smiled, feeling completely at ease now that he knew his uncle well enough to be comfortable around the man. If he were being technical, Joseph was actually a . . . cousin, he believed, but the man had insisted he was an uncle, and since he felt like the Anderson kids were his cousins, he'd fallen right into calling him that.

This was a family that didn't take no for an answer to anything they needed, wanted, or demanded. That's why the Anderson empire had grown so huge through the years with Joseph at its head. The man might technically be retired now, but everyone knew he was still at the helm. He just did things from behind the scenes, sitting in a comfortable lounge chair with a cigar and scotch instead of behind his massive desk on the top floor of the Anderson headquarters. But he wasn't as sneaky as he might like to think he was.

It had only been about a year since Noah had learned he was one of "those" Andersons. And though he was still somewhat in awe to be a part of the Anderson empire, he was growing more comfortable with it by the day. For one thing, the family might be richer than Bill Gates, but they in no way looked down upon people. For another, family truly was something special in the huge mansion Joseph called home. In a world where the word *family* meant little to a lot of people, it gave Noah hope to see it so intact with his blood. He'd also discovered in life that family didn't have to be blood related. He'd served with men he'd forever call his brothers. A strong bond could make family just as much as blood did.

"You're late," Joseph said as Noah moved forward.

"I'm ten minutes early," Noah corrected.

"In my book anything less than thirty minutes early is late," Joseph said before he took a sip of his fine scotch and then picked up a cigar, taking a whiff and sighing with pleasure.

"Didn't you tell Katherine you weren't gonna smoke as many of those?" Noah asked with a devilish gleam in his eyes.

"She's out shopping right now, so there's no harm in having a few puffs," Joseph said before his eyes narrowed. "And no one needs to mention it."

Noah chuckled. "It's quite adorable how you think you won't be busted."

Joseph reached into a drawer in the table next to him and pulled out a tin of breath mints. "These are mighty strong. I eat about a dozen when I'm done, and then I have minty-fresh breath," he said proudly.

Noah didn't argue any further. If Joseph was getting away with smoking his cigars, it was because his wife was allowing it. The relationship between Joseph and Katherine was exceptional. They had a love most people aspired to have. It was something Noah had never seen before. They truly made each other better people, and the way they looked at one another sometimes made anyone watching feel as if they were intruding. The rest of the world faded away when they were together. A love that strong was a rare thing. Noah wasn't sure it existed beyond the two of them.

Though the more he hung around his newfound cousins, the more hope he had in love and marriage, because each of his family members seemed to have found the perfect spouses. They were all so in love with each other it really did seem like Noah had stepped foot inside a perfect Hallmark Channel movie marathon. Maybe he had. Maybe he'd gone to sleep and woken up in a *Truman Show* type of universe. Should he be searching for a secret door to the outside world?

Nah. If he'd woken up in this new universe, he really didn't want to find his way out, because he kind of liked it. Of course, that made him think about Sarah. She was exasperating and amazing all in one. She'd let him in a little bit, and then she was right back to pushing him away.

He'd never had to chase after a woman before, and he wasn't sure he wanted to now. But no matter how much he told himself to pull away from the beautiful, intriguing, frustrating female, he couldn't seem to talk himself into doing just that. He was drawn to her.

When she'd been in her accident a while ago, he'd been truly scared. Yes, he'd been with her, but the thought of her being hurt had terrified him. When she'd had complications that had nearly taken her life, he'd known he couldn't walk away from her. Because the thought of her dying had taken his breath away.

"So, Joseph, tell me what was so important that I had to rush here ASAP?" Noah asked.

"I want to know how the plans are coming with the veterans center," Joseph said. He clipped his cigar and lit up, his eyes sparkling as he took the first puff. "Perfection." It was a rare moment his voice came out as a sigh versus the normal boom that tended to make people jump.

"We meet all the time about the center. What really has you beckoning me?" Noah said, not allowing Joseph to get away with his normal sneaky behavior.

"I'm hurt you think I have an ulterior motive to having one of my favorite nephews here," Joseph said, not at all looking hurt or offended.

"You tell each and every one of us that we're the favorite every time you see us. That's a lot of favorites," Noah said with a chuckle.

"You know it's also okay to simply chat *and* have new favorites every other day," Joseph said, losing his smile. "And can you tell me why you young people are always in such a hurry? Maybe I truly just value my time on this earth and want to spend it with the people I love most as often as humanly possible."

Noah laughed as he grabbed a beer from the fridge and sat down across from Joseph, getting comfortable. This could take a while. He was learning more each day about this man, and he had a sneaking suspicion the meeting had more to do with his personal life than his professional.

"You know, Joseph, life is supposed to be an adventure. I do value my time and spend it with the people I love. I have great siblings and a whole new family. What more do I need?" he asked. He didn't necessarily believe this, but it was fun to goad the man. Judging by the narrowing of Joseph's eyes, he was succeeding.

"And how long do you expect to just float through life? Your poor mother would want to see you settling down, enjoying all the simple pleasures to be offered."

"Really? You're *really* gonna bring my mom up as a segue to try to get me married and producing?" Noah said with another laugh. "I've been warned about your matchmaking abilities and of all the ways you'll go about getting what you want."

"Warned?" Joseph said, sitting straight up as the word came out as a roar. "I'm offended."

Noah didn't even try to hold back his merriment now. He laughed harder than he had in a very long time. The pure indignant expression on Joseph's face was priceless. It was taking all he had not to pull out his camera and snap a few pics to share with his siblings and cousins. But he was sure they'd seen the exact same look on Joseph's face many times before.

"Oh, come on. You're telling me no one ever calls you out on your meddling ways? I find that nearly impossible to believe," Noah said.

"I'd never offer my assistance where it's not wanted or appreciated," Joseph said. But as if he was finally beginning to realize Noah was toying with him, the look fell away, and he sat back, eyeing Noah with a look that appeared slightly respectful. "You're a little smarter than I realized."

"What's that supposed to mean?" Noah said, now the one feeling slightly insulted.

"I just might have underestimated you," Joseph added.

"Hmm, many people have. I like to sit back and assess a situation before jumping in feetfirst."

"I see." Joseph didn't add more, and Noah wanted to demand what he had seen. But then Joseph would realize he was getting to him, and he wasn't going to give the man that much power. He had enough as it was.

"Okay, let's get to the point. I do have a lot of work to do," Noah told him, not having as much fun with this game now.

"There's no point. I just wanted to make sure things are going well," Joseph said.

"Well, things are on schedule. Sarah and I are meeting at the site next week to get an idea for the final layout. Hudson and his crew are getting anxious for the final plans, but as you're at the site nearly daily, you know how the first building is going, so I don't know how much more I can add."

"Is Sarah doing well?" Joseph asked.

Sarah was brand new as an architect, but Noah would be lying if he said she was anything less than exceptional. She was meant to do this job.

"She's got great ideas and spends a lot of time on this project. Someday I wouldn't be surprised if she's designing for the best of the best. She's a true artist," Noah said, meaning it.

"That's great to hear. I knew from the beginning she'd be excellent for this project."

"And you don't hire anyone but the best," Noah said with another chuckle, feeling more at ease again.

"Of course not. I wouldn't be where I am now if I settled for medio-cre," Joseph told him.

"All kidding aside, Joseph, I'm truly thankful to be a part of this project. Our veterans don't get nearly as much respect and help as they deserve. Thank you," Noah said.

"I'm proud of you and your siblings for serving our country. I knew you'd be the best men to make sure this project is exceptional, and it will be the new standard for more facilities like it all across the United States."

"I hope that's the case. I hope it gets so much publicity the public will rise up and demand we do more for those who keep us safe."

"I agree, son."

They talked for the next hour about the project, and Noah managed to dodge every single question Joseph threw his way, trying to dig out information about his and Sarah's relationship.

It wasn't hard to do, as he couldn't actually explain his relationship with her. Yes, the two of them had been like two magnets drawn to each other from the moment they'd first met, but lately it was more as if they were bombs with the fuses lit and ready to explode.

They were either going to go up in flames together, or they were going to turn out to be duds. He wasn't sure what was going to happen in the end. He just knew he was more than willing to play it out and feel the explosion, if or when it came.

CHAPTER FIVE

Noah stepped from his large Ford F-350 truck and looked up at the massive walls of his brother's home. It was a far cry from the small three-bedroom house they'd grown up in. Though it had been cramped, he couldn't remember ever feeling miserable there. He'd been with his wonderful mother and four siblings, and he hadn't minded being stacked on top of one another.

It was still odd to see how far all of them had come since those early days, though. Sure, there might've been some bad times, but what he recalled with clarity was all of the good. The stories he could tell of some of the adventures he'd had with his siblings could probably fill a novel—and entertain whoever chose to read such a book.

Though his childhood had been filled with good memories, he'd still had a need to escape home. He'd wanted to find adventure, see the world, travel, find out what life was like on his own. He'd been a brother and a son, and he'd wanted to find out what it was like to be an individual.

He'd found that and more when he'd signed up for the navy at the tender age of eighteen. He'd barely graduated high school when he'd said goodbye to his family and run off to boot camp. His brothers had each done same. It wasn't that they'd had an example to follow; it was just that they'd been called to serve. Maybe it was because they'd had such an awful father and a wonderful mother. He wasn't sure why. He was just grateful he'd done what he'd done.

After one contract, though, he'd decided not to make a military career his focus, and he hadn't reenlisted, but that didn't take away his respect for the armed services, and it certainly didn't take away his love for the project he'd been asked to help with. He was honored to be designing the Anderson veterans facility. And he was glad to do it with Sarah.

Noah's mother had been gone now for over a year, and the shock of her death still hadn't worn off. Maybe that was why he was currently at his brother's place. Since they'd lost her, they'd all been spending more time together, realizing that life wasn't eternal. In the blink of an eye someone they loved more than life itself could be gone. They'd never gone through a period in life when they hadn't liked one another, but at the same time, they'd all grown busy and complacent in their lives, and sometimes it would be months before they realized they hadn't spoken.

After losing their mother, they'd promised to never let that happen again. Now Noah didn't go more than a day without talking to at least one of his siblings. He honestly couldn't say he favored one more than the other. It depended on the day and the mood he was in to determine who he wanted to speak to more.

Each of his siblings had different personalities. It was kind of amusing how they could grow up in such a tight-knit family and all be so very different. They each had a strong work ethic, but they were as different as night and day. Their personalities ranged from almost too serious to romantic to humorous to easygoing. But he had noticed the older they got, the more each of them changed. Maybe life was about adapting to new situations and experiences. You didn't have to fit neatly into a mold and stay there forever. Breaking away from the bonds of life was quite therapeutic.

Noah began moving toward Finn's front door. He looked down at his expensive work boots and the fine cut of his slacks and smiled.

He liked wearing a suit. His concession to that was a designer pair of jeans and a polo shirt. Noah couldn't remember the last time he'd put on a pair of sweats—not even to sleep in. Maybe he needed to loosen up a little, experience more freedom. Sarah seemed to bring that out in him. She was tightly wound, and wanting to help her unwind was making him want to be more free. He was determined right now to make a change.

The funny part about the way he dressed was that he did it all for himself. He couldn't care less what anyone thought of him. Noah was a confident man, had been all his life. He worked hard, and though he'd never been a wealthy man, he'd known his place in the world and had always known he'd be a success. Impressing strangers was the last thing on his mind.

But now that he'd received what Joseph Anderson said was right-fully his, he had more money in his bank account than he could possibly ever spend. That money hadn't changed who he was. It had fast-tracked him on his career; having the Anderson name meant something, but he was still the same man he'd been before he found out he was one of *those* Andersons.

He knew this new identity wouldn't change his siblings, either. They'd been raised by a beautiful, wonderful, humble mother who would spank their asses even as adults if they ever thought they were better than another just because of what was in their wallet or what their name was.

He was eternally grateful for the values she'd instilled in each of them.

Noah was confident for sure, but standing at six feet three and weighing 190 pounds helped a little with that. When you added in his crystal-blue eyes, chiseled jawline, and fit body, he had little to feel insecure about. His dark hair and easy smile had made finding dates a little too easy his entire life.

But since he'd met Sarah, his desire to date anyone else had disappeared. She intrigued him more than any other woman he'd ever met. And he still wasn't quite sure what to think about that. Should he fight the feeling? Or should he follow in Finn's footsteps and make her his wife?

Well . . . if she agreed.

And he wasn't sure she would. He had no doubt she was attracted to him. That was more than obvious, since anytime they were in a room together, he could practically smell the smoke rising from their overheated bodies. But she seemed to be even more afraid of commitment than he was.

That was saying a lot.

They were hot and heavy; then they'd both freaked out after the accident. They were drawn together like two powerful magnets; then they ran as fast as they could when it was too intense. They had to figure it out before they drove everyone around them utterly crazy.

Noah stepped up to Finn's door and smiled. He couldn't help but think about how opposite he and his brother were. While Noah loved suits and ties, Finn preferred ratty jeans and hoodies. Noah also kept his hair short and neat and used gel. Since Finn had retired from the military, his hair had become slightly unruly, and he rebelled at any kind of uniformity. All the siblings had similarities that made it more than obvious they were brothers if they were together. But their personalities couldn't be more different.

Their mother had told them how much she valued their differences. She loved how unique and talented each of her sons were. Knowing that gave them the courage and pride to go after their dreams, knowing there was nothing they couldn't accomplish if they put their minds to it.

Noah didn't bother knocking on his brother's front door. They were family, and there was no need for that. Luckily Finn had married a woman they all loved and who loved them as well, because she didn't care about the normal conventions, either. If they did knock, she was offended they didn't feel at home enough to treat it like their own house. His brother had truly lucked out when he'd gone after Brooke. She was a one-of-a-kind female.

When he stepped inside the large house, he was hit in the face with the most delicious smell, which instantly had his stomach growling and his pace quickening as he headed straight for the kitchen. He thought back and couldn't remember the last time he'd put food in his body.

One negative of being a bachelor was he'd get busy and forget to stop and eat. Food was a necessity of life, and he certainly took pleasure in eating well, as long as he wasn't the one having to do the cooking. Brooke didn't always cook, but when she did, it was definitely good.

He found Brooke in the kitchen, stirring something on the stove. Maybe there were times in life he didn't make the best decisions, but he doubted that. He crept up to her and leaned in.

"Whatcha making?" he asked in a loud voice.

She jumped about three feet in the air and let out an ear-piercing scream before turning around and giving him a death glare with her hand placed over her heart. He started laughing, unable to control himself.

Damn, it felt good to have a great belly laugh. He was still bent over as Brooke scolded him when his brother Finn skidded into the room, his eyes intense as he assessed the situation. It didn't take long to figure out what was going on.

"Your brother's a pain in the ass," Brooke said, shaking her finger at him. "He doesn't get fed."

"Whoa, now there's no need for that," Noah said in between chuckles.

"You never want to piss off the cook," Finn warned. "But I see you've arrived in style. I about came in here with an arsenal when I heard my wife's scream."

Noah was sure his brother wasn't kidding. "I almost feel sorry for a person stupid enough to mess with your wife."

"Damn straight," Finn said. "He'd never be found."

"I don't need anyone protecting me. I can certainly take care of myself," Brooke told them both.

"I have no doubt about it. You took down Finn the first time you met him. I've been a bit in love with you ever since."

"Quit flirting with my wife," Finn said before grabbing Brooke and giving her one solid kiss. "And I *let* her take me down."

Now it was Brooke's turn to laugh. "You keep telling yourself that, darling,"

"I will," he said. The way he looked at Brooke was so intimate Noah felt like an intruder. There was no doubt how much the two of them loved each other. It made Noah want things he'd never wanted before. He wasn't sure what he thought about that.

"Have you forgiven me enough to feed me?" Noah asked, trying to look as apologetic and helpless as possible. He really was hungry, dang it.

"I don't know," Brooke said. But she moved over to the cupboard and pulled down three bowls and began dishing them up.

"I love clam chowder," Noah said as he accepted the bowl and moved over to the breakfast bar and sat. The smell of the soup was pure heaven. Brooke set out some crackers, fresh bread, and butter before she sat with them.

He was eating too quickly, and some chowder dripped down on his shirt. He got up and grabbed a wet rag, quickly cleaning up the spill. Finn laughed as he sat back down next to him.

"Shut up," Noah told him, swiping at the spot again. He couldn't stand stains. It was so trashy.

"Better be careful, brother. People might think you're not perfect if you go out in public like that," Finn told him.

"I'd rather be a bit uptight than a hobo like you," Noah said as he looked at the ripped jeans and faded shirt Finn was wearing.

"Hey! I was in a uniform for seventeen years of my life. Now I want to be comfortable," Finn said. "It's a much less stressful way to live. You should try it sometime. Why don't we get dirty and go shoot some Tannerite?"

The desire to take the afternoon off and do just that was so damn tempting Noah found himself close to saying yes.

He shook his head.

"I have too much work to get done right now to play hooky today, but it's tempting. Some of us can't live like bums and sit around the house in ripped-up clothes," Noah said. Finn just smiled, not seeming offended at all. "Besides," he added before his brother could say anything, "I have nothing to prove to anyone."

"Come on, little brother. We'll have a blast, and we haven't had a day like that in a long time," Finn pushed.

"Yeah, your adventures usually end up with someone in the ER, and I can't afford a week off of work," Noah pointed out.

"That only happens once in a while," Finn told him with a laugh.

Brooke was watching the two of them with a smile. She didn't have any family left and had told them several times she loved that by marrying Finn, she'd inherited an entire new one. Noah was glad to call her his sister.

"You two enjoy the rest of lunch. I just got paged to the clinic," Brooke said after her phone went off.

"It's Saturday," Finn said with a pout that cracked Noah up. His brother wasn't normally the pouting kind.

"I'll be back as soon as I can," she told her husband. "You hold down the fort until I'm back."

"Deal," he said before kissing her so intimately Noah once again felt like an intruder.

"Don't let the children escape," she warned before stepping out of the room.

"Where are my nieces?" Noah asked. He was a lot in love with them.

"Sleeping. It's a rare event," Finn said with another laugh.

"Brooke trusts you on your own with them?" Noah questioned.

"I'm a hell of a dad," Finn said as he puffed out his chest. "But those little girls do give me a run for my money," he admitted. "And with Brooke back to work part time, we've hired a nanny. *Not* that she doesn't trust me," he quickly added, "but because we both realized sleep deprivation was beginning to make us slowly lose our minds."

Noah laughed some more. "You're getting outwitted by a couple of infants. I love it."

"You just wait," Finn warned. "You'll be on this side of life before you know it. Then my girls will be sleeping through the night, and I'll be laughing at you," he promised.

A shudder ran through Noah. "No way. I'm not that dumb," he said.

"Mm-hmm. That's what I thought. Now I can't even imagine how lonely I'd be without Brooke and those girls. They're my world."

"Damn straight they are," Noah said. "And my nieces."

"Yeah, we're all pretty blessed."

There weren't more true words spoken. They'd always been a blessed family. Some people might forget that, but Noah vowed to always remember and always be grateful. His mother had reminded them too often of how fortunate they were for him to dishonor her by forgetting.

He said goodbye to his brother after another hour. It was time to go find Sarah. He wasn't even going to pretend he didn't want to see her. And he had some soul-searching to do. Maybe it truly was time to trade in the suit and look at life like an adventure. Maybe if he could do that, he could do anything.

CHAPTER SIX

Dreaming was essential to the human existence. If people spent more time with their dreams and less time in reality, the world would be a happier place. Sarah firmly believed this. Why was it so damn important to grow up? Why did she feel she had to always be in control of her life and her experiences? She didn't want to grow up, didn't want to be responsible. Yet even knowing this and having a desire for freedom, she couldn't seem to let her hair down and let it all go.

She wanted to be one of those people who decided to be in Neverland forever and think to hell with anyone who had a problem with it. But no matter how much she desired that, she couldn't seem to get herself to act on her own wishes.

Sarah had spent so much time in school in uptight clothing with glasses on and her brain active while trying to portray a person who had it all together that she hadn't known anything about life. She was beginning to figure that out, but she was still a little lost. Now she was twenty-seven and just now starting to know who she was.

On her days off she lived in a favorite pair of sweatpants and a camisole. But she wouldn't dare show up in public like that. While working, she often wore a pencil skirt and cotton blouse. She wanted nothing to do with silk or satin or any clothing that would take too much time to coordinate. The more time she spent on grooming, the less time she had to do her actual work.

She did have a love of fitness, though, and there was always a gym bag in the back of her car, because she never knew when she'd need to go for a run. Her brain never stopped working, so sometimes the only way she could begin to shut down was to push her body to the breaking point and then go a little farther. Just because she could. She loved the Cam Hanes saying of "Nobody cares. Work harder."

Being an architect was about the greatest job a person could have. She'd always been a creative person, but there were so many fields she could've gone into with her love of design. When she'd looked at the architectural degree, there'd been no more looking. She'd found her passion, and she couldn't wait to see her creations all around the world. But it was still a predominantly male-driven field, which made her feel the need to work that much harder.

As much as Sarah did love dreams, there was a time and place to feel them. This wasn't it. Right now she had a lot of work to get done. She sat in her small office and tried to focus on the design she was working on. This project was difficult because it was the first one that her name would be attached to that the world was going to be critical of. Whenever the Anderson name went behind something, it became a media sensation.

She had to force herself not to panic as she erased another line and fought herself not to throw the entire paper into the garbage can. It wasn't only that this was an Anderson project; it was also the fact that she was working with Noah Anderson, who was driving her *and* her hormones absolutely crazy.

She'd been more than willing to take her time making a name for herself, but now she wasn't going to be able to do that. This job could make or break her career. That was a lot of pressure for someone who already was so critical of themselves. She wanted to be a superstar in this world of art and creation. But she wasn't sure she'd ever feel she was good enough, because there was always something she could do to make it better.

She lost track of time as she continued working, so when someone tapped on her door, she about jumped out of her seat. Then she was annoyed with herself. There was no reason to be jumpy or irritated at a distraction. Maybe it would refresh her mind enough to finish this dang drawing.

When her door opened and she found Noah standing there looking far too sexy as he took up the entire width of the doorframe, she felt her heart stutter. His sparkling blue eyes gazed at her so intensely she had to force herself not to look away. She didn't want him to realize the power he had with nothing more than a look.

There were days she wished she never had to see him again. And then there were moments she wanted to find reasons to be with him, to hear the sexy smooth sound of his voice, to feel his hot breath on the back of her neck as he looked over a drawing she was doing, to feel the touch of his fingers against her skin in a casual brush. She was a hot mess, and she knew it, but there didn't seem to be a whole lot she could do about the situation.

She was working with the man, whether she wanted to or not, and he wasn't the type of guy to be easily intimidated or back off from what he wanted. And he'd made it more than clear he wanted her—at least for now.

"How are you today, sexy?" he asked in a voice so smooth and hot he could melt butter with it, even on a cold day.

It drove her absolutely insane how he took her voice away with a few simple nondescript words. But all the man had to do was be in the same room with her, and she was a mess. That alone was a reason not to date him—or sleep with him anymore.

"My name is Sarah, not *sexy*, not *darling*, not any other pet name you think of to annoy me," she said in the haughtiest voice she could come up with. The smirk he gave her made her want to jump from her chair and get in his face. Sarah had never been a violent person, but the emotions this one man raised in her were insane.

"You have a very beautiful name; I can assure you, though, that I have many nicknames that suit you just as well," he said with a wink.

"Look, Noah, I've been sitting at this desk all day with no breaks. I don't have time to have a verbal spar with you. What do you need?" she asked. She hated being this girl—so uptight and to the point. Life was too short to live it stressed. But this one man made her so out of control she couldn't help herself around him.

He took his time sauntering forward, and she tried not to watch. He moved with grace and beauty, which was odd, since he was such a large man. But then again, there wasn't a single thing she'd found wrong with him so far, so of course his movements would be utter perfection, just like the rest of him.

He stopped right in front of her desk, leaving the most appealing parts of him very visible and *very* nearby. Her fingers were practically shaking with the need to reach out and touch him. She clenched them into fists and prayed she'd get through this impromptu meeting quickly and with her brain fully functioning.

He didn't say anything for a long time, just caressed her face with his beautiful eyes, making her breath come out in short little pants. He looked at her with such familiarity she felt as if they'd known each other their entire lives instead of only a year. There were just some people in life you clicked with right away. Apparently she'd clicked with him, though she *would* continue to fight it.

"I haven't spoken to you all week. How are you doing?" he asked. The words came out with sincerity, as if he really did care how her week had gone.

Sarah had spent an afternoon once thinking about all the things people said to one another. People greeted each other, asking how they were doing, asking about their families, dates, lives, and careers. But most people asking those questions didn't really care about the answer you gave. It was just so ingrained in people to be polite they went through the motions.

But that made no sense to Sarah. Why pretend to care when you didn't? When she asked a question of people, it was because she truly wanted the answer. One thing she'd stopped asking many years ago was "How are you?" because it only took seconds of reading someone's body language or facial expressions to get your own answer to that question. Something she liked to ask a lot more that came with some fun answers was "Is there anything new going on in your life?"

Sarah tried to do something new and exciting once a year. That way she didn't feel guilty about being so in control the rest of the time. Plus, she needed a thrill once in a while, when her job was so dang sedentary. Her favorite part of working was when she got to be out in the field. That got her off her butt and doing something she truly loved.

"I'm bored with sitting all day long," she answered honestly. "I love what I do, but there are times I wonder why I didn't go into archaeology or medicine, something that would stimulate my mind *and* body."

At her last words his lips turned up, and her stomach clenched. Of course the man was thinking about how capable he was of stimulating her body. She had to admit, if only to herself, he was very, *very* good at stimulating her in all sorts of exciting ways.

His body leaned forward as if he wanted to make contact, and she pulled back. If the man touched her, she was a goner. She knew she'd melt in his arms and not only let him do anything he wanted to her but be an active participant, even going so far as to beg him to never stop. She craved this man like a runner desired water.

"Anytime you want an adventure, I'm more than willing to give you one," he told her as he leaned against her desk. At least he wasn't looking as if he was going to touch her again.

"What are you doing here, Noah? I have a lot of work to get done, and it's not going as well as I'd like," she reminded him. He obviously wasn't in a hurry to get to the point, so she'd have to lead him in that direction.

"We need to do something completely different," he said with a long pause that had her intrigued. "I'm stumped," he finally admitted.

"Is that true?" She didn't take him as a man to get stumped, and if he did, she really didn't take him as the type of person to admit it. She wondered if this was another ploy of some sort on his part. She might not know him really well, but she had never taken him for the type of person to lie, though.

Noah stepped back and pulled a chair forward. He had this cute way of sitting on chairs. He never sat in them correctly. This one he plopped down on sideways so he could lean his right arm over the back, as if he had all the time in the world to sit there and lounge about.

He pulled out a folded paper from his pocket and plopped it on her desk. She gazed at it for a moment before looking at him again. She waited, but he didn't say anything. Finally she sighed and pulled it toward her.

"What is this?" she asked.

"It's our first layout. I made a few changes, but I don't like how it's going. I haven't been in the field in a while, and I think we need to explore. Maybe go to the site, maybe somewhere else. But this isn't working. I'm thinking about taking a couple of trips to look at other facilities. Yes, there's a lot wrong with the services and buildings provided for our vets, but there's some things that are being done right. We need to figure out which is which and put all the good into this one place. We need to set the standard for the rest of the buildings created in the future."

Sarah's curiosity was now officially piqued. She loved how much thought and effort he was putting into this. And it wasn't just because he was now one of the famous Andersons. It was because he truly did care about veterans services and wanted to give them an absolutely beautiful place to spend their time when they were recovering from one injury or another.

She opened the paper and looked at it. Yes, they'd done a fairly good job, but she agreed with him that more could be done. They had time. Joseph wasn't rushing them. Noah's brother was anxious to get going on other stuff, but the main facility had been designed first, and he was building that now. They could make sure and get the rest of it right and not make Hudson fall behind on his work.

Noah rose from his chair, too active to stay sitting for long. When she looked up, his eyes met hers, and her breath caught again. There was fire in his gaze, and she had a feeling he was doing all he could not to close the small gap between them and lay his lips against hers. She wasn't surprised at how much she wanted to close that distance herself.

Instead of doing just that, she broke away from the intense look and scooted back, placing her gaze safely on the paper in front of her. It was much smarter to do that than play with fire.

"I don't know if we should take so much time away from the actual drawings to go exploring," she told him.

He smiled at her, that impish look back in his eyes. Noah didn't ever take no for an answer. Normally, neither did she.

"Let's meet tonight for dinner and go over it. Then the next day we'll get in the field," he said, as if it was a done deal. Technically he was the senior architect and therefore in charge. She'd be a fool not to listen and learn from him—at least professionally.

"I don't know . . . ," she said, feeling as if she was getting tricked into something.

"Yes, you do. We've got this," he said. He gave her one scorching look, then turned and began walking from her office. Part of her wanted to call out to him and tell him she was her own person, and he couldn't tell her what to do. But the rest of her wanted to go on an adventure with him. But she'd already been on some adventures with him, and it hadn't gone well at all—it had been downright dangerous.

But one thing she could almost guarantee by working with Noah Anderson was that she'd never be bored. And Sarah despised being bored.

She let out a sigh as he left her office without turning back. It looked like the next step in her adventure with the Anderson family was starting. Maybe she should just accept it and go along for the ride.

CHAPTER SEVEN

Noah couldn't keep the smile from his face as he kicked his motorcycle into full throttle and flew through the back roads, taking a corner a bit too fast. His laughter rang out as he felt more free than he had in a long time. There was nothing better than a sunny day and speed. Well, maybe that wasn't true. A good woman beneath a man was pretty damn amazing, too.

He'd decided to go back to his youth and loosen up. And he never did anything at half measure. Why do it halfway when you could go all the way?

From the time he'd been about twelve, he'd had a need for speed. They hadn't had the money then to buy recreational vehicles, but he'd found friends with them. By the time he was sixteen, he'd been an expert at driving. The adventure had only just begun then. He'd never lost the need for a good thrill; he'd just put it on hold for a while. But he truly didn't want to settle in life. Why should he, when there was so much adventure to be had? He was always in control, so driving too fast was a release he greatly needed.

And now that he was working on this project, for the first time in years he and his brothers were all in close proximity to each other. It didn't get much better than that. He loved his family. It was easy to let life get in the way and to let too much time pass with little communication. He loved being together again. Life was falling into place exactly how it was supposed to.

Of course thinking like that had him thinking of Sarah. She'd stormed into his life like a summer hurricane. And he wasn't afraid. That shocked him. He'd always loved women. What was there not to love? They were soft to his hardness, kind to his sarcasm, and beautiful to his ruggedness. He loved how they felt in his arms, loved how they made him smile, and loved how silky they felt against him.

But Sarah was different from anyone he'd ever been with before. She was all of those things he'd ever wanted and so much more. She was exactly what he'd been searching for without realizing he'd been seeking anyone. He'd been with many women and had walked away without looking back. He had a feeling he wouldn't be able to do that with Sarah. She was a one-of-a-kind woman, and he wasn't going to easily let her get away. He'd tried to leave her, and he'd failed horribly, quickly running right back to her.

His ride ended much sooner than he wanted it to as he pulled up to his brother Crew's place. Crew was the family psychologist, and they all liked to flick him a bunch of shit about it, but they also were incredibly proud of him. Of course, Noah had a master's degree as well as Crew, but Noah knew how much time and energy his brother had put into his profession. Crew had gone a step further and had gotten his doctorate, and he was damn good at what he did.

Noah took his career and himself seriously, but Crew made him look like an utter playboy. Crew was far too serious about life. It was all of the brothers' mission to loosen him up, to get him to laugh a little more. Sure, life had to be taken seriously, and they all had to grow up at some point. But they didn't have to do it at the expense of their happiness. It wasn't too crazy to believe they could have it all and laugh while doing it.

Noah got off his bike and looked at the large house, which seemed so odd for his brother to own. It was a farmhouse with about fifty acres to it. Crew had only owned it for about six months, and when he'd brought the family up to see it, they'd all been shocked. Maybe Crew felt he was missing something in life and wanted more adventure, but he didn't know how to express it. Maybe he didn't even know he wanted it. Noah wondered if his little brother was going to make a farm there. He just couldn't imagine Crew on a tractor or shoveling horse manure. But it would be a picture-perfect moment for sure if that were to happen.

He tried the doorknob and smiled when it opened. Open doors were important when it came to family. Maybe it was time for Noah to buy his own house so his brothers could come and stay with him anytime they needed. It seemed that was the thing to do at his age. It scared him a little, though. If he settled down completely, would he lose himself? He wasn't ready for that—or at least he didn't think he was.

Walking through the hallways of his brother's large home, he smiled. The place was still so empty. It needed paint and furniture and pictures on the walls. He did notice how very clean the floors were, though. And since Noah was a dusty mess from his ride, he knew he'd drive his brother slightly crazy with the dirt he was tracking in the otherwise pristine home.

He made it all the way to the kitchen before he found Crew, who looked at his attire with a bit of disgust, shaking his head. Noah didn't say anything as he moved to the fridge and smiled when he found ice-cold beer inside. He was trying to embrace Finn's attitude of worn jeans and a T-shirt. It wasn't completely comfortable for him, but the reaction from Crew made it totally worth it. Crew was far more uptight than Noah had ever been.

"Go ahead and make yourself at home," Crew said with only slight sarcasm.

"Of course I will," Noah told him. He popped the top off his beer and took a long swallow, letting out a sigh at the smooth taste. "Delicious."

"My cleaner isn't going to like you visiting," Crew said before he moved to the fridge to grab his own beverage.

"Nah, she'll love it, since it's job security," Noah told him. "I love this place. If you get sick of it, let me know. Maybe it's time I put my own place on the map." He was a bit shocked when the words came out. But the thought became more appealing by the second. He really did love the house, and the property had many possibilities of what he could do on it.

Crew looked thoughtful before he spoke. That wasn't unusual. Crew never spouted anything. He liked to compose his words carefully. He never allowed himself to get drunk, and he never lost control. It would be great to see what would happen if he did.

"I like this place. I don't really have an explanation as to why, but I feel at home here. I won't be selling," he finally said, as if he'd considered doing just that for about five seconds.

For the first time Noah noticed some changes in his brother. Maybe all of them were growing up. Noah had never looked at Crew like he was a lost soul, but maybe his brother had gone into the degree he'd chosen because he was seeking answers about his own life. Who really knew another person if that person wasn't willing to share? Even if a person did share, they didn't give you everything. If they did, there'd be nothing left of themselves.

"I think it's a good idea for you to settle down," Crew told him when Noah didn't say anything for quite a while.

"I don't know why I even said that. I've just been sort of thinking about it lately. Maybe all adventure or all work is where I fail. Maybe I can have a balance and have more than one thing."

"There can be adventures to be had in one place," Crew said. "And just because you own a home doesn't mean you aren't allowed to leave it."

"I know. I know," Noah said. "But buying a house is a big step for a confirmed bachelor who likes to wander the world looking for the next adventure to be had."

"Let's move to the den. I got new furniture," Crew said.

Noah followed his brother through the house and was impressed when they stepped into the huge room. It was certainly a man's dream space, with a bar, a couple of couches, and a nice fireplace. Noah headed toward the liquor cabinet and glanced at the expensive labels.

"Hmm, good stuff," he said as he pulled out a bottle of scotch and took off the lid, giving it a smell. "Yep, gotta try this."

"It's a little early," Crew pointed out.

"Nah, it's never too early to quench your thirst," Noah told him. He put some ice in a glass and poured the smooth liquor on top, then took a sip. "Heaven," he said with a sigh. "Want some?"

Crew cracked a smile. "No, I'm good," he said. "But help yourself."

"I'd rather ask for forgiveness than permission," Noah said.

"Are you ever going to grow up and act your age?" Crew asked as he sat down and sipped slowly on his beer. "Of all our brothers I've taken you as the most serious other than me . . . until lately."

"Why should I? Just because someone tells me I need to do something doesn't mean that's what I'll do," Noah said. "I'm liking this new carefree attitude. It's making my suits a lot less tight. I might give them up altogether."

"I don't know why I bother with any of my siblings. You guys don't listen to me worth a damn," Crew said.

"Maybe we'd listen more if *you* loosened up a bit," Noah said. "You take life too seriously."

"And you don't take it seriously enough," Crew countered. "You've changed. Every one of you have changed in the past year."

"So have you," Noah pointed out. "Maybe what we all needed was change." He thought for a few more moments, then spoke again before Crew could say something. "Maybe we could meet somewhere in the middle." He moved to the couch across from his brother and sat. He wasn't in a hurry for anything today, which was a wonderful novelty.

"I don't think I need to change," Crew told him. "I have responsibilities that I take very seriously."

"Maybe I have a fear of becoming someone I don't know or like. Maybe I want to have less responsibility. Maybe that's why I have the need to wander. I'm afraid if I settle, life will become boring and one dimensional. If I see the world that way, I'll never be able to do my job."

"By living that way, you might one day wake up and realize you've wasted a lot of time. It's okay to find a bit of peace in a crazy world," Crew said. "I can honestly say I have nothing to feel regret over."

"Well, for me to offer a compromise is a big step. I don't like giving even an inch. So if I can do it, then I know for sure you can," Noah told him.

"Yeah, one thing all of us have in common is we don't easily back down."

"Are you saying that's a good thing?" Noah asked.

"I wouldn't necessarily say that's an asset. It depends on the situation. Strength of character can play a big role in life. But too much stubbornness can hold us all back. It's good to shake up the normal day-to-day routine."

"That's true, I guess," Noah admitted.

"How are things going with Sarah?" Crew asked. "I've never seen a woman get under your skin like she does."

"I don't know why she gets to me so much. She's completely wrong for me. But even knowing that, I can't get her out of my head. I want to be with her all the time. I love how I feel when I'm with her."

"Maybe you're falling in love for the first time in your life," Crew suggested.

"Nah. We haven't spent enough time together to fall in love," Noah said. "But I tend to send mixed messages." There was no way he'd convince his brothers he was a happy single guy if he wasn't able to convince himself.

"Hmm," Crew said, and Noah suddenly felt sorry for his brother's patients.

"Sometimes your little sounds drive me absolutely crazy," Noah told him.

"You've known her for about a year now, so this isn't new anymore. You should really know what you want by now. If you're just toying with her, I'd suggest you let her go. She's not the kind of woman to be played with."

"I'm not playing with her. It's just a physical thing," Noah said. He wasn't sure if he was trying to convince himself or his brother of this.

"For someone who doesn't want commitment, you seem awfully attached to this woman," Crew pointed out.

"And you're getting this from just a few words I'm saying?" Noah questioned.

"No. I'm getting this from hearing you speak about her for months."

"Maybe I should keep my mouth shut from now on," Noah said.

"You know none of us are judging you. I know this is a process you have to work through," Crew said.

"I know that, but I'm not sure what I'm thinking or feeling, so it's impossible to put it into words," Noah admitted.

"Just tell me what's on your mind right now," Crew suggested.

Noah thought about it for a moment. "She fascinates me. I love being with her, and I love how she sparks my imagination *and* my hormones. She's got so many dimensions to her I don't think I'll ever truly know who she is. And I'm not scared of how I feel. That's enough right there to scare the hell out of me, but it doesn't. I've just screwed up a lot. I don't know if I can make it right."

"I'd say you're on the right path if you want something and aren't afraid to accept it. You can either run in life or embrace what's in front of you," Crew told him.

"Is this how you talk to your patients?" Noah asked.

Crew gave a rare chuckle. "Some of them, especially the more stubborn ones."

"Well, don't use your shrinky magic on me. I'm doing just fine."

"I have no doubt you are," Crew said. "The guesthouse is finally fixed, so you can move your stuff out there anytime you want. Stay as long as you need."

The gesture made Noah smile. "I appreciate it. Until I figure out what I'm doing, I don't want to rent a place."

"Well, the guesthouse is much better than a hotel. I can't believe you've stayed there so long."

"Hey, it's convenient, and I don't have to clean up after myself," Noah said. "But I do miss having a back porch to kick back on."

"Yeah, I've never been a fan of apartments, and a hotel is worse than one of those."

"It hasn't been so bad, but I'm over it. I'll move in tonight." He was feeling better already. "But for now I'm going to shower. I have a date with Sarah, and I can't be around her all dusty and stinky."

He stood up and began heading from the room. He had clothes in Crew's and Finn's places. He really was a hobo of sorts.

"Glad you have priorities. At least you clean up for a girl, even if it's after tracking crap through my entire house."

"Of course I have priorities. You aren't nearly as pretty as Sarah," he said with a chuckle.

"That hurts my feelings," Crew said.

Noah laughed again as he walked from the room and went down a few more hallways until he got to the guest room with its own bathroom. This house truly was great. Maybe he'd find something like it, or maybe he'd design his own place.

He stripped and jumped in the shower, his thoughts on Sarah the entire time, which made him rush through it. The sooner he was done, the quicker he'd see the girl.

Yeah, he was pretty much a goner when it came to her . . . and he didn't even care.

CHAPTER EIGHT

Sarah's nerves were in a jumble as she drove up the long driveway to Noah's brother's place. She never should've agreed to meet him at the house. It was supposed to be in a public place where she could count on many people around them. She didn't trust herself to be alone with the guy. It seemed every time they were one on one, they ended up naked. She was trying to tell herself that wasn't a good thing.

But he'd sounded professional on the phone when he'd called her and asked if she could come to the ranch instead of a restaurant. He said he didn't want anyone overhearing them as they talked about the project. The more they kept away from the media, the more the place got publicity because it was such a mystery. That was logic she couldn't argue with.

She'd decided after Noah left her office that all she really needed with this man was closure. She'd been fascinated with him from the moment she'd met him and had stupidly believed that if she slept with him, then she'd get over her infatuation. That had totally backfired. So what she really needed to do was spend more time with him, and then maybe she'd get over her fascination with the man. That was it. She was sure of it. He wasn't as perfect as he'd seemed in the wee hours of the morning.

She'd spent far too much time thinking of this man. He was smart in how he kept her interested. He knew how her brain worked and knew that if he kept her intrigued about things, he'd have her hook, line, and sinker. It worked well for him but wasn't so good for her. But she was determined to get over the man. This fascination with one guy was something totally new for her.

As she pulled up to the house, her heart thumped a bit too quickly. She'd been to this property before. A friend who'd moved away many years ago had owned it. She'd had her first kiss on the ranch, come to think of it. That had been a long time before. She smiled at the memory. Neither of them had known what they were doing at the tender age of fifteen, but thankfully kissing had gotten better the older she'd become. Kissing Noah Anderson was extraordinary. He was fantastic no matter what he chose to do.

No. No. No. She wasn't supposed to have those types of thoughts anymore. If she wanted to get herself under control and finish this damn project, she had to pull it together.

But being at this property was messing with her head. She'd had good memories at this place, and she couldn't help but think of how many more memories she could make with Noah. She'd always dreamed of making love beneath a star-studded sky, and this was the perfect location for that.

The last summer she'd spent at this ranch, she'd been eighteen and in a crisis of what she'd wanted to do with her life. She'd broken up with her high school boyfriend, and she'd been so lost. If it hadn't been for Chloe and Brooke, she might've spiraled out of control. But they'd pulled her back in, and she'd gone to college, and now she was living the dream. If only she didn't feel like there was something missing.

But Sarah had grown up a lot since she was a teen. Sometimes that depressed her. She liked to be free and let her hair down. She liked to run on the beach in a bikini with laughter trailing behind her because she was feeling so much joy.

Maybe being a professional was what was making her so damn vulnerable. She needed to loosen up again and take the time to run and laugh at the same time—to be free. The accident had almost taken her life. She couldn't keep being afraid.

Shaking off those thoughts, she stopped her car and took a deep breath. Then she stepped outside and took in the fresh country air. It was so different out here, not that far from the city. But it was far enough to relax and feel as if you were in another world. She clung to the straps of her computer bag and tried to decide where she was supposed to go.

Noah had told her he was staying in his brother's guest cottage. But she didn't know if he'd be up at the house or in the cottage. The house seemed a much safer location for the two of them to meet. She hoped at least his brother was around so they wouldn't be alone. She wasn't sure she could control herself if they were.

She heard a noise coming from the direction of the guest cottage, and she let out a sigh. She knew that was where he was. It seemed luck wasn't her friend on this pleasantly warm evening.

She moved down the path, knowing exactly where she was going. There was a huge yard in front of the cottage that couldn't be seen from the main house. It was intimate and private and not what she needed right now.

"You're a little early. I like it."

The voice came from behind her, and Sarah turned to see Noah walking up, confidence in each step he took.

"I can't stand being late. It shows disrespect," she told him. The man was getting far too close to keep her hormones under control.

"Nah, it just means you're a busy person. No disrespect intended when a person is running a little late," he said.

"You can keep telling yourself that all day long," she assured him. She really didn't do well at small talk, but any conversation she had with him was always so easy. That was another thing that drove her slightly insane.

He smiled, and her heart stuttered. She had to look away from the man, so she began playing with the strap on her large bag that had her plans in it. She'd do just about anything to keep herself distracted from Noah.

"So are you ready for some fun adventures?" he asked.

His good humor made her want to relax and fall into him, so instead she felt her body stiffen. She was fighting this feeling every step of the way.

"I'm not up for an adventure. I want to get this job done," she told him.

"I've come up with a new philosophy in life," he said. She waited, but he was quiet.

"Fine. I'll bite. What is it?" she said with an eye roll.

"Life doesn't have to be all about work. I want to do this the right way or not do it at all. You're either all in or not in at all," he told her. There was such intensity in his eyes; she wondered if he was telling her she was about to get fired from this project, like she'd already attempted to do. Maybe the best thing she could do would be to walk away, but everything inside her rebelled at doing just that. She was a competitive person, and she didn't easily walk away from anything. And now that she was truly in, she needed to finish.

Instead of just easily complying with the man, she narrowed her eyes and stiffened her spine. She wasn't going to be a pushover. No way, no how.

"Let me know more of what you have in mind, and I'll tell you if that's acceptable or not," she said.

He was quiet for several long moments before he smiled, his eyes sparkling. He knew a challenge when he saw one, and she was certainly challenging him right back. She wasn't even 100 percent sure of what she wanted, but she knew she wasn't ready to give up.

"What I have in mind about the project or about us?" he asked, his expression almost mocking.

"There absolutely, positively isn't an *us*," she said with a glare.

"I'm not going to even justify that response with an answer," he said. He looked slightly ticked at her reply. Had she somehow offended him or hurt his feelings? That was impossible. Sure, they'd slept together a while ago, but that didn't mean they were in a relationship.

He took a step toward her, and she nearly panicked. She absolutely couldn't allow this man to touch her. She'd go insane in a heartbeat. She needed to stay strong and not let him see that he intimidated her or affected her, but she also couldn't allow him to touch her. She was definitely in a quandary.

He stepped forward again, and she felt herself taking another step back. It was irritating her.

"What are you afraid of, Sarah?" he asked, his voice softer.

"Not you," she said with a glare as she stopped and stood her ground. He was getting too many wins lately when it came to the two of them. "But we need to focus on the project at hand, not on what's happened in the past between the two of us."

"Man, do you know how to make your voice grow cold when you're trying to get a point across," he said with a chuckle. "Are you putting me in my place?" He didn't seem as if she'd put him anywhere. She had a feeling the man wasn't easily intimidated or controlled. A lot of guys she'd dated had been far too weak for her. She didn't want to be a bully, but sometimes she came across that way. Her stubbornness made her too controlling sometimes. Maybe one of the things she liked about this man was the fact she couldn't control him. That gave her a liberation she couldn't explain.

He reached toward her, and she glared at him. He backed off before he'd touched her, and she was glad for that.

"We need to set some ground rules right here and now, Noah," she told him.

His lips turned up into a brilliant smile. She didn't like feeling as if she was getting laughed at, but she couldn't call him out on every little thing. They'd never get through this day if she did.

"Hmm, I've never been good with rules. Isn't there a saying about rules needing to be broken?"

"Rules are a good thing," she countered. "We're both working on this project, and I think we need some firm boundaries while we finish it."

"Well, I've never been good with boundaries," he said with a shrug. His smile was still firmly in place.

"Maybe I do need to quit," she said with a sigh. "Maybe it's impossible for us to work together."

He reached out and touched her arm, making a shiver run through her. She didn't pull away this time. "I'm sorry," he said, sincerity ringing in his voice. "I can be an ass. I know it. But sometimes breaking molds in life can give us the biggest advantages."

His voice had softened with an edge of huskiness that made her knees go weak. It was so strange the effect he had on her. If it was anyone else but him, she'd be embracing the relationship, taking it wherever it led. But he was dangerous to her sanity, and that was too scary for her to play with. It was worse than fire.

She pulled away from him, though it was hard to do. Then she looked in his eyes, keeping her expression serious. He was going to agree to her rules, or she was walking, even if it did set her way back in her career. At least her sanity was going to be okay, and that was more valuable than any job.

"Are you agreeing to listen to me or not?" she asked.

"We've been working together just fine up to this point, so I'll listen," he told her. There was a bit too much mischief in his eyes, and that worried her, but she decided to move forward in the conversation.

"Okay, then let's go over the rules," she said again.

He looked at her with humor, as if he was indulging her. She once again had to get over her irritation, or this conversation was never going to end.

"Okay then," she said with a smile. "There's to be no more flirting or innuendos. We are going to keep it professional. That means no touching and definitely no trying to have sex with me." She took a deep breath, glad she'd gotten all of that out smoothly. She ignored the smile on his face. She knew she had to continue. He wasn't saying a word.

"This is a working relationship, and we're to keep it that way. Nothing but professionalism from here on out. I love that I'm on this project, and I love your trust in me and *really* love Joseph Anderson's trust, so we're going to stick to these rules, or there are going to be consequences," she warned.

He still wasn't saying anything as he looked at her as if he were a parent indulging a mischievous child. That got her back a little bit more straight. He was going to take her seriously if it was the last thing she accomplished in her entire lifetime. Several long moments passed as she grew more and more impatient.

"Do you have anything to say?" she asked.

"I have plenty to say," he told her. The smile had never left his face. She didn't trust it one bit.

"Well, what is it?" she huffed out.

He paused long enough to let her know he was in total control of this situation. She wasn't prone to violence, but she was thinking of making an exception right about then!

"I'm going to give you a counter offer," he said in a smooth, sexy voice that had her knees once again shaking. "I won't do anything you don't want to happen."

He didn't add anything else. There were no stipulations on his part, no response to anything she'd just said. He was closing the conversation in a few choice words that had her stomach clenching. He wasn't a man to be intimidated, but she was feeling pretty damn intimidated herself right then. She might've hated him a bit for that. She wasn't giving him the satisfaction of knowing how much he'd gotten to her, though.

"Well then, I guess we're a hundred percent okay, because I don't want anything but professionalism from you. Our working relationship can continue," she told him in the haughtiest voice she could manage. His smile didn't budge one bit, but she didn't care. She'd made herself more than clear, and he'd said he wouldn't break her rules unless she was willing to break them. She wasn't worried she would. She was a strong woman who'd made men's knees shake before. This one man wasn't going to bring her down, not one little bit.

"Now that we got the boring stuff out of the way, let's get to work," he told her. She ignored his snide little remark. It wasn't boring stuff. It was electric stuff that had her heart racing and her body shaking. There was no need to admit that out loud.

"Let's see the plans," she told him instead.

He nodded and turned to head toward the cottage. She absolutely didn't want to go inside there, but she didn't really have much of a choice. She'd agreed to meet him there, and they'd come to terms with things, so she could suck it up.

They stepped inside the small cottage, and Sarah glanced around, memories of her time on this property flashing through her brain. It was mostly good memories that sent a little pang through her. But that was the past.

This was the present, and she needed to stay fully focused. If she didn't, she feared she'd be consumed by Noah, and she wouldn't even realize it was happening. And once she got caught in the eye of the storm that was all him, she feared she'd never find her way out.

CHAPTER NINE

Noah wiped his palms on his pants, shocked to realize they were sweating. He'd been in places where bullets zipped past him, nearly taking his life, and he hadn't felt as nervous as he did while Sarah sat across from him. Especially when she was talking about what they could and couldn't do together.

What was it about this particular girl? He wasn't sure. They'd had such a short amount of time together, and she was fighting him every step of the way, so why in the world was he worried about what she thought of him? He'd left women's beds before without a thought of them ever again. But not this girl, not this time.

There was something special about her, and spending more time in her presence only added to her appeal. Maybe this romance would end in a blaze of glory . . . or maybe it would lead to more. Only time was going to tell. He did know for sure that she wasn't going anywhere anytime soon—not with this massive project to be completed. Because of that, he had no doubt that their chemistry together was going to make them explode in the near future.

"This is everything I have so far. You've seen most of it, but we really do have to go to the site and work on things. Then we need to travel to other locations to make sure we get it right. We've got to get this right," Noah said as he pushed the papers toward Sarah.

"How much have you changed from the beginning?" she asked.

"I've kept the locations the same but changed some of the ways the buildings line out. I'm still not liking it, though," he told her.

"What aren't you liking?" she asked.

"I can't answer that. I don't know; I just know it's somehow not working, and I'm growing more frustrated by the minute. I create art," he said. She raised a brow. "I want to design things that people talk about long after I'm dead. I can't do that with something ordinary, so this project means a lot to me. It's a huge one for you as well, and so we need to get it right."

"I've seen things you've designed. You do have true talent, Noah. I'm actually pretty honored to be invited in as part of it all. I'm sure you could do it without me," she said. The awe in her tone made his chest puff out the slightest bit.

"I like what I do, just as I know you love what you do. I think it shows in your work," he said. "We just have to stop fighting each other so we can get it exactly right."

"Maybe we need to quit thinking about it in terms of greatness and go back to the basics. Let's go on a treasure hunt for the best buildings, take pictures of them, document the process, and show it at the grand opening. The whole process can be there for the world to see. Our pictures can hang on the walls. We can show people what buildings and places have inspired us." The more she talked, the more animated she became. She was getting excited about the idea of traveling. If it took her looking at it like a treasure hunt, he certainly wasn't going to complain.

"So you like to hunt for treasure?" he asked.

"Who doesn't want to find treasure?" she responded. The guarded expression she'd been wearing since she'd arrived evaporated as she got into her idea of searching for gold—or her version of gold, that was.

He drank a long swallow of beer before he smiled. Maybe a treasure hunt would be the thing to bring them together. Maybe it would tear down the walls she'd so carefully erected against him, and maybe it would give him a chance to find out if they had a real connection or just mind-boggling sex that would eventually end.

"Ugh, sorry. I get an idea in my head, and then I lose all reasonable thought. But there's so much art out there in the buildings that have already been created that I think we could truly be inspired. I don't like feeling stuck, and I don't want this project held up because of us," she told him.

"First of all, there's no need to apologize. Secondly, I love the idea of a treasure hunt. I wasn't sure what exactly I wanted to do, but I love this idea," he told her.

"Do you have any ideas on where to begin?" she asked.

There were so many places Noah wanted to go. But he knew each one had to be special. The first place had to draw her in so she'd want to continue this hunt, want to continue spending time with him. And he knew they really would be inspired. This was a win all the way around for both of them. For a moment he was at a loss. He wanted to keep her intrigued, keep her interested, and he couldn't do that by taking her somewhere less than extraordinary.

"Let's pull out a map and go from there," he told her.

They did just that, and over the next few hours, they studied the map and the prints they'd drawn. But as they continued studying their designs and the map, they were both intrigued by a couple of places.

"I remember being in this place once. It's a small country town, but there are buildings over a hundred years old that have been maintained. It might be the exact inspiration we're looking for," he suggested. "Let me think some more on it, but let's be ready to go tomorrow. Sometimes we just need to take a leap."

"Tomorrow won't work for me. I'm teaching a class and can't cancel. But we can go the day after."

She stood up and began packing her bags, and he had the ridiculous urge to stop her. He wasn't ready for their night to end. He never was when he spent time with her. But they'd discussed all they'd needed to today, and he wasn't going to be able to stop her without breaking one of her ridiculous rules. This rule thing was going to end real quick, if he had anything to say about it.

"Okay, then we'll get started in a day and a half," he finally said when he couldn't come up with a valid reason to delay their night.

"This is either going to be a lot of fun or a big waste of time," she warned. He found it amusing she was now the one consoling him if they didn't find what they were looking for.

"Looking for treasure is never a waste of time," he countered. "We'll find something; it just might not be what we're expecting." It might not be at all what he was looking for, but it might be exactly what he needed. Maybe Crew was getting too much in his head, because he was starting to think like a damn psychologist.

She gave him an unguarded smile that had his heart thumping. She really was one of those women who believed in magic even when she didn't want to. She might try to fight that side of herself, but when her guard was down, she couldn't help but dream. His new goal in life was to see that look of wonder and excitement in her expression every chance he could get. Whether Sarah liked it or not, she was in his life.

He had a feeling it was where she would stay. Their journey together might take them down some uncharted paths, but in the end they'd find themselves exactly where they were supposed to be.

And he had a feeling that X was going to mark the spot.

CHAPTER TEN

Sarah had always been a person to come to decisions quickly but then question herself endlessly about what she'd decided upon. Sometimes she felt good about the choices she made, and at other times she'd kick herself. Living that way could be exhausting. Why couldn't she be more carefree? Wouldn't that make life so much easier? Probably. But it might also make it pretty boring as well.

She was also a person who wanted to see the entire picture before the art was finished. That was why this veterans project was so consuming. It wasn't something that could be completed in a day. It was going to take a lot of time, and she had to allow herself to look at it like one big adventure that was to be taken in steps instead of a day-by-day thing where she had to get a certain amount done in a timely fashion.

But even if she gave herself a thousand lectures, she also knew she wasn't going to lighten up. And she knew being with Noah Anderson for any length of time was going to alter how she was feeling as well. The man flustered her. She wasn't used to that. She was used to being in control, and there was no way for her to achieve that with him. She couldn't seem to concentrate anymore—even if he wasn't there. He was constantly on her mind.

Her day had been long, and she felt weary as she strolled into a café. It was time to meet her friend for dinner. She was sure she'd forget all about Noah within seconds of being with Chloe. No one had ever been able to come between her and her best friends. If anyone had tried, they'd been quickly schooled on what true friendship meant.

"Hey, Chloe. Sorry I'm late," Sarah said with a sheepish smile. She normally was on time for everything. If it weren't for her head being in a fog right now, she'd have been early even.

"It's okay. I don't have anything else happening this evening. I'm free for us to catch up on gossip," Chloe told her as she approached.

Chloe threw her arms around Sarah, and the two of them hugged. She wished relationships with men were as easy as they were with besties. Then she wouldn't have all this indecisiveness running through her brain.

"You've been so busy lately; I feel as if you've forgotten all about me," Chloe said with a pout as she pulled back.

"I'm sorry. This project really is consuming me, and working with Noah isn't exactly a picnic," Sarah admitted.

"I know, and I totally get it, but if I go too long without seeing each other, I get cranky," Chloe told her. "And you do realize our souls are aligned, and the light begins to fade if we don't see each other's faces?" She was laughing as she said this, but there was actually some truth to her words.

"I know. I need to do better at multitasking. I can do my job and not fall off the face of the earth," Sarah assured her bestie.

"Good. Now that we have that settled, there's a reason I asked you to come to this particular location," Chloe said with barely concealed excitement.

"What's happening?" Sarah asked, feeling the excitement flow from her friend through her. It was always that way with Chloe and Brooke.

"This is mine," Chloe told her as she jumped up and down. "The name will change when we come up with a good one, but I signed the papers this morning. Brooke was supposed to come, too, but those babies weren't cooperating, so she has to wait to know. I finally have my own place! And what makes it even better is we used to come down here when we were kids. It's now all mine to do with whatever I decide."

"You bought it?"

"Yep. It's mine, *all* mine," she repeated, looking more like a teenager in her excitement than a woman. "And it will do amazing. I know it's completely meant to be," Chloe said.

"Oh my gosh, Chloe, I couldn't be more happy for you," Sarah said. She looked around the room with new eyes, excited for the possibilities. "Are you going to change it up in here or keep it the same?"

"Of course I'll make changes," Chloe said, as if she were crazy to suggest otherwise.

"I'm so proud of you for taking this step. I know it's going to be amazing because anything you put your touch to turns to gold."

"Thank you. I'm a little proud, too, and the reason things turn to gold is because I have the best people in my life to support me, encourage me, and help me every step of the way." She then turned toward the hovering waiter. "We have a special guest tonight. Give her anything she wants."

"Don't be intimidated by her. I'm low maintenance," Sarah assured the man, who smiled.

"She's lying to you," Chloe told the waiter, who was fighting not to chuckle. "But she might try to be on good behavior tonight. We'll see." Chloe turned back to Sarah. "I'm assuming you'll want our best wine." The waiter handed her a menu as soon as the words were out of Chloe's mouth. Wine sounded pretty perfect after the day she'd had.

"How about a nice glass of cabernet?" a deep male voice said from behind them, making a shiver run down Sarah's spine. Slowly, she turned and found her gaze locked with a seemingly amused Noah, who winked at her before smiling at the waiter.

"Of course, Mr. Anderson," the waiter said before he turned to go and get a bottle without waiting to see if she was going to confirm that choice or not. It was just another reminder of the power the Andersons carried.

"I don't need wine," Sarah tried to call out, but it was too late. She'd just been thinking that was exactly what she needed, but she didn't like Noah having the power he had, and she really didn't like him taking over and ordering for her, even if that would've been exactly what she would've ordered. He was observant, that was for sure. And they had spent enough time together for him to know exactly what drinks she preferred.

"Live a little," Chloe said with a smile as she turned her head to look back and forth between her and Noah. The restaurant might as well have been empty, as alone as she suddenly felt with the man she'd been avoiding all day. She wasn't supposed to see him until tomorrow. She'd been counting on the night to work up her courage. She could remain professional with him if she gave herself enough pep talks—and read some more self-help books as well.

"Are you making my help run for you?" Chloe asked before she leaned in and gave Noah a side hug. "It's good to see you."

"I always enjoy a visit with a beautiful lady, and it's good to make people run. It keeps them in shape. Did I hear correctly that you're the official owner of this place now?" Noah asked.

"You heard right," Chloe said, her smile so big she almost looked like a clown.

"How did you hear?" Sarah asked. "I just found out."

"Good news travels fast," Noah told them.

"Yes, it does, especially in a small town," Chloe said. "But I do have to run into the kitchen for a little bit. We're going to be closing down in about a week for the remodel, but I want to have people excited this week, so everything needs to run smoothly. All the staff has agreed to stay on. I can't wait."

"Well, I'm starving, so feed me something great," Noah said.

"Mmm, go with the pasta primavera. The cook made a special sauce that's amazing," Chloe suggested.

"Don't be gone too long," Sarah said, a bit of desperation in her tone. She was now avoiding looking into Noah's eyes.

"I'll hurry, but I'm sure Noah will be more than happy to keep you company in the meantime," Chloe said.

Sarah wanted to call the woman a traitor, but since she hadn't been around much, she couldn't be mean. Chloe turned and left, leaving her standing there with Noah. She didn't even want to sit. She was trying to decide if she should turn and walk away. Feeling awkward, Sarah finally did sit, and Noah smiled before taking the seat across from her.

"You, Chloe, and Brooke have a special bond not many other people share," Noah pointed out.

"Yes, we really do," she said. "But I haven't been around enough lately, and I'm missing my friends. You don't need to sit here and eat with me. I'm fine with being on my own until Chloe gets back," she added.

"I need to eat, too, and I've always liked this place." The smile he gave her was enough to make her knees weak again. The waiter returned with the bottle of wine, and Noah took it from him. "I'll pour." The man left, and he filled both their glasses.

"Thank you," she murmured, picking up the glass and taking a big gulp.

"I have a suggestion," he told her with a wink. "Why don't we play a little game?"

The wine was perfection, but if she wasn't careful, she was going to start talking too much. Alcohol did strange things to her, and though she was always an honest person, alcohol made her a freaking open book.

"What are you talking about?" she asked as she stupidly took another big swallow of the delicious red.

"If we are going to have an adventure, we're gonna spend a lot of time together. Let's see if we can get through a single meal first," he challenged.

"That's a game?" she asked.

"*Life* is a game," he replied with a smile before he sipped again while his eyes trailed down the V of her neck. That made her breathing instantly deepen.

"I don't believe that," she said sadly.

There had been times in her life she'd laughed a heck of a lot more. Growing up really sucked sometimes. Being responsible wasn't a barrel of fun, but it was what you had to do—or so she'd been told.

"So you aren't willing to bend?" he asked, challenge in his eyes.

That made her hackles rise. He was challenging her, and it wasn't easy for her to walk away from a challenge. She knew he was doing it on purpose, knew he wanted a reaction from her, but even logically knowing this, she couldn't seem to stop herself from playing right into his hands.

"I can sit here and behave just fine. It's you who can't," she told him, lifting her glass only to realize it was empty. She'd polished that off way too quickly. Still, she didn't complain when Noah reached out and refilled the glass. Maybe it would take the edge off. Maybe she could learn a bit of control and keep the zipper closed on her lips.

"To mutual understanding," Noah said as he lifted his glass. She only hesitated a moment before she clinked hers against his, almost feeling as if she were making a deal with the devil. She probably had done that the first time she'd met this man.

Noah leaned a bit closer, and Sarah felt that urge to run again, but at the same time she wasn't sure if she wanted to run *to* him or *away* from him. It was killing her not knowing what to do.

"I failed to mention how sexy you look," he said, his eyes stripping her dress away, making her feel as if she were waking up in one of those nightmares where you're nude in front of the entire school. "You look as good clothed as naked."

There was no doubt her next sip went down wrong, making her choke. Noah's low growl and hooded eyes were causing her to shiver and sweat at the same time. He didn't know the meaning of playing fair. He did know how to send her into a puddle at his feet.

But she was an adult, and she should be able to stop him with nothing more than a look. She'd laid out the ground rules, and she needed to enforce what she'd said the night before. If she allowed him to continue in this train of thought, he'd think it was acceptable the entire time they were on this adventure she'd come up with. She still wasn't quite sure how that had happened. She'd gone to the house more determined than ever to keep things professional, and then in the blink of an eye, she was asking him to go on a treasure hunt with her.

The man was good. He was so smooth she wasn't even sure anymore which were her ideas and which ones were his. He had a way of getting her to do something she hadn't wanted to do without her realizing she was not only doing it but doing so with a smile on her face. Was this what it was like to have the kind of power he had? She couldn't imagine how good the man must feel every single day of his life. She wondered if he'd ever been told no with emphasis and meaning behind it. She'd rather walk through fire ants than tell him any of the thoughts she was having. Luckily the waiter returned, giving Sarah a few extra moments to figure out what to do next.

"Have you decided on dinner?" the waiter asked.

Sarah tried to reply but found her voice gone. That was something she might be grateful for soon, but not at this particular moment. Not once Noah began speaking.

"We're both going to have the pasta primavera, thanks to the suggestion of Chloe. We'll also have salads with house dressing, stuffed mushrooms for an appetizer, and the house-made bread, please."

The waiter looked at Sarah, and she thought about ordering something completely different from what he'd just said just to assert her independence, but what he'd ordered actually sounded pretty great. She just gave the man a nod so he'd know it was okay.

Once they were alone again, Sarah looked over and got caught in Noah's gaze. She wanted to correct him for ordering for her, but she could only call him out on so much before she felt like she was always complaining. She didn't want to be that person. Besides, the smirk he was wearing told her he was waiting for just that. She refused to be predictable, so she simply picked up her glass and took another sip and tried to let her irritation with the man fade.

It was time for a conversation not involving anything to do with the two of them, though. She didn't mind finding more out about the man. He had an interesting story to be told.

"So did you stay in contact with your family over the years before this project?" Sarah asked. Maybe a change of subject was just what they needed. She was going to prove just how civil the two of them could act around each other. The fact that they'd slept together didn't need to dictate how they now behaved.

"We've always been close, but there were times we went too long without talking. I've vowed to never let that happen again. The past year has been too great to let that feeling go again."

"That's good," Sarah said, meaning it. "How do you like being an uncle?"

"Those girls are amazing!" he said with a brilliant smile. "I wouldn't mind a few like them, but that would require me staying in one place for a very long time, and I'm not sure I have that in me," he told her.

His words shocked her. Sarah didn't know how to respond. She decided it was nothing more than words. He didn't at all seem like the fatherly type. She didn't take him as the marrying type, either. Of course, that was what she'd always assumed about herself as well, but the older she was getting, the more she was thinking about her future. Did she really want to be alone the rest of her life? Did she want to watch her best friends get married and have perfect little families while she remained the crazy aunt who made the kids kiss her on the cheek? Was she going to be that cat lady the town folks talked about? A shudder ran through her. She didn't generally care what people thought about her, but she was beginning to wonder if her independence was so valuable to her that it was worth the loneliness that ensued.

"You seem too adventurous to settle down and have kids," she finally said. She wasn't quite sure how long the silence had lasted that time. She could get lost in her own head for hours on end.

"I love adventure," he admitted. "Which is why we're going to have fun on this treasure hunt. I think you need and want some thrills of your own. You're trying to hide it, but the more I look into your eyes, the more I see how much you want it. I promise you that's not a bad thing."

"Maybe I do want to do something I haven't done before," she said almost defiantly. "That doesn't mean I don't love what I do or my day-to-day life."

"So you've come to me for adventure?"

"*You* came to *me*," she pointed out.

"But *you* chose to stay," he said with such intensity she felt glued to her seat. "And the treasure hunt was *your* idea. I was just planning on hanging out at the construction site. I like your idea much, *much* better."

The waiter set down the bread, salads, and mushrooms before quickly disappearing again. She took the opportunity to compose herself and take a few needed breaths and a couple more sips of wine. She was trying to slow down, but it was having the effect she wanted, and her nerves were calming. She just needed to find the sweet spot where she wasn't so nervous, but she wasn't so over the top Noah would be able to draw any information he wanted out of her.

"I did choose to stay, Noah, because I like the idea of creating something that's never been created before. And I *am* inspired by things around me. I don't think anyone can do a creative job by sitting in an office. I think it dulls our brains and, even worse, our hearts, which we need to do art. But this has nothing to do with wanting an adventure, and it *really* doesn't have to do with a need to spend time with you," she scolded.

Feeling much better at getting that off her chest, she lifted her fork, forced herself to spear some lettuce and tomato, and took a bite. She was sure it tasted amazing. Right now she was having a hard time enjoying the meal, though.

"I think you're protesting an awful lot for someone who came up with the idea," Noah said, his posture lazy, his eyes crinkling as he smiled before taking a bite of his food and sighing. "This place has never disappointed. It will get even better with Chloe here. She's a perfection-ist in the best way possible."

It was unmanageable for Sarah to stay irritated with the man when he was complimenting one of her two best friends. If a person wanted to get close to her, loving her besties was a good way to do it. If she was being perfectly honest with herself, she would have to admit there were some pretty great qualities about Noah. He was a positive person who treated others pretty dang well. But that didn't mean he was a good mate to have. It was just an excellent quality he possessed.

"You don't look like you eat too much," she said, not able to keep her eyes from scanning his hard chest and flat abs. He might enjoy food, but he was obviously incredibly active as well.

"Baby, I know exactly how to burn off my meals," he said, giving her another wink. She glared at him.

"Stop turning everything I say into a sexual innuendo," she said. She speared a mushroom and stuffed it in her mouth. It was a bit too hot, and she wanted to open her mouth right away, but there wasn't a chance she was giving him that satisfaction. She just chewed and tried not to concentrate on the burning heat on her tongue.

For a moment Noah's eyes narrowed the slightest bit, and she saw an edge of temper in his expression. That was fascinating. It took her mind off her hot food as she finally swallowed and waited to hear whatever was on his mind.

"We have something. I just want you to quit fighting it," he said.

"I agree there's chemistry between us. But our time came and went. I want it made clear we're no longer lovers."

"Maybe we haven't been in a long time, but we've definitely burned up some sheets," he told her. She looked around as her cheeks flamed. No one appeared to have overheard him. She wasn't sure why she was letting it embarrass her. They were single people who'd done nothing wrong in sleeping together. But it wasn't something she wanted announced to the world, either.

"Can you act a bit more professional?" she asked. His smile grew.

"You're allowed to let go and act a bit unprofessional," he countered. "I'd be more than happy to help you with it. It's a new lesson in life I've been embracing, and I don't think I have any desire to go back to who I was. I'm having a lot more fun with this new philosophy in life."

She took his words seriously. She chewed on them for a few moments as she considered what he was saying. She didn't want to be so stubborn that she wouldn't hear good advice even if she considered the person giving it to be the enemy.

"I do let go sometimes," she said. Then it was her turn to give him a sassy smile. "But I'm very picky who I do it with." Her smile grew bigger. "It won't be you."

"I think I'll change your mind. There's a tigress inside you that's begging to be set free. I'm making it my mission to be the one to release it."

Surprisingly, Sarah found herself chuckling. "Is that a line you've used before?" she asked. Maybe it was the wine, and maybe he was simply wearing her down. She was beginning to find this conversation amusing. Yes, he turned her on, but he also intrigued her and challenged her. She was beginning to like that a whole lot. She never had been able to resist a challenge.

"I've never needed to use it before. I've also never had a woman so resistant to me, though, so this is all-new territory for me," he said with a shrug. He didn't appear at all fazed by her repeated rejections. The man was damn confident. She wasn't going to tell him how much of a turn-on that was for her.

"I bet you've had many women fall at your feet," she said.

"Just as I'm sure you've had men following you around like obedient puppy dogs. I'm sure they didn't even need a leash," he countered.

She laughed again, feeling completely at ease. She couldn't help but enjoy a conversation with someone who not only sparred with her but challenged her, made her laugh, and wasn't in the least intimidated by a thing she did or said. She'd chased many men away with nothing more than a simple look.

"I've dated and possibly made a few men quake in their pretty little leather shoes," she told him. That wiped the smile from his face, and she laughed again as she held up her glass. "Let's toast to new adventures and lost puppies." Surprise popped into his expression, making her glad she was growing so relaxed. It was good to not be predictable.

"Yes, to adventures and . . . puppies," he told her as he clinked his glass against hers. "*And* hot, sweaty, exciting nights."

She didn't try to argue with him. If he wanted hot, sweaty nights, he could have them. She wasn't agreeing to be a part of those nights, though it wasn't an unpleasant thought. Not an unpleasant thought at all.

"Now that we've gotten as many innuendos and flirting attempts out of the way as possible, can we talk about work, or do you not know how to do that?" she asked. She was completely relaxed now and didn't care either way how the conversation went in reality. But she did find that she enjoyed pushing his buttons.

He sat for a long moment as he sipped on his wine and analyzed her. She was tipsy enough that she didn't mind. She could tell he was thinking deeply. There was no need to ask him what it was about, because she knew he was going to either tell her or ask another question soon enough. When he opened his mouth to speak, she just smiled.

"Would it have made a difference this past year if I'd simply held you captive for a week or month straight?" he asked. He said this with such seriousness it took several times of running his words through her brain before the words processed. The man was utterly shameless, and though she thought she had no filter, she was beginning to think he had even less than her.

She wanted to tell him it wouldn't have made any difference at all, but she wasn't sure that was true. If she was locked away with this man, she feared she'd never be able to willingly walk away. If she told him that, though, the amount of power she would be handing over would be something she'd never recover.

"Since that didn't happen, I guess neither of us will ever know the answer to your question," she said with a bit of sass and a lot of satisfaction at his shock. He recovered much more quickly than she was able to, though.

"Maybe. But sometimes if you don't think of the past or the future, the present doesn't matter," he said slowly. "And you never know when a good kidnapping is going to take place. Be careful of the challenges you throw out there, Sarah. I never have been able to resist a good one." She had no doubt it was a warning. But it was one that made her instantly want to challenge him. The man turned her on unlike anything she'd ever felt before.

She sat across from him as he put kinky thoughts into her head. Would their bodies still slide perfectly against one another's? Would he kiss his way down her shoulders, cup her breasts, whisper in her ear, and cause havoc through her system? Would his mouth make its way between her cleavage and latch on to that sweet spot at her hip that drove her to madness? No other man but him had found it, and just thinking of that made her wet and eager. It had been nine months since she'd last slept with the man. That was far from a lifetime, but it was long enough that she was seriously hurting at the thought of not having him buried deep within her.

Judging by the satisfied look on Noah's face, she had no doubt that he was very aware of the thoughts he'd put inside her head. He had a large enough ego he was obviously pleased with himself. She wanted to shoot him down, but she was now aching too badly to come up with something good enough to do just that.

He'd wanted to play a game—and he was doing very, *very* well at it. She was definitely losing this battle of words and looks. However, she was surviving the evening, and she could definitely give herself some major credit for that. It passed by in a blur, and before she knew it, the dinner was finished.

The waiter brought out coffee with dessert, and she gratefully sipped it, needing to clear her head as Noah stayed abnormally quiet. It was much wiser for her to keep her mouth shut now and try to sober up. If a winner had to be called for the evening, he was going home with the gold medal.

"Since we're starting so early tomorrow, I think we can definitely call it a night," she finally told him. Had five minutes passed? Ten? She wasn't sure. He was just as good at knowing when to stop talking as he was at using his words wisely for maximum impact.

He smiled. There was so much behind that expression she wondered what it was he was thinking. But she wasn't going to ask. If he wanted to tell her something, he certainly would. If he wanted to keep a secret, she was more than confident he'd do just that, too.

"I'll let us call it a night. We do have an early day tomorrow," he said, as if he was bestowing a gift upon her.

When he rose, she tried to do the same, but her knees were shaking. She found him leaning over her as she tried to tell herself to breathe. He affected her so much—it was insane.

"I'll walk you out." He was standing incredibly close as he said this, and his heated breath caressed her flushed cheeks.

"I can get myself to the door," she replied.

"I'm very aware you can take care of yourself, but I was taught much better than to let a lady walk herself out," he said before pushing a lock of her hair from her face and letting his fingers trail down the side of her cheek.

She inhaled sharply before calling herself a few names. She was a grown woman in control of her emotions. Noah had clearly been in charge this entire night, and she was going to have to give herself some major talks before falling asleep, because she wasn't allowing that to continue to happen. They had a partnership, and it was time she stepped up beside him instead of constantly being a few steps behind.

"I need to go, Noah," she said, her voice a bit more steady.

He held out his arm. She rolled her eyes but took his elbow. It was going to happen, so she'd rather it was slightly her choice rather than having him take her hand and place it through the crook of his arm. She'd forgotten Chloe was supposed to come back out and join them. Her friend was an utter traitor.

When they made it outside, the streets were empty and quiet as he walked her to her car. Her slight buzz was long gone, but she wasn't sure her trembling legs were going to allow her to drive. She might be sitting there for quite some time. They didn't talk as they moved down the street. She took in plenty of cool breaths, glad for the coffee she'd consumed.

"Thank you for dinner," she said. He'd paid so quickly she hadn't had a chance to pitch in.

Noah didn't say anything else as he turned her body, causing her to face him. He looked into her eyes, and she caught her breath, waiting to see what was going to happen next. If he kissed her, she wasn't sure she'd stop him. He pulled her against him, not with force but with confidence. She allowed it, though she offered a minor protest.

"You're breaking the rules," she warned.

"Rules are always made to be broken, and this is long overdue," he countered.

The desire in his tone matched the hunger in her body. His gentleness ended as he closed the gap between the two of them. There was zero hesitation on her part or his as his lips finally touched hers again. She quickly forgot why she'd been fighting him so much.

The first time the man had kissed her, she'd forgotten her own name. It was even more intense now. Knowing his touch and what he could do to her was an aphrodisiac she couldn't resist. Her hands reached over his shoulders, and she tugged him closer as her mind shut down and her body awoke.

He smelled of sweat and musk, and she wiggled against him as she tried getting closer. It was just a kiss—just one kiss. It couldn't hurt anyone. But it could bring a lot of pleasure and a lot of pain later. Maybe the pain was worth it.

Before she could even think of getting too lost in his embrace, though, he pulled back from her. It took a few moments for her to realize the kiss had ended. She opened her eyes and saw fire in his expression. He was looking at her with such intensity it made her sway into him, causing him to groan.

She'd been so resolved, so intent on being strong, and then with one simple touch, all of her convictions had flown out the window. Panic invaded her as her throat closed. He seemed to feel the difference in her, because he let her go and took a step back, as if he didn't trust himself not to touch her if he wasn't farther away.

"I'll see you in the morning," he said. He didn't look at her again, just turned and walked away. She didn't budge from the spot as he moved down the street and disappeared from sight. She wasn't sure how long she stood there, but eventually the cool night air got to her, and she climbed into her car.

She feared it was going to be a very long, restless night. He'd begun the evening wanting to play a game she hadn't wanted to play. She was also aware she'd gone along with him and even more aware there'd been a winner and a loser.

And she most definitely hadn't been the winner.

The most surprising thing of all was she didn't mind all that much. Sarah had always been a very black-and-white person with an undertone of believing in magic, fairy tales, and Santa Claus. But one thing had never changed her whole life, and that was she wanted to win at all costs.

Suddenly she found herself not knowing what to do because she didn't mind losing to him. But maybe that was because even if she felt she was losing, she also knew deep down inside that she was also winning.

Yep, she was in trouble . . . big, huge, monstrous trouble.

Chapter Eleven

Sarah knew she should assist Noah as she watched him loading up the sleek airplane with more supplies than they could possibly use. But instead, she sat back, out of sight, and watched. He truly was a treat to behold. And since she wasn't able to turn off her thoughts, she might as well go with it.

His hair was ruffled as he grinned while singing along to a song he had playing loudly. He looked far too charming in his aviator sunglasses and sun-kissed skin. It was so effortless for him to look good she was sure he didn't even think about it anymore. Maybe he'd been one of those typical teens who'd primped in front of a bathroom mirror for hours, but now she pictured him as a man who climbed from bed and grabbed the clothes on the closest hanger before running his fingers through his hair and calling it good.

He was gorgeous. No effort was needed. Today he wore a pair of dark jeans and a blue polo shirt that she knew matched his piercing gaze. He grabbed another bag and set it in the back of the plane, making the muscles in his arms tighten, stretching the fabric of his shirt in the most delightful way.

He literally took her breath away. He was rugged and handsome but sleek at the same time. And he made her entire body burn. His looks didn't hurt in the least, but it was the total package of the man that had her so intrigued.

If the man hadn't walked away from her the night before, she wasn't sure she'd have been able to keep on telling him no. She felt such a strong pull toward him that if he pushed her much more, they'd both get what she truly wanted. She might be smart enough to know Noah was bad for her, but she was also a woman with needs, and she knew beyond a shadow of a doubt he could satisfy any cravings she was having.

Her stomach clenched as her mind flashed through the last time they'd made love. Going on a treasure hunt with Noah hadn't been one of the brightest ideas she'd ever come up with. But it was too late to back out now. She needed adventure, needed to spread her wings more, and needed to not live in fear. She wasn't used to feeling that emotion. She *really* needed the heck out of her small office.

And she needed to give herself a break. He was a beautiful man, after all. And what harm did it really do to take a peek or two at him? As long as she was smart enough to keep her dang hands off of him, she'd be just fine. She could look her fill, have a few lustful thoughts, and then be the professional she'd spent a lot of time, money, and energy to become.

She'd tried reading one of her favorite self-help books the night before, but instead of the words inspiring her, they'd disgusted her. Normally she was a perfectly reasonable and logical person. She could be impulsive, but not where it truly counted.

Noah loaded the last bag into the plane, and Sarah couldn't stand there staring at him any longer. He'd wonder where she was, since she wasn't ever a person to be late.

With a sigh, she pushed away from her semihiding place and began walking across the private jet strip. She had a feeling it was going to be a very, *very* long day. The excitement brewing in her stomach betrayed how much she wanted to be there, though. She might be afraid of what she was feeling with Noah, but at the same time, she was embracing this adventure the two of them were taking together. She truly couldn't make up her mind about what she wanted or needed.

She drew closer, with Noah's back still to her. There was a restless energy about him that told her more than anything that he wasn't a man to sit still. Even if she were to let her guard down, she wasn't sure where that would leave the two of them. She might have an adventurous soul beneath her professional demeanor, but she was also a homebody. She'd never be able to leave her friends and family—not even for true love. She feared too much the love she felt for those left behind would end up making her feel resentment toward anyone who tried to pull her away.

Sarah was still several yards behind Noah when he turned and smiled. She hadn't made a sound, but she wouldn't be surprised if there were waves coming off her body, alerting him she was there. That magnetic pull between them seemed to only grow stronger the longer they circled one another. She had a feeling that sensation would last a lifetime—or possibly take them both down until they couldn't get back up.

"I think this might be the first time you've ever been late for something," he said as he licked his bottom lip, sending a little thrill straight to her core. The combo of his deep voice and solid jaw was one that had melted her on more than one occasion. Wet lips just added to the overall perfect picture the man made doing nothing more than standing in front of her. This really was going to be a torturous plane ride. The thing wasn't big enough for the two of them. Then again, she had a feeling a 747 wasn't big enough to calm her hormones, even with them on opposite ends of the plane.

"I got caught up in traffic," she said, which was a lie. She'd been at the small airport awhile, but she'd been enjoying the view for far longer than she'd ever admit.

His smile grew wider, and she wondered if he had known she'd been standing where she'd been the entire time. She shifted on her feet as she grew more and more nervous by the second. Noah might like to come across as a lighthearted playboy, but she knew the amount of intelligence he possessed. She decided she was sticking to her story, and there was nothing he could do about it.

He didn't say anything to counter her, just walked over to the passenger side of the small aircraft and opened the door, then held out a hand. She stood there, unable to make her feet move.

"We're losing daylight," he told her with a small chuckle.

She let out another sigh as she moved forward, ignoring his hand as she gripped the small rail beside the door. She stepped up and climbed inside the compact plane. It was definitely small, but not uncomfortably so. She glanced behind her and saw two rows. It could comfortably carry six people for a weekend getaway or a sightseeing flight.

Her door shut, and she had only a moment alone inside the shiny plane before his door opened, and he climbed inside. The space considerably shrunk with him in there with her. His legs spread out a bit, and his thigh brushed hers. He seemed utterly comfortable in his space as he began to click on buttons and prepare for their flight. She was trying to slowly shift her leg away from his without him noticing. She didn't want him to know it was bothering her. But there really wasn't anywhere for her to go.

She watched as he grabbed his seat belt, and she did the same, trying to figure out how the buckle worked. Of course it couldn't be simple like the ones in a car. She looked at him out of the corner of her eye and then tried to do the same. She failed.

"Have you been in a small plane before?" he asked.

She was still busy fiddling with her seat belt. He didn't say anything, just leaned over and grabbed it, latching it into place in less than a second. She didn't bother thanking him, as she hadn't asked for his help.

"No, I haven't," she told him, her breath just a tad husky. He'd been fast buckling her in, but his fingers had brushed her hip, and anywhere the man caressed her made her skin burn, whether there were clothes in the way or not. She knew what it felt like to have nothing between the two of them. She also had no doubt he'd touched that particular place on purpose, as every time his lips went there, her hips had arched, and she hadn't been able to control the moan. They might not have slept together for a long time, but he'd learned her body as well as a violinist learned their instrument.

"Do you get sick or have any fear of flying?" he asked.

"No. I fly commercially some, and I'm not a superfan of turbulence, but I get through it," she said.

"Well, we couldn't have picked a better day for a nice flight. The skies are clear, and the winds calm. We have about a two-hour flight since we're going to take a scenic route. We can speed it up on the way back."

"Where are we going? I know there were a few places."

"I researched the ghost towns, and the best one is Shaniko, Oregon. It was abandoned in the mid-twentieth century, but several of the old buildings are still standing, including the jail, city hall, water tower, chapel, and more. It's definitely a tourist destination, and they've revived the town in recent years to encourage visitors, but they protect it, so if we start at the beginning, we will have a good idea of where to go from there," he said.

"I think that sounds perfect. I've never been there, and I've made it a mission to visit as many historic places around the United States as I possibly can," she said, feeling instant excitement. "Let's go."

He chuckled as he faced forward and began messing with the controls on the plane. There were so many of them she wasn't sure how he could keep them all straight. It seemed like an impossible task to her.

He started the plane, and she was pleasantly surprised how quiet it was. She'd heard that small planes could be obnoxiously loud. He handed over her headphones and then began taxiing out toward the runway.

"Hold on tight, and prepare for takeoff," he said through the headphones.

"Aren't you going to demonstrate the safety features?" she asked with a smile. She was getting more and more excited, even enough to not let his leg pressing against hers distract her . . . too much. She was always aware he was touching her.

"Hmm, you might have to play the flight attendant and demonstrate those for me," he said as he faced her for a moment and gave her a wink.

"Your mind went straight to the gutter, didn't it?" she said, trying not to smile.

"Yep," he admitted, his lips turning up into a huge grin. She had a hard time not enjoying the flirtation and easy banter with him.

Sadly she decided she'd better stop now before the conversation got too out of hand. They were only at the beginning of their trip, and the sexual tension was already almost too much for her to take. They didn't need to add in wordplay and make it worse.

It didn't take long for him to reach the head of the runway, and then they were lifting up into the sky in one smooth motion. Her lips spread wide as she watched the ground grow smaller beneath them.

She might fly commercially for work and pleasure, but never had she been in a small plane. There was freedom inside one that she could see could grow addictive. She wanted to see everything below them. It was magical, and she was a person who believed magic was something everyone needed in their life. It had gotten her through some difficult times.

"Are you having fun?" Noah asked. She glanced at him and saw he wore a matching grin.

"This is amazing," she admitted. If she could always travel this way, she might enjoy going places a heck of a lot more.

He didn't turn away from her, and their gazes locked together. The pull was so strong she wanted to close the slight gap between them and run her tongue across his bottom lip, as he himself had done earlier that day. It was amazing how quickly this man made her want. She could go from eager excitement to burning desire in the blink of an eye. He opened those beautiful lips to say something, and she finally had the strength to turn away from him. Her hormones were positively out of control.

"If you keep looking at me like that, I'm likely to crash," he warned in a low growl that had her stomach clenching.

"I'm working on it," she told him. There was no use in denying it. There was something to be said about a person protesting too much.

He let the subject go, and she focused instead on the ground below them. She wasn't sure how high they were, but the animals in the fields underneath seemed like tiny ants, so it was high enough that if they did crash, it wouldn't go well. It was safer for both of them for her to keep her eyes glued to the window.

After several minutes of silence Sarah began to relax again. Yes, his leg was still pressed against hers, but he was a skilled pilot. She'd never even thought to ask him how much time he had flying or what had made him decide to get his license before she'd hopped into a plane with him. Maybe that was because she trusted the man more than she cared to admit.

"What made you decide to become a pilot?" she asked, thinking talking would be wiser than this intense silence between them.

"I had several friends who flew, and it always looked fun, so I decided to give it a try," he told her with a shrug.

"And, of course, anything you try, you excel at," she said with a smile.

"Of course," he answered cockily.

"Isn't it expensive to become a pilot?" she asked.

"I had friends who helped me, so it didn't cost much at the time," he told her.

Money would never be a problem for him again, as he was an Anderson, but she knew he'd grown up as poor as she had. His family was even more impressive because of their humble beginnings. Each of the brothers had made something out of their lives when the odds had been stacked against them. There was a lot to be impressed about when it came to Noah Anderson.

"I think it's something I wouldn't mind attempting," she told him, feeling a bit unsure as she said the words.

"I can give you a lesson right now," he said.

She looked at him, and he was still smiling, but he looked serious. The funny thing was how tempted she was. But she wasn't an impulsive person. She'd have to study it first and see if it was something she truly wanted to do.

"No." She felt a bit of panic at how much she wanted to take him up on it. "I'd have to read everything about it first," she said more calmly. She needed to remember that. Noah made her want to do things she'd never have thought about doing before. She wasn't sure how she felt about that. Was it a good or bad thing?

He chuckled. "If you can drive a car, you can fly a plane. It looks a lot more complicated than it is," he assured her.

"I'll take your word for it. You go ahead and fly us for now. I'll read up on it and see if it's something I actually want to do."

"Your loss," he said, sounding slightly disappointed. It surprised her that that bothered her. She found she didn't want him to be disappointed in her. "But if I get knocked out, you're going to have to figure it out real quick."

She turned and glared at him, and he chuckled again. "I'm glad to see you amuse yourself so much," she huffed.

"I've learned that life's too short to not laugh often, especially at ourselves."

"I actually agree with that. I still have a hard time letting go sometimes," she said with another sigh.

"Yeah, that can be difficult," he told her, seeming to understand.

"Well, at least I'm getting an adventure while we're working on this project," she said. This might not be nearly as exciting as the adventures he took on a regular basis, but for her it was pretty great.

The more relaxed she became as they continued to fly, the more she noticed their bodies aligning. The back seats had a bit of space between them, but these front seats seemed made for lovers to cuddle. That didn't seem the wisest idea for the person responsible for keeping them all alive.

She turned, finding his eyes on her again. She pulled in a breath, inhaling his musky scent. How long had they been in the air?

"I've warned you about that look," he said in a husky drawl.

Maybe if she were on a true adventure, she'd lean in and run her tongue over his bottom lip before gently biting down on it. Maybe if she were a seductress, she could take pleasure in making his pants tight and his body throb. But she wasn't that. All she was currently doing was torturing herself.

She turned away and let out a shaky breath. They'd been in the air a long time. "How close are we?"

She could feel the grin he was wearing as he answered her.

"We have about thirty minutes," he told her after a significant pause. He'd waited long enough to let her know he wasn't completely letting her off the hook. He was so much better at playing these games than she was.

She tried focusing on the outside of the plane, but the longer they went without talking, the more she internalized in her own head, and right now that wasn't a very safe place for her to be.

"I *am* grateful to get this new perspective, Noah," she finally told him. "I know I was resistant to the entire plan, but I need inspiration. I don't know what's been going on with me lately, but I'm not doing my best work. Thanks for not giving up on me. This job truly does mean a lot to me."

He reached over and squeezed her thigh. It was an assuring touch, a friend comforting her. But there was no time Noah touched her that it didn't make her burn. She didn't look him in the eyes this time, or she feared they really would crash, because the simplest touch from him had her insides burning, which she was sure would reflect in her expression.

"I needed the inspiration as well, so I'm glad we came up with it together," he told her. "Don't thank me. You were hired for this project because Joseph knew you were the right person for the job. He knew we'd make a good team. And we do. We push each other, and we expect as much greatness from ourselves as from each other, so that means we're going to give the best facilities these men can possibly have and deserve. Besides, I hate sitting all day. It's much better to move."

"Thank you," she told him, meaning it. She wanted to reach out and squeeze his arm, let him know how much his words meant to her, but she was already tense enough at the sexual tension between them.

She wondered if the two of them would actually be friends if that tension wasn't there. She did like the guy. She could tell herself all day long she didn't, that he was a playboy Casanova, but she'd been around him long enough to know that wasn't the case at all. He was a great friend. Maybe she'd get over her hormones, and they could have a friendship.

But if they did, that meant she'd have to deal with watching him with other women, and that wasn't something she thought she'd ever be strong enough to handle. Maybe. The world could also quit spinning.

"Are you still glad you became an architect?" Noah asked.

"Sometimes I annoy myself at my poutiness when I should be grateful for the fact that I graduated college and I get to work in a career I want. I shouldn't need anything more," she told him.

Noah laughed, and the sound was so carefree she couldn't help but join him. He was just so easy to be with most of the time. She could almost imagine what fun it would've been to grow up in his family. The love and laughter must have always freely flowed.

"It's okay to not be satisfied all the time. We'll never push forward and try to achieve more if we get too comfortable with where we are," he said.

"I can agree with that," she said. "And I like looking at it that way a whole lot more than my way."

"Good. We're starting our descent now, so be prepared for some ear popping."

She hadn't realized so much time had passed. It really did fly by when she was with this man. He made everything else melt away. That was the thought that popped into her head more than anything else.

He was quiet as he guided the plane smoothly closer and closer to the ground. Maybe if she could climb out of this small space and have a little bit of distance from this man, she'd be able to think more clearly once more.

Maybe not.

She wasn't sure she'd ever be the same person again—not after knowing and making love with Noah Anderson. She had a feeling he was the type of man who impacted a person for the rest of their life.

The plane landed with barely a bump. She was stuck inside her head as they taxied up to a small building where a large SUV waited for them. He'd thought of everything for their trip. She hadn't had to do a thing. It was pretty nice to be taken care of, actually. She was so used to being the one who had to be responsible; she could understand the appeal of being with a man like Noah, who she was completely confident would get things done.

He stopped the plane and then looked at her. She began to fiddle with her seat belt, needing to get out into the fresh air. But he laid a hand against hers, and she stopped, looking at him and the intense expression he was wearing.

"I'm trying desperately to give you the space and time you're asking for, but there is something special between the two of us, Sarah. The sooner you quit fighting it, the more we can explore it. I'm a patient man, but we all have a breaking point."

Sarah inhaled sharply as her gaze was lost in his. She didn't know how to respond to him, and she didn't think her throat would loosen enough to do so, even if she did have words to say.

Their stare lasted a long time before he finally looked down, breaking the spell. She finally took in a breath, realizing she was a bit light headed. Her belt finally unsnapped, and she desperately reached for the handle on the door.

He was throwing out a new challenge to her.

And she wasn't so sure she wanted to turn it down.

CHAPTER TWELVE

Noah could be a gentleman if he needed to. But most of the time he chose the other route. Being the good guy was dull and didn't offer much. His patience in waiting for Sarah to realize they were made for each other was growing thin.

He'd enjoyed their plane ride together, but it had also been pure hell in another sense. Her leg pressed against his for nearly two hours had left him hard and terribly uncomfortable for the entire ride. When she sneaked those sexy glances at him, it had taken all his control not to grab her and kiss her like her eyes were begging him to do.

He climbed from the plane and walked over to help Sarah out, but she was on the ground before he could. It might be better not to touch her for a while. He needed to get his body in control again, or this was going to be one hell of a long day.

There was no one at this small airport, and he had some fantasies about taking her right there against the side of his plane. He'd never wanted to bring a woman to his plane before, had never fantasized about all the positions the two of them could try in and on it, either. But Sarah made him want it all. Hell, thoughts like that weren't helping the bulge in his pants disappear.

It wasn't like he was some hormonal acne-riddled teenage boy. He could control himself a hell of a lot better than he'd been doing. But dammit, that kiss the night before had nearly done him in. It had been months since he'd had her beneath him, crying out in pleasure as her body clenched around him.

That kiss had reminded him of everything the two of them were missing out on because she was being so damn stubborn. He never would've chased after a woman so hard—never before Sarah, that was.

Maybe it was the intensity of their relationship, and maybe it was the fact that she was a treasure all by herself. But whatever it was, his hormones weren't evaporating as he'd like them to, and he simply wasn't interested in anyone but her.

Noah didn't try saying anything else as he moved to the back of the plane and grabbed their bags, moved over to the SUV, and found the key right where it was supposed to be. He loaded their things inside the vehicle, then moved away from it. They'd been cooped up in the plane for nearly two hours. He needed to stretch his legs before climbing into another box, even a roomy one.

"Where are you going?" Sarah asked when he walked farther away.

"I need to walk for a minute. We have about an hour drive from here, and I want to stretch my legs for at least ten minutes," he told her.

She moved up beside him. "That's a good idea," she said with a happy sigh. She stood a good two feet away from him, but he could still smell her sweet perfume and practically feel the heat coming off her body in waves. He picked up his pace—she easily matched it.

"You're a really great pilot. I didn't have one moment I was afraid at all," she told him.

"I'd never want to scare someone who goes up in the air with me. I have an awe and respect of flying."

"I can see that."

The two of them went silent again, and Noah felt his fingers twitch with the need to reach out and clasp her hand in his. She was so easy to be with. If she'd quit fighting this feeling between the two of them, they could so be making magic together instead of having all of this tension between the two of them.

After about ten minutes Noah turned to move back to the vehicle. They only had so much time in the day to get things done, and they'd get to walk around plenty in the ghost town they were headed to.

They got to the SUV, and Noah pulled out his map and looked.

"Don't you have GPS?" she asked as she checked the bars on her phone, then looked at him with confusion.

"Yes, I have GPS, but it doesn't hurt to study a map. It's becoming a lost art," he told her.

She laughed a bit sheepishly. "It's easy to get lost in technology," she said.

"And then no one knows what to do when the electronics go down," he replied.

"That's true. I can read a map, though," she said with a shrug.

"Good, then you can be the navigator," he said as he climbed into the driver's seat. She pulled out her phone. "Without the phone," he added.

"Seriously?" she said with a wry grin.

"I like maps," he told her.

"Fine." She picked up the map with a slight roll of her eyes. He'd mapped out the roads they'd need to take, making it very easy for her to give him directions.

"I get the need to do this, but it's ridiculous when the car can just tell us where to turn," she said after they'd been driving for about five minutes.

"I plan on exploring many areas that don't have access to satellites and navigation."

"I don't know if I ever want to be quite that remote," she said with a shiver.

"Sometimes it's amazing to go to a place the rest of the world has no clue exists. It can be paradise to swim naked and cook with nothing more than a fire."

"That's called camping, though I've never understood the appeal of being in the middle of nowhere with few luxuries from home. I do like a good bonfire, but why would a person leave a perfectly warm house to go sleep in the wild? We've made advances so we don't have to do that anymore," she pointed out.

Noah laughed. "I think there's a natural part of all of us that appreciates and craves the basics in life. The less and less we live off the land and learn survival techniques, the more lazy we get. I love camping."

"I've never done it," she admitted.

Noah was shocked. "You've never once camped?"

"Nope. No need to. I have a place with a warm bed I can climb in and out of."

"Oh, Sarah, you've seriously been deprived. I might just have to prove to you how amazing camping is," he said.

"No, thank you," she primly told him.

He laughed. She really did amuse him.

"We'll see," he said.

He was remembering why it was worth it to be a patient man, and with this woman he had a feeling he could do just about anything. Even when he was frustrated beyond compare, it didn't last very long. He was beginning to think there wasn't anything he wouldn't do for her. He wondered if that was how his oldest brother had felt when he'd met Brooke, if he'd just known she was now his world.

He never would forget Finn walking into that room and announcing he was getting married. He'd only known Brooke a single day, but he'd been sure he was going to marry her. Was that going on with Noah? Was he in love with this woman and just fighting it? That was a terrifying thought. He had to get out of his own head before he blurted something he didn't want to blurt.

"Are you ready to be inspired?" he asked.

This time she gave him a huge grin that reached her eyes. "I sure hope so."

"I've always hated the word *hope*," he said. "I like to just know. I know we'll be inspired. I think if we use the word *hope*, we're setting ourselves up for failure, and I don't like to fail."

Sarah laughed. "I've never thought of it that way before. You make me think of things in a whole new way," she told him.

"Good. I like to make people think, just as I like to push myself."

They chatted back and forth as they drew closer to Shaniko, and he could feel the excitement rolling off Sarah as they began seeing signs of the town ahead. Her grin grew.

"Are you inspired yet?" he asked with a chuckle.

"I think I am," she said. Her beauty when she let down her guard was something incredible to behold. It took his breath away. "I know I can be a pain in the ass sometimes, but I'm so glad you keep pushing me. I'm incredibly glad to be here."

That shocked him. He wasn't quite sure what to say in reply.

"You don't have to say anything," she said, as if she were reading his mind. "I just want you to know that I appreciate what you're doing."

He took a deep breath. She made it nearly impossible for him to keep his feelings and thoughts to himself. He reached over and grabbed her hand before she could pull away from him. He squeezed her fingers.

"There's so much I could give you," he said, meaning each and every word.

"You've given me plenty," she said with a wink that once again shocked him. She was flirting a bit. Damn! This woman was confusing the hell out of him. "Now tell me more about Shaniko."

She was switching topics so fast she was making his head spin. He parked the car, then turned and looked at her.

"I don't know everything about it, but I believe it was founded by businessmen in the early 1900s. The hotel, city hall, jail, church, and stable, along with a few more original buildings, are still standing. It was known for its huge wool production in the beginning. In the last ten years they've revived the town, now providing lodging, places to dine, and shopping for tourists, which is good and bad at the same time."

"Tourism is a necessary evil," Sarah said.

"I agree with that. But I remember my mom bringing us here when we were young, and we thought we were Old West cowboys. My brothers and I took over this town as the long arm of the law. If any bad guys came along, we'd have surely taken them down," he said as he puffed out his chest.

Sarah laughed. "I'm sure you'd make an adorable little sheriff," she said.

"Hey! I wasn't little even when I was young," he told her.

This made her laugh so hard he reached over and patted her back. He wasn't sure if he should be offended or not. He decided if she was laughing, it was always a good thing, though, so if she found him humorous, at least she wasn't bored.

He also realized the amount of influence this one woman held over him. There was nothing he wouldn't be willing to do to keep her laughing, to keep her happy. He wanted to hear the musical sound of her voice every single day. He wanted to be the one to put that smile on her lips, then to kiss it away and make her moan.

This was about so much more than good sex. Yes, the sex was phenomenal, but it was the total package of Sarah that appealed to him. He was in big trouble—big, big trouble where this woman was concerned—because he truly was falling in love with her, and he wasn't sure he'd be able to get her to let down her guard long enough to fall in love with him. He wasn't sure he could stay in one place long enough to give them a fighting chance.

Her laughter finally began to die down, and he gave it a couple more seconds before holding out his hand. "Ready?" he asked.

She looked a bit longingly at his hand before she nodded and then fell into step beside him, leaving his fingers sadly empty.

"Let's get an ice cream," he said. She perked back up.

"Most definitely," she agreed as she looked around. There were a few people here and there, but not in great quantities. He knew the tourists started coming in droves later in the season, but it was still early in the day and the season, so they were in luck.

"I'm excited to get to check another ghost town off my list," Sarah told him as they approached the ice cream shop.

"How many have you been to?" he asked.

"I don't know. I'd have to look, but a couple dozen at least," she replied.

"I'd love to check some off with you, so we'll have to do that," he said.

She paused in her steps as she looked at him. He knew it was to try to figure out if he was just saying the words or if he meant them. Surprisingly he had. He liked spending time with this woman.

"You know, Noah, you should be careful with words. I might just say yes," she warned. He felt his heart skip a little beat. She was capturing him, whether she knew it or not, and the biggest surprise of all was that he wasn't scared about it.

They stepped inside the ice cream parlor and each got a cone, then stepped back down into the streets. He wasn't sure which way he wanted to go, so he let her lead the way.

"Where to first?" he asked as he ate a large chunk of Oreo and sighed. He always got the same kind. Maybe he was slightly a creature of habit, as much as he wanted to be this big adventurous man.

"The hotel," she said as they approached the huge building.

They walked inside, and it felt as if they were going back in time. It was a functioning hotel, but the history of the building had been kept fully intact, with original flooring and pictures hung on the walls showing the families who'd initially settled in the town. There were brief descriptions of who they were and what they had done in the small community.

Sarah took her time exploring the hotel before they came back outside and spent the next few hours looking at the rest of the town. She took notes and jotted sketches, and it was late in the afternoon before they even thought about leaving.

"You know, we could just stay overnight at the hotel and explore more tomorrow," he suggested, really liking the idea. There was only one room available. He wasn't telling her that until she agreed.

She hesitated as if she liked the idea, and he felt his heart thump and his pants tighten. But then he was sadly disappointed when she shook her head.

"No. I've taken a lot of pics and notes. There's no need to stay another day," she said. "Let's just finish our walk, then head out."

This time when he took her hand, she didn't fight him, and he felt as if he'd just won a freaking gold medal as they looked at the old barns, school building, and jail. They turned a corner and found a cemetery with hundred-year-old stones inside that instantly fascinated Sarah. She let go of his hand and moved through the well-maintained grounds.

He heard the sound before Sarah did, but he was a bit slower than her as she jumped backward with a little squeal. He quickly caught her and pushed her behind him as the two of them looked over to where a rattler was giving them the evil eye.

"I didn't think they had rattlesnakes in Oregon," she said, wide eyed and scared. She wasn't wearing good enough shoes to protect her from a bite.

"Let's just slowly back away," he said, not taking his eyes from the poisonous snake.

"Okay," she said, and she began retreating with him. They didn't say another word until they were a safe distance away. Then a shudder passed through her. "Damn! My heart is racing," she admitted.

He let out a chuckle. "Yeah, I've run into snakes before, and it always gives me a bit of a scare," he admitted.

"I'm a lover of nature, but I'll take my lush green areas anytime over the desert. There's too many deadly creatures where it gets too hot. I think it's because the heat makes everyone cranky," she said.

That made him laugh again. This woman sure made him laugh an awful lot. He loved it. Yes, he got irritated at times, but she also made that evaporate. He was deciding he liked himself a lot better with her around.

"I've always been a fan of heat," he said.

"Well, I'm not. I get cranky when I'm overheated, so I can understand the animals feeling that way."

"You don't look too cranky right now," he said as he pulled her against him. He couldn't help it. He'd been good the entire day, but she amazed him. He had to touch her, had to have one more little kiss, or he'd never make it back in one piece.

She didn't pull away from him, didn't chastise him, and didn't tell him no. The lids over her eyes lowered as her lips turned up the slightest bit.

"You know this shouldn't happen," she said, but her words came out softly as she reached around him, her hands splaying across his back.

"One kiss doesn't hurt a thing," he said. Then he stopped talking as he leaned down and gently caressed her mouth with his. He was so hungry for her his body was on fire, but he didn't deepen the kiss.

Their day had been perfect, full of flirting and laughter and wonder. He wanted that to be first and foremost in her mind. He didn't want the focus to be all about sex, because he was realizing it was so much more than that with this woman.

Though he didn't want to, he pulled back, gently cupping her cheek as he watched her eyelids rise. She gave him the sweetest smile, and he grinned back at her.

"You are so beautiful," he whispered, and a small giggle escaped her as she looked at him dreamily.

He caressed her cheek for a second longer, then pulled back. He wasn't going to mess this moment up, and if she kept looking at him like that, he was going to find the nearest building to take her to so he could make love to her for hours on end—something they should've been doing for the past few months nonstop.

There was so much about this woman that fascinated him, and all he knew was he didn't want this day to end, didn't want this project to end. Maybe if the two of them spent enough time together, it would become natural. Maybe in the end it couldn't be stopped, because it was just as simple as that it was meant to be.

Chapter Thirteen

Sarah was quiet as the two of them began their drive back to the plane. That kiss had been beautiful and a perfect way to end their time in the quaint little ghost town. It had also left her head spinning and her heart racing.

Every time she was with this man, she got to know so much about him. And though she wanted there to be reasons not to like him, he was making it increasingly difficult for her to find flaws.

After about ten minutes the silence between them was getting to be too much for her. She had way too good an imagination to be locked inside a car surrounded by his scent. If they didn't have a conversation soon, she was going to have a complete breakdown and end up climbing over the divider between them and attacking him.

She'd never done it in a car before. She searched her memory for her high school years, and yes, she'd made out in a couple of vehicles, but that was all she'd done. She'd never had sex in one and never felt the need to reach over, undo the guy's pants, and take him in her mouth.

She was feeling that urge right now. Her mouth watered at the thought. She wanted this man with a desperation that was making her slightly insane. She wanted to please him, to make him cry out, to make him hers.

"I think this is a great time for you to tell me about your time in the navy," she said, jumping at the sound of her own voice; it was so loud and panicked sounding.

He looked at her with a bit of worry in his expression. "Are you okay?" Of course he needed to ask her that. She had practically screamed at him.

"Yes, just restless," she told him.

He chuckled but thankfully faced forward again and concentrated on driving. She focused on getting her breathing back to normal.

"So do you have any good stories?" she asked. At least her voice was a little more normal now that she was breathing in and out.

"I have plenty. What do you want to hear?"

"Something entertaining." She didn't want to add that she definitely didn't want to hear about all the women she was sure he'd picked up while he'd looked amazing in his uniform.

"Hmm," he hummed as a smile grew on his face. "I remember one adventure when I was pretty new to the crew." He chuckled as he thought back to those days. She began to relax.

"I was a deck seaman, and I had the job of painting the waterline on the side of the ship."

"What's a waterline?"

"There's a large black stripe that goes all the way around the entire ship that's about two feet up from the water. That's called the waterline. It has to be repainted every year or so. It was my job to work on this, but it was a bitch to do."

"Doesn't sound too hard to paint," she said with a bit of mocking.

"Mm-hmm, easy for you to say. You weren't the one in a little twelve-foot boat that wouldn't stay where it was supposed to because I was having to use brooms as oars."

"You were a navy man, and you had to use brooms as oars?" she said, truly laughing now. "Why?"

"There weren't any oars for the boat," he replied with a shrug.

"On an entire navy vessel you couldn't find a single oar? That seems absolutely absurd."

"Nope. Not one oar, but I'm creative, so I used brooms," he said proudly. "But that wasn't the problem. The problem was that I'd paint a little bit, and then my boat would move out in the water, so I'd have to row back and paint some more, over and over again."

"It seems like the job would never get done at that rate," she said.

"That's the conclusion I came to," he said. "Until I looked up and spotted the pad eyes and came up with a plan of action."

"Pad eyes?" she questioned.

"They are these hooks that are up about eight feet from the waterline that are welded into the side of the ship about every fifty feet. So I figured if I got a boat hook, which is a long wooden handle with a hook on the end of it, I could hook it into the pad eye, climb up the pole, and hook a rope through the pad eye, then make myself an anchor."

"Oh, I can see this going very, very badly," she surmised.

"Nope. It went smooth as butter. I got the hook in, ran the rope through the eye, then climbed back down and did it again at the next eye. I worked on this for weeks, and it was all going smoothly."

"Well, that's not a very interesting story," she said, disappointed he hadn't fallen into the sea. Maybe there was a devilish side to her she hadn't been very aware of until interacting with this particular man.

"Just wait for it," he told her with a chuckle.

Her attention was properly gained again.

"I got promoted to petty officer third class, so it was no longer my job to paint the side of the ship, but I had to teach a new guy how to do it."

"That's not so hard," she said.

"You would think," he said with another laugh and a roll of his eyes. "However, not everyone in the navy is a water expert."

"Ohhhh," she said with a big grin.

"I was with a guy named Speedy, and he didn't have the name because he was fast. We got down in the boat, and I explained to him that I was going to put the hook in, and his *one* job was to hold the end so the boat didn't float away."

He went quiet for a moment, and she waited.

"It was all going smoothly. I hooked the pad eye, climbed up and got the rope through, and then looked down."

He went silent again, and she began laughing. She could already tell where this was going. "The boat was gone, wasn't it?"

"Oh, the boat was about fifty feet out, and I'm there dangling on the stick above the water." He glared at her when she laughed again. "So I told him to row back to me. So Speedy starts rowing, but apparently I was supposed to teach him how to row, because he's rowing on one side of the boat and going in a circle as my arm begins to wear out."

She was laughing so hard at this point her stomach was beginning to hurt. She could just see the look on his face as he tried to figure out if the guy was messing with him or really that dumb.

"In his defense," she said between chuckles, "he was rowing with a broomstick." She could barely get the words out.

The look he gave her she was sure was the same look he'd given the poor man rowing himself into a circle, getting dizzy.

"I yelled out to him to row on the other side," he said, then smiled. He must be realizing how humorous this situation was. "So he did and then started turning in a circle the opposite way."

"Oh my gosh, you have to stop. My stomach is killing me," she told him as tears began running down her face.

"I realized there was no chance of me not getting wet. So I reached in my back pocket, secured my wallet, and dropped into the water. I had to swim out to him, where he was looking sheepishly at me while I was cussing him out."

"Where were your other crewmates?"

"Doing their own jobs."

"So you totally could've drowned right there next to a huge navy ship, and no one would've known?" she questioned, a bit confused.

"In their defense, we were navy men and should be able to handle the water," he told her.

"That's true. I hope Speedy swam better than he rowed."

"Me too. But he learned real quickly how to row 'cause he brought us back to the ship after his lesson."

Sarah chuckled again as they approached the airport. The drive had gone by much more quickly with him sharing his adventures with her. She reached over and patted his leg.

"Thank you for that. I can't remember the last time I've laughed that hard," she said as she wiped away her final tear. "That was great."

"I'm glad I was able to entertain you with my painful memory," he said with a smile.

They continued to chat as they loaded their bags into the plane, and then Sarah sat back and watched as the sun began to set. It had been a perfect day, and it was ending with a perfect sunset.

She was done for. Maybe she should just admit that to herself and give in. Or maybe she'd continue to torture them both. She really wasn't sure what would happen next.

She wasn't sure she wanted to know what would come. Maybe there was truly something to be said about living in the moment. Only time was going to tell how this was all going to turn out.

Chapter Fourteen

Three days.

Three very long nights.

It was funny how a person looked at time when they were miserable versus when they were happy. When a person was in a good mood, time sped by far too quickly. When they were miserable, it dragged on and on and on and on.

Sarah hadn't seen or talked with Noah since their trip to the Oregon ghost town, and she missed him. She didn't want to miss him, didn't want to want to see him, but she did indeed miss him, and she was more confused than ever about what that meant. They'd done a lot of drawings on their own since the trip, and they were planning on going to the work site, but after their trip they'd separated and hadn't had a chance to get back together.

Then out of the blue he'd called her the night before and said he'd found their next place of inspiration. The only thing he would tell her was to bring a good pair of shoes.

She'd asked him what that had to do with the project, and he'd only said she'd have to wait and see. She could push it and prove it had nothing to do with their work, but maybe by going she'd be inspired. And the bottom line was that she did indeed miss him.

This newest trip was to an island off the coast of Washington. She was always up for a good hike, and she hadn't been getting enough exercise lately, so truly this was a win all the way around. But at this particular moment she was restless and cranky and shouldn't be near anyone.

How was it that she'd always been so independent and secure on her own but in the space of such a short time had learned to depend on this one man for a bit of peace and happiness? How was it that she'd rather fight with the man than sit alone in quiet and read a book? And how could she possibly make it stop? Did she even want to make it stop? She honestly couldn't answer that.

Her fingers twitched on her phone as she ached to call him, as she searched for a reason to do just that. That kiss had been amazing, and then he'd looked as if he'd wanted to do it again when they'd said goodbye at the plane, but he'd just given her a sultry look, then turned and walked away . . . again.

It was so dang easy for her to get lost in the beauty of Noah's incredible blue eyes. All logic flew right out the window when she was around him. He made her feel things she'd never felt with any other man—made her want things she'd never wanted with anyone else.

When she found herself close to caving and dialing the man up, she forced herself to call Brooke instead. Her best friend answered on the second ring and enthusiastically invited Sarah to come over. That was a much safer option for her sanity.

After putting her phone away, she tucked her drawings into her bag and jumped into her car. It didn't take her long to arrive at Brooke's place. The home was everything Sarah had once wanted. Maybe she just needed to accept that her life had taken a different path than she'd planned and appreciate the journey she was now on instead of looking at what other people had. And maybe she should accept that fate might have a different plan in mind for her now versus what it had in mind even a year ago.

Brooke answered the door immediately. Her best friend looked rumpled, but she was wearing a bright smile.

"That was fast," Brooke said as she held open the door.

"Thankfully, because it seems I can't be on time for anything these days," Sarah said after giving Brooke a big hug. "I don't know what's happening to me."

"Well, life sometimes happens," Brooke said with a laugh. "We aren't alone, though. The neighbor had an emergency and asked if I could babysit. Her daughter is absolutely adorable . . . and a terror, so it'll make visiting a bit difficult, but I think we'll manage if the twins stay asleep. I can't guarantee anything peaceful these days."

Though it might sound like a complaint from most people, Sarah could see the love shining in Brooke's eyes. She was made to be a mom, and she'd embraced that role wholeheartedly.

Just then a little girl ran up to Brooke and latched on to her leg as she looked up at Sarah with big brown eyes filled with curiosity. Acting on instinct, Sarah knelt down and smiled.

"What's your name?" she asked.

"Eliza," the small child answered in a tiny voice. "I'm three," she added with a sweet grin.

"That's a perfect age," Sarah said, feeling a tiny pang at this life her best friend now had. She'd never been jealous of mothers. She'd actually always felt sorry for them, since they appeared to be so tired most of the time. But since her head was screwed up these days, apparently she was feeling the need to have a child as well. She hoped that passed really, *really* soon.

Eliza lost interest in the conversation, and Sarah stood up and looked at her bestie, who didn't appear at all fazed at the chaos her life had become.

"You're keeping mighty busy these days with the twins and babysitting duty," Sarah told her. "Is it what you were expecting?"

"I'm living the dream," Brooke said. The funny thing was there was zero sarcasm in her friend's voice. She really was living a dream life—or at least her idea of a dream life. "I'm definitely keeping busy, but no, it's nothing like what I would've expected. Of course I never thought I'd be a mother and wife or have ideas of PTA bakes and neighborhood parties. But I do love it all. I think I was lost and had no clue who I was or what I truly wanted and needed. And in the end what I needed was a family." She was quiet as she grinned a satisfied smile. Then she shook her head as if clearing it. "I think you might be having more chaos in your life than me right now, though." She led Sarah into the living room. It was clean but definitely cluttered with toys.

"I used to absolutely love being busy. Now there are times I want to slow down and other times I want to speed up. I don't think I know what I want half the time," Sarah said.

"We can keep on wasting time with idle chitchat, or we can get to the good stuff," Brooke said with a sly smile. Sarah knew what that meant.

She stalled. "What good stuff?" she asked as Brooke gave Eliza a toy before giving Sarah her attention again.

"You and Noah are spending a lot of nonwork time together even though you told me the affair was over, and you were one hundred percent done with him," Brooke told her.

Sarah's cheeks heated as she looked over at the young child, who wasn't paying them the least bit of attention. She never had been able to lie to her best friends. None of them could pull it off.

"We're just trying to figure out how to make this project the best it can be. That's all," Sarah said way too defensively. "And to do that, we're doing some unconventional stuff."

"Hmm, why am I finding that difficult to believe?" Brooke said with a laugh.

"Because you've always been a meddler," Sarah told her.

"That's *so* not true," Brooke said with a mock gasp.

"Noah has grand ideas that by doing things a bit differently, we're going to make a dream center. I want it to be the best. I want this to really enhance my career," Sarah said.

"Yes, Joseph Anderson picked the two of you, so he obviously has a lot of trust in you," Brooke told her. "I have no doubt this will be fantastic when it's finished. I love what I see so far. And I love that your name will be on it."

"My name isn't front and center, and I shouldn't care as much as I do, but I can't help but want perfection," Sarah said. "And I want *some* credit. I hate that I do, but I so do."

"Your name is on this project, so it's as much yours as Noah's," Brooke defended. Of course her best friend would say that.

"I feel as if I'm just along for the ride. Noah is the big name, and I'm a little resentful of that. I'm working as hard as him on this, and his name will be front and center, and I'll just be a sidenote. There's so much holding me back from being with the man, but sometimes I have no idea why I'm fighting it. And then other times I think I'm doing the right thing. I'm a mess," she admitted.

"So if you really don't expect anything out of this, why spend so much time on it? And why spend the extra time with Noah?" Brooke pointed out. Eliza let out a squeal of joy when a puppy came by and licked her on the cheek before going over to his bed and curling up. The scene made Sarah smile, made her nerves calm.

"I have to work on this because I committed to it. And therefore I have to spend time with Noah, which is what's leaving me in an utter hormonal mess," Sarah insisted.

"I don't think that's *all* it is."

"I swear the only reason I'm doing this is that I'm invested now," Sarah said. She couldn't look her friend in the eye. She was 98 percent sure she was lying.

"I think the man's completely infatuated with you. He might be fighting it as much as you are, but the way he looks at you tells me he's falling in love," Brooke said. "Maybe you just need to accept it."

"Don't go there, Brooke," Sarah told her, but the words made a funny little tingle start up in the pit of her stomach.

"I know you were hoping for a carefree fling, where you forget all about him the moment it's over, but I think the two of you connected, and I don't think that connection can break. You're falling in love with him—and though it seems impossible, he's falling in love with you. Don't you think that's worth exploring?" Brooke asked.

"I've never wanted to risk falling in love. It's not that I don't trust it or believe in it. I just see too many failed romances," Sarah told her. She was now twisting her fingers on the hem of her shirt.

"Why?" Brooke asked. "I know Noah can be a pain in the ass, and he hasn't had the smallest inkling of settling down in the past. But he's also a wonderful man who donates to abused kids and schools and who holds my babies like they're the most precious beings on this planet. There's a lot of good in him—enough to risk your heart for."

Sarah found herself on the verge of tears. She had to push them away quickly. This was a road she'd sworn she wouldn't go down. "I love that you love him, and I'm glad you've gotten close this past year. But I can't do it. I can't give up what I've achieved and risk it all for a relationship that isn't meant to be. He is known to walk away. He's done it before."

Brooke shrugged, but the look in her eye was telling her she didn't believe Sarah had a choice in the matter. She didn't want to admit even to herself that she thought Brooke might be right. She could keep on fighting it, but it was like punching herself in the face while looking in a mirror.

"Okay, I'll lay off. Tell me what you've been up to this past month while I've been nursing nonstop," Brooke demanded.

"I'm just working, working, working," Sarah told her. It was difficult for her to switch topics so quickly. Her mind was still on Noah.

"You guys have been full steam ahead from the beginning. I'm surprised you aren't done yet."

"I know, but we're both perfectionists, and that makes it more difficult to ever call it good enough."

She rose and paced the large room. She'd always been a somewhat restless person, but lately it was getting worse.

"There's nothing wrong with having it all, Sarah," Brooke pointed out. "You can do your job *and* give yourself time to enjoy life *and* a sexy man."

"I love my job, though, so isn't that enjoying life?" Sarah asked. She really wasn't sure why she was trying to convince Brooke she was so happy when she obviously wasn't.

"What would make you the happiest? What would bring you back to yourself?" Brooke asked with knowing eyes pointed straight at her.

Could anyone ever answer those questions? She wasn't sure.

"I love my job," she said instead.

"That's evasive," Brooke pointed out.

"As you well know, life isn't always black and white. There are many colors to each and every day. I'm not unhappy," Sarah assured her.

"That's true. Do you think you'll be able to finish this project, when you feel the way you do about Noah?" And they were back on the man Sarah didn't want to think about.

"Yes, I can," Sarah said.

"He's incredibly gifted. And I think he can help you achieve your dreams," Brooke said with a smile. "Finn has some of his buildings on the wall. He's very proud of his brother."

Sarah looked over and immediately recognized the framed shots. She'd looked into Noah's other work when she'd been hired for this project. Sarah looked at one of the images, her heart pounding as she imagined looking at her own work hanging on a wall in people's houses.

"Yes, he is," Sarah said in a whisper as her eyes caressed the beautifully captured images.

"Don't give up on him," Brooke told her. Sarah's gaze snapped back to her friend.

"I think you actually believe the two of us belong together," she replied with a small chuckle.

"I think you are meant to be. I hope it lasts for eternity," Brooke admitted.

"We have totally separate lives. It can't work in the end," Sarah told her.

"Not necessarily. I still believe in magic, and so do you. You just have to find it within yourself, and you have to chip down that wall you've built." She paused with that knowing look on her face.

"Aren't I the one who's always believed in magic?" Sarah asked.

"Yes, you are, but you're too close to realize how good a man he is," Brooke told her.

Brooke let Sarah process her thoughts without interruption. Then Eliza stumbled and fell, letting out a scream. Brooke jumped up and grabbed the little girl.

"She didn't really get hurt. It's just past her nap time," Brooke assured her.

"I'll get out of here so you can lay her down," Sarah said as she stood.

Brooke tried assuring her she didn't need to go, but there was nothing else that could be said at this point. The best thing Sarah could do was pull her thoughts together while taking a nice long walk.

She told her bestie goodbye and practically ran for the door. Each moment she was with Noah, she wanted him more. Each time she was away, she craved how she felt when she was with him. Maybe she should see how it played out . . . and maybe she should run as far and as fast as she could. She honestly didn't know which direction she was going to take. She was playing a game that she didn't know the rules of. So in the end she wasn't sure how they'd determine the winner and loser. Maybe each of them would be both.

CHAPTER FIFTEEN

There was something about the sound of the ocean that had always given Sarah peace. Whenever she'd been searching for enlightenment, she'd find her way to some form of water, whether it was the ocean, a lake, a river, or even a creek. Somehow she'd been able to find answers with her toes in the water when no other way seemed to be presenting them.

Now she needed answers more than at any other time in her life. She was torn on what step to take next. She didn't enjoy being this indecisive. So she made her way to the same beach she'd visited many, *many* times before. One of the greatest things about the Seattle area was the sheer amount of water surrounding it. The city itself was claustrophobic, but if you just went out in any direction a little way, you could find peace.

There were mountains, streams, water, and wildlife. There were answers in the streams and the stars. If she took her time and paid attention, she might find what she was seeking. Maybe she'd even experience some of the magic she still believed in.

Visiting with her best friend had left her more confused than before. Neither Brooke nor Chloe loved someone easily, especially if that someone was trying to enter one of their lives. So for Noah to have both Brooke's and Chloe's support was making this situation even more confusing for Sarah.

Maybe she should listen to them, listen to her own heart or hormones or whatever it was that was pulling her toward this man. She might find the peace she'd been struggling to experience since first meeting Noah.

Being a part of Noah's life was like being caught up in a huge thunderstorm. There was definite beauty and magic in the moment, but in the blink of an eye the situation could turn deadly, like the car accident. Being with him was also making her realize she might be missing something essential in her life. Did she want something she'd never thought she'd wanted before? Was a happily ever after in her future? Or was she being submerged into a world she didn't want to be in and being tricked by her hormones to continue?

She wasn't sure which was the right answer.

In the time she'd known Noah—about a year now—there hadn't been one single day that had passed where he hadn't popped up in her mind at least once. That was frustrating for a woman who'd been so perfectly content to flirt and date and then walk away without ever looking back. Maybe there'd been a time in her life she'd dreamed of romance and marriage and kids, but that had been a long time ago. She'd grown more cynical as she'd gotten older.

And then Noah had come along, and she was suddenly envisioning playground equipment in the backyard and a puppy nipping at their toes. She was jealous of her best friend for being tired because she was up for days on end taking care of her beautiful babies. This wasn't who Sarah was. But then again, she wasn't sure who in the heck she was anymore.

The sky was darkening as Sarah continued walking along the shore. Waves crashed harder and harder with each hit as a perfect storm began to form. She loved being on the beach when the weather turned. The view was spectacular. If she couldn't find magic during a storm, then she was a lost cause and should throw in the towel.

She kept her gaze pointed toward the sea, but Sarah knew the moment she was no longer alone. She also knew it wasn't just anyone who was approaching. There was no difference in sound, and no smell carried on the breeze. She wasn't sure she'd be able to hear over the sound of the wind and waves even if someone was to call out to her, but she knew Noah was there. She didn't turn. She was afraid of how she'd react if she did.

But even without turning, she could feel his gaze boring into her, feel the tingles on the back of her neck. She told herself she should walk away, pretend she didn't know he was there. Her heart thundered out of control, and she felt frozen to the spot.

She was still as he stepped behind her. He was so close she could feel his body heat. No words were spoken, but she knew that he was very aware she was in tune to his presence. There was no denying her response to this man. She could try to pretend, but that would just make her more of a fool than she already felt.

Slowly she turned. And then she was instantly caught in the intensity of his gaze. She didn't try to look away, but she wasn't sure what his expression was telling her. There was more emotion in this one look than any she'd ever seen before. She was caught, and nothing was going to pull her away. Why was she still fighting this?

The wind picked up speed, and she could smell the rain in the air. The storm was coming closer, waiting to unleash its power on them. It couldn't have been a more perfect moment if she'd asked for it. She was with this man she desired on the beach with a storm brewing. Was this the answer she'd been looking for?

She wasn't sure how long the two of them stood there gazing at each other without a single word being uttered. They weren't needed. Their bodies and eyes were doing the talking. It was the most intense conversation she'd ever experienced.

He reached up, and this time she didn't flinch away. Why should she pretend she didn't want to feel his touch? She craved it more than she needed oxygen, more than she needed food or water, more than she needed to stay strong.

His finger swept down the side of her cheek, and his palm cupped her chin, and she didn't turn away from him. She still hadn't come to a decision about what she was going to do, but in this moment she didn't care. She just wanted him, wanted what only he could give her. She wanted to say something, but she wasn't sure she could trust her voice. Her control was incredibly close to snapping.

"Tell me what you need," he finally said. There was so much power behind those five complicated words, and there wasn't even close to an easy answer.

"I don't know," she finally admitted. She was afraid of what he'd have to say about that, but she watched as his eyes softened.

"I know," he told her. "I'm sorry you're confused. I'm sorry this is so difficult for you."

She felt on the verge of tears. Who was this guy? Was he truly this understanding, truly this wonderful? She'd been indecisive and wishy washy from the beginning of their first time meeting. It hadn't gotten better in the past year. And still he was standing there with understanding in his eyes. It made this so much harder.

"Why do you keep trying?" she asked.

His lips turned up the slightest bit. His hand didn't move from her cheek, but his thumb caressed her jaw and lip. He finally shrugged as if he was the one confused. But there was nothing indecisive in his expression as he opened his mouth to speak again.

"You ask that like I have a choice," he said. "There is no choice when it comes to you. I've tried leaving, but I come back because I'm drawn to you. I need you just as you need me. I think when you realize how true that is, it will be so much easier on both of us."

His tone never changed, but the intensity in his eyes grew as he spoke. She knew this wasn't a line, knew that he meant what he was saying.

"I can't seem to let go," she admitted.

"Maybe if you did let go, you'd set yourself free," he responded.

His words and touch were making her fall apart, no matter how much she tried holding herself together. The touch of his fingers on her skin was making her body burn. The storm surrounding them only amplified it all. She was about to be swept away.

"Maybe you don't have all the answers," she finally said. She had to say something, had to bring some calm to this situation, because right now she felt as if she were being swept farther and farther out to sea, and their feet hadn't moved a single inch.

He didn't counter her words, but his eyes told her he knew she was bluffing, knew she was fighting to hold on to the last of her control. She wanted to rile him, wanted him to be as swept away as she was currently feeling.

She glared.

He smiled.

"I won't pretend to know it all," he finally told her. "But at least I don't run from what I feel and want. At least I'm not afraid to live."

It was a clear challenge, and her shoulders stiffened.

"You don't know me," she said. "And it doesn't matter to me what you think you know."

"I do know you. You're wrong to think I haven't spent this past year learning more about you than any other woman I've ever known. I'd know so much more if you allowed me in. Stop fighting this feeling. Stop fighting us," he said.

Finally some of the calm he'd been portraying slipped. That slip in self-control calmed her. This mattered to him. She wasn't sure why, but it did matter. Maybe it wasn't just a game. She didn't know.

She was about to respond when his eyes narrowed, and his hand shifted. His touch on her cheek moved, and he wrapped an arm around her, pulling her tightly to him, bringing their bodies as close as they could be without brushing together. It was the most beautiful torture.

"I don't know, Noah," she said, her voice barely above a whisper. The longer they stood like this, the more her body ached and the more her hormones and heart triumphed over her logic. She couldn't take this—couldn't fight *him* and herself. Maybe that was the answer. She needed to simply let go. She just didn't know how to do that.

The wind picked up speed, making her hair whip around them, giving them a sort of cocoon, as if they were in the eye of the storm. She was begging herself to let go, begging herself to give in to what she truly wanted. But she couldn't seem to do just that.

"Sarah, you know what you need. You know what I need. I want you. Let me have you," he said. His words begged her to give them both what they wanted, but he didn't push it further than that. He was giving her a choice and making her stand by the decision she was going to make. "Take away the pain from both of us, and say yes."

It would be so easy to give him what he was asking for. She had a feeling she wouldn't even have regrets, but still she was unable to give him the words he needed to hear. What was wrong with her? She'd never been this woman before.

"If I do this, I won't be the same again," she said. That was more truth than she'd been willing to give him before. It was this moment, this time, this storm, and this water. It was him and the situation, and her defenses were crumbling.

"Neither of us will ever be the same again. That's what you've failed to realize," he said. She saw the warning in his eyes moments before his head started to descend. He didn't want to ask anymore. But still he was giving her time to stop him if it wasn't what she really wanted.

His lips were so close to hers she felt his hot breath brush her trembling flesh. He hesitated, but he wasn't going to wait for long. She didn't want him to wait, didn't want him to give her too much time to think. Maybe talking was the last thing they should be doing. She'd been struggling with what to do, struggling with making the right choice, and she couldn't seem to make up her mind, so maybe she'd do best to listen to her body, to listen to the response she felt as he neared her.

She didn't always need to be in control. For once in her life she wanted someone else to have the power. She didn't trust her own mind to make the best decision for herself. She needed him to make the indecision she was struggling with disappear.

The storm exploded around them as thunder boomed, and the waves reached closer. He didn't close the final half inch between their lips, and she knew it was to force her into making that final decision.

She hated him a little—and she despised herself even more.

"You will never control me," she said, her voice a shudder, her body on fire.

"I never want to," he said. "I want you—all of you—nothing more and nothing less."

The fight went completely out of her.

"Kiss me," she said. She didn't even try to think about her decision. She didn't try to fight it. How could she when he was giving her a piece of himself? When he was being vulnerable with her? He was giving more to her than she'd ever been willing to give to him. She couldn't resist that. She had no desire to.

The reward for her words was a satisfied savagery in his eyes that made her stomach clench in pure desire. Her core pulsed, and her body ached. She'd made the right choice. She had no doubt whatsoever.

The wait was over as Noah leaned into her, closing that miniscule gap between them. His lips took her own in a kiss that made her moan against him, the sound being lifted away by the storm. She opened to him, needing his tongue tangling with hers. He consumed her in the most delicious way, and she let it all go—all the thoughts, all the fight, all the reservations.

She was his—at least for now. And it was exactly where she needed to be. This was where she'd belonged from the start. She'd been foolish to think otherwise.

The power of Noah's kiss was unlike anything Sarah had ever felt before. Each time he kissed her, it felt new and exciting. She couldn't get close enough to him, couldn't feel enough, climb high enough, or take enough. There was nothing she wasn't willing to give or take when in his arms.

His kisses promised wild passion and excitement. They promised to fill all her needs. They were the type of kisses books were written about and songs were made for. They were the kind of kisses movies couldn't portray properly. They gave her everything and took it all.

He wrapped both arms around her, and she could feel the power of his excitement, feel his arousal pressing into her, telling her where he needed this to lead. She didn't want to tell him no. She wanted fulfillment. He was hard to her soft and rough to her gentle. He was everything she'd ever needed without knowing it was what she'd been craving her entire life.

She couldn't get close enough. She pressed into him, wanted more, needed more, demanded all he was willing to give. And right now, she knew that was the sun, the moon and the stars, the entire universe. They were made to come together.

Noah gave her desire and freedom and put her safe world at risk. And none of that mattered. All that mattered was feeling total and utter satisfaction. She needed this man, and she was finally ready and able to take what she should have months before.

He broke their kiss, and she cried out as she grasped for him. She wasn't ready for it to end. But he was in more control than her, and he knew exactly what he wanted to do. He kissed his way along her jaw, then sucked on her neck, where her pulse beat out of control. Her stomach clenched, and she felt her core pulse.

"I want to take you right here and now," he said before his hand slid up her shirt and his fingers squeezed her sensitive breasts, making another cry escape her tortured lips.

She didn't say anything. She didn't think she was capable of sound at this point. Instead she let herself feel all he was doing to her, and she enjoyed every single moment of it.

She barely registered it when he picked her up in his arms. The rain began soaking them both, and she felt as if she was floating as he moved across the beach. She didn't care, as long as he kept his lips on her neck, her jaw, her lips, and her temple. His hands caressed her back as he moved away from the power of the crashing waves.

Then they were in a cave. There was no chance of her denying what she wanted now. Their clothes were soaked as he set her on her trembling legs. But she was far from cold. She reveled in the feel of his hands touching her all over. His lips took hers in a possessive caress that had her crying out his name.

Somehow he managed to strip away their clothes as the thunder rattled the walls of the dark cave. There was just enough light for her to see his utter perfection. She ran her fingers over his hot, wet skin and sighed as he consumed her mouth.

And finally he was lifting her, pressing her back into the stone wall as he lined up their bodies. It had been so long, far too long since she'd been in his secure embrace. There was no resistance as he pressed forward, burying his thickness deep inside her wet folds. She wrenched her lips from his as she screamed out his name, then buried her face in his shoulder and held on tight.

She didn't want slow and easy. She wanted their lovemaking to match the fury of the storm blazing a few feet away from them. He gave her what she wanted as he pounded her flesh. She was so tight, so needy, and so hot. She came as the sky darkened and thundered, as lightning flashed across the clouds, and as the sea reached for them.

He let out a growl as he released his pleasure deep within her. And then they were done, both of them utterly spent. Neither said a word for several long moments. She took one more second and ran her lips across the rough skin of his neck, and then she pulled away from him. He only resisted for a moment.

No words were spoken as she found her wet clothes and struggled into them. She didn't face him but assumed he was doing the same. When she was finished, she finally was able to look at him. She turned, resolution in her eyes.

"I won't say I regret that. I wanted it," she told him.

"You might not be saying the words, but your body is telling me right now you wished it wouldn't have happened." His tone was defensive, his body stiff.

"I don't regret it, but it probably shouldn't have happened," she said with a shrug. "But I needed it." She felt weak and vulnerable right then. She didn't like it at all.

Fury flashed across his eyes, and she watched as his fingers clenched together in a fist. She knew the words he wanted to say. She was impressed with his self-control. He was holding back when he wanted to let go on her. She didn't blame him. She couldn't seem to make up her mind, and that wasn't fair to either of them.

"We're meant to be together. It's more than just sex, Sarah," he finally said. He didn't move toward her, though. She was grateful for that. She was feeling too much in this moment to think straight if he touched her.

"I don't know if it's hormones or more. I just know that if it was meant to be, then I wouldn't be fighting it so much," she said, sadness consuming her. If they were supposed to be together, wouldn't she know without a doubt? It seemed like that would be the case.

"I haven't done anything you haven't wanted me to do," he told her. He was barely managing to keep his fury under control.

The storm kept on raging, and it seemed more than fitting, as he looked as if he was ready to explode, and she felt as if she was being pulled out to sea. This situation was messy and complicated, and they'd just made it that much worse. She couldn't regret her moment of weakness, though. It had felt too damn good—until reality sank back in.

"You're right. I wanted to be with you. I don't regret we did it. I just don't want to continue doing it. Should I quit right now?" She was asking him with no ulterior motives behind the words. This project was his first and foremost, and she'd walk away if that was what he needed her to do.

He was silent for several moments, and she had to fight the urge to cry. She hadn't realized how much it would hurt to lose this opportunity. Not only would she not get to see this project to the end, but she'd never see this man again. That seemed almost unbearable.

She wasn't sure how long the two of them stood there. She didn't cry and didn't look away. She'd asked him a question, and she needed to wait for an answer. The wait seemed impossibly long.

"You'll stay," he finally said. "I won't let you take the easy way out." His words almost seemed a threat. She didn't know what to think about that. "You can look at me as we work together, knowing how much I want you and also knowing your pride and foolishness is the only thing stopping us."

She flinched as he finished speaking. Her tears were so much closer to the surface, but she refused to allow them to fall. There was no way. She also didn't have anything else to add to his words. They could keep on throwing things at each other, or they could walk away before something was said that couldn't be taken back.

She chose to walk away.

He chose not to stop her.

She left the cave without looking back and focused on the crashing waves as she drew farther and farther away from him. She didn't stop moving. She was afraid if she did, she would run back to him, beg him to forgive her foolishness.

He might be right about her—about them. She might need him more than anyone she'd ever needed before. She might be damning both of them by continuing to deny what was right in front of her.

Still, she kept on walking. She didn't know how to do anything else. She didn't know what would come next. So all she could do was put one foot in front of the other, and maybe a new day would bring the answers she so desperately needed.

CHAPTER SIXTEEN

Noah sat in his truck and blared the music as loudly as it would play. He might not have any eardrums left when it was over, but that was a risk he was willing to take. With the mood he was in, it was probably safer for everyone for him to risk hearing loss rather than be around actual humans.

This train of thought led him to many, many questions on life and all that entailed. But one stood out above the rest.

Why in the hell did people choose to fall in love?

People actually sought it out. He was utterly perplexed by this fact. There were dating sites that individuals *actually* signed up for, put their pictures on, and listed things about themselves on to try to attract another individual.

It made no sense to him. None at all.

Not only that, but the flower market made a killing off of love and romance. Mostly men, but some women, too, bought flowers for their lovers to tell them how much they loved them or to say they were sorry or to celebrate a special occasion or even for the simple reason of letting them know they were thinking about them.

There were cards and trinkets, lingerie and poetry, sexy games and chocolate, and on and on and on, and he didn't even want to think about the wedding industry. All of these things were geared toward love and romance. He could understand the sex part of it all. That made sense to him. He couldn't understand the *love* part.

Why would anyone put themselves in a situation where they were vulnerable, where they were dependent on another person for their own happiness? From what he had witnessed, all of that led to nothing but pain and frustration.

In his own defense, he hadn't been looking for love. He hadn't wanted anything to do with it. For that matter he hadn't really believed much in it at all. It wasn't as if he'd had a shining example in his parents to go by. He'd been more than content to roll around many, many, *many* different beds, feel the varying textures of multicolored sheets, and then happily walk away the next day, fully satisfied. He hadn't even had to remember the girls' names.

But then Sarah had blown into his life like a freaking summer storm, and he hadn't been able to shake her. She consumed his thoughts, his emotions, his feelings. She had him begging her to be with him like some pathetic teenager who didn't know the first thing about heartbreak, and she had him so frustrated he wasn't fit company for anyone.

He hadn't been seeking love, but somehow he'd found himself in a situation where it was utterly consuming him. It was all he thought about. He wanted this woman, and he didn't want to want her. He seriously didn't want to *need* her. He wanted to run in the opposite direction of her, but he couldn't make himself do that.

So that all led him back to his original thought of why in the hell would anyone seek out love? He didn't get it. If someone was just minding their own business and love slapped them in the forehead, there wasn't a lot they could do about it.

He finally understood why people sought enlightenment in the far reaches of the world. If a person was completely on their own, then they weren't going to be in the range of Cupid's damn poisonous arrow. Love made a lot of money around the world, and it was all a bunch of hogwash.

Yeah, when things were great, that love spell worked out mighty fine. But when things weren't so great, it caused unbearable pain. He'd heard the saying that it was better to have loved and lost than to never have loved at all. He was disagreeing with that in a big way. As a matter of fact, he was in the mood to call some of those damn radio advice stations and give them a piece of his mind.

It was much better to not have a damn clue about love and the consequences of loving someone. He'd be much more content right now if he'd never met Sarah and her constantly changing mind. He could've been dating Betsy or Barbie or Jane Doe, having a nice night, and then skipping to his truck in the morning.

But no! He didn't get to do that because he was in love with a woman—or thought he might be in love with a woman—who was consuming him to the point of madness. He'd tried convincing himself it was nothing more than hormones, but it had been two days since she'd walked away from him on the beach, and it wasn't sex he was thinking about.

No, it wasn't sex at all. It was her. He wanted to see her smile, hear her laughter, and feel her touch. Yes, she made him harder and hotter than any other woman before could've even dreamed of making him. But it was so much more than that.

He could describe her beauty and the way she moved down to the minutest detail. He could pick her voice out of a recording of one hundred thousand people. And he could know her touch even if that same mob were all laying their hands on him.

It was more than sex. It was passion and understanding, and it was love and sacrifice. He was willing to give her anything she needed. But what she wanted was time and space. That was something he was having a hell of a time conceding to her.

If a day went by without her at his side, he felt lost. But he still didn't know what all of this meant. He still didn't know how to proceed. Maybe he should go back to one of the things he'd said to her and just kidnap her. If he had her trapped in a room with him for a week straight, he was sure they could come to a mutual understanding. That thought was very appealing.

A knock on his truck window startled him so badly he jumped in his seat and smashed his head against the roof of his truck. With a wince and a glare, he turned to see Joseph Anderson staring in at him. Dammit!

This so wasn't what he needed right now. He was too messed up to keep it all to himself, and the last person on the planet he wanted to tell his woes to was his uncle Joseph.

Joseph didn't budge when he hesitated to roll his window down. Noah let out a sigh, knowing he wasn't left with much choice but to comply. Finally, he turned down his music, ignored the buzz in his ear, and pushed the button to roll down the window.

"I thought I saw your truck up here. What are you doing? I could hear the music a mile down the road," Joseph said as his knowing gaze bored into Noah.

"I just needed a place to think," Noah replied, trying to keep his voice light. He couldn't hear properly, but he was pretty certain he'd failed.

"Mm-hmm," Joseph murmured, and Noah had the urge to smash his fist through the front window of his beautiful truck. "I see."

"What do you see?" Noah snapped. Nope. He wasn't doing well at all at keeping calm and composed.

"Got women trouble?" Joseph said with a chuckle. "I can spot that look on a man's face twenty miles away."

"I have zero women troubles," Noah said with a low growl.

"We can do this the hard way or the easy way," Joseph said with an almost-taunting smile.

"Has anyone ever told you to mind your own business?" Noah snapped. He waited for the man's wrath. He got laughter instead.

"I can't recall anyone ever being that bold," Joseph said. "I'd ignore it, anyway," he added with a shrug. The world was truly Joseph's oyster, and he could do whatever the hell he wanted. Noah wondered what it would be like to live a life like his.

"Well, I don't want to talk about it," Noah told him.

"I might be able to help. You never know. I have been around the block a time or two," Joseph said. He leaned against the window and looked like he wasn't going anywhere for a very, *very* long time.

Noah chewed on his last words for several moments. He had a feeling he wasn't getting out of there until he gave the big man something. Why had he chosen a hill so close to Joseph's place to have his pity party? Was he seeking punishment?

"I just can't seem to see eye to eye with Sarah. It's not a big deal, and it won't affect our work," Noah said with a grumble.

Joseph surprised him again when he laughed.

"Son, you will never see eye to eye with a woman. They always have the upper hand. The minute you learn that valuable lesson in life will be the time you find peace."

"Why would you say that?" Noah asked. Joseph wasn't helping at all. Not that he'd expected him to.

"Why is Sarah frustrating you?" Joseph asked, ignoring Noah's question.

He sighed. "Because we have something, and she is trying to act like we don't." Maybe a bit of honesty would end this conversation a lot sooner.

Joseph looked as if he was thinking for a moment, so Noah sat there quietly, though it wasn't easy for him to do in his current frame of mind. Finally Joseph spoke again, just when Noah didn't think he was going to.

"When you run into a problem in life, what do you normally do?" Joseph asked.

Now it was Noah's turn to think for a moment before he spoke.

"I find a solution," he finally said.

"Exactly," Joseph told him as he reached in and patted his shoulder so hard it sent him forward a little. He was lucky he didn't get his head slammed into his steering wheel.

"What does that mean?" Noah asked when Joseph didn't add more.

"Don't let a little roadblock stop you from getting what you want," Joseph said.

Noah let out another sigh. "I can't force the woman to be with me," he told him.

"Does she want to be with you?" Joseph asked.

"I would bet everything I own she does," Noah said without hesitation.

"Then make her realize it," Joseph told him. "I better get home before Katherine sends out a search party. If you still need some advice, come down to the house instead of killing your eardrums."

He didn't give Noah a chance to respond. He just disappeared as quickly as he'd arrived. Noah sat there for the next fifteen minutes considering his uncle's words. Could it really be that simple?

He finally smiled for the first time in two days. Yeah. Maybe it was.

CHAPTER SEVENTEEN

Noah let a few more days pass before he decided to put his new plan of action into place. He was missing her like crazy, so he was assuming she'd be missing him just as much, and he needed her to realize she didn't want to be away from him for his new plan to work.

The negative to this new plan was that it had put a crimp in their work. They hadn't been able to go on any new adventures together, and the project was now behind. Maybe no one was upset about it, but Noah was a workaholic, and he knew Sarah was as well. The fact that she hadn't called him told him she was worried he'd changed his mind and didn't want her working on the project anymore.

He wasn't that guy. Even if they weren't going to be lovers, he'd never take this away from her. It was too important to her career, and she was doing an amazing job. He just felt they could do that much better as a real team without all the sexual tension. If they just came together—multiple times—their work would greatly improve.

There was a small part of him that had the feeling to just run away again. He'd get over her if she was out of sight and out of mind. But he couldn't even stand a few days apart from her. He'd discovered that firsthand.

So instead of denying how he felt—even to himself—he'd found out where she was, and he was currently pulling up to a small community college. He smiled as he parked in front of the building. This could end up being a lot of fun. He couldn't deny he had a few fantasies about the teacher's desk.

Apparently Sarah didn't have enough on her plate already, so she was working on her doctorate and teaching a summer course at the college. She might just go further than he'd ever dreamed of going in his career. He couldn't have been more proud of her for it. Thanks to her friends, he'd found out exactly where she was and what her schedule was.

He'd arrived early enough to hear her speak. He wanted to see how she was doing without her knowing he was there, and he wanted to see how she interacted with the students. If he'd had a professor as hot as her when he'd been in school, he was sure he wouldn't have gotten a single thing done. He'd have been too busy mentally stripping the teacher's clothes away. Hopefully he was a bit more grown up now. But it was doubtable, since he knew exactly how good Sarah looked in the nude.

It was far too easy to find the classroom Sarah was teaching in, and it was even easier to slip in the back door and slink down into a seat in one of the back rows. He could observe her without her ever being aware he was there.

Damn! The woman was phenomenal.

She stood at the head of the class in a pencil skirt and fitted green blouse, wearing a nervous smile that he was sure he was the only one to notice. He knew she wasn't confident in this position of teaching, but she was giving it her all, and there was no way she'd show her fear to this classroom full of students who'd probably rather be at a lake somewhere than in a stuffy classroom in the middle of summer.

Of course with her as a teacher, he thought there was no better place to be than right where he was. He might have to reenroll in school. He was so smitten with this woman there wasn't much he wouldn't be willing to do to spend time with her.

She had the class mesmerized as she spoke of the joys of creating something that had never been made before. Her enthusiasm was contagious, and though there were a few students who looked less than thrilled to be sitting in a classroom instead of on a lake, the majority appeared as if they were right where they'd always dreamed of being.

With Sarah as the teacher, he could fully understand why they felt that way.

"I bet you all had no idea that architecture was once an Olympic sport," she said.

Two kids who had been talking in front of him stopped at her words. She had the entire classroom's full attention.

"What? How?" someone asked. She chuckled.

"In the early decades of the modern Olympic Games, there were one hundred fifty-one medals awarded for such things as music, painting, sculpture, literature, and, of course, architecture. The original founder, Baron Pierre de Coubertin, of the International Olympic Committee, considered art an essential part of the competition. It did have the caveat that every submission had to have a sports theme to it."

"That's amazing," someone said.

The class was now wide awake and hanging on her every word. Noah had loved his time in school. Yes, he'd been somewhat restless, as he'd wanted to be out there in the real world experiencing life, not learning about what other people had done with theirs. However, he'd loved learning more about how to bring his craft to utter perfection. Yes, he knew an education was key to that. But he also knew nothing great could come out of sitting and listening. You had to eventually rise and follow through on the thoughts floating around in your brain.

"Here's something else that might make you think," Sarah said with a waggle of her brows. "The supervisor of the original Ouija board company fell to his death from the roof of a factory that he'd said the board told him to build. He made his fortune making and selling the boards—and then lost his life to them."

There were a few chuckles in the class and a few students wearing horrified expressions on their faces. Noah was somewhere in the middle of both and might not admit it, but a shiver ran down his spine. That was just plain creepy.

She continued speaking, and Noah didn't realize how much time was passing as he sat mesmerized by this woman he was completely smitten with. He was low in his seat as he watched her talk with animation and intelligence. She had learned quickly how to do her job, and she was as good as she was because she had a true passion for it. The way she spoke clearly told a story of who she was.

There'd been so many times they'd been together when she'd had her guard up that it was a real treat for him to sit back and get this time to observe her when she was giving fully of herself, holding nothing back.

"Roman architecture was at its peak during the Pax Romana period, which lasted over two hundred years. Rome was responsible for some of the most influential innovations in architecture that are still used to this day. Can you name some examples of how this influences us now?"

The class was actively involved in this discussion.

"They created concrete, didn't they?" someone said.

"Yes, very good. They found that it was stronger and easier to use than marble and that they could carve things into it."

More questions and answers were asked and answered, and the entire class participated. He was in total awe.

Noah had thought he'd known this woman pretty well up until this moment, but he was learning that he'd barely begun to scratch the surface. This moment, though, told him he wanted to know so much more about her. Each layer that got peeled back made her that much more appealing to him. He was beginning to realize he wasn't going to let her go without a serious fight.

Noah found himself slightly disappointed when the class came to an end. He'd been utterly captivated by Sarah the entire time she'd been lecturing. Probably because she invited so much participation from the class. He'd had to sink lower in his seat so she wouldn't see him, as she looked out on the audience so much to call on the students. That kept them actively involved and eager to participate. If she wasn't such a great architect, he'd think she'd be better suited as a college professor. Maybe she could do a bit of both, if that called to her.

Some of the kids stopped and talked with Sarah as she gathered her materials. He sat up in his seat and waited for her to notice him. He no longer needed to hide. There wasn't a chance he was leaving until the two of them talked . . . and hopefully more.

After the final student had passed by him, and Sarah was at her desk putting the last of her items into a backpack, he stood up and stretched. The chairs weren't exactly made for a guy his size, and since he'd been slouched on top of that, he felt a few aches through his legs and back.

He didn't make much noise, but she stopped what she was doing, and her head slowly came up until their gazes locked. For the briefest moment joy flashed in her eyes, and he knew in that unguarded moment she'd missed him as much as he'd missed her. She might have her guard in place, but at the end of the day, she craved him just as much as he did her.

It wouldn't be long until he was getting her to admit that to both of them. Being apart for less than a week had been hell on him. He couldn't imagine going a lifetime. It had been good for him, though, because it told him that this was about so much more than an obsession or a fling. It was about lasting for a lifetime. Did a person know that about another in such a short time? His brother Finn had known in a few minutes that he'd met the woman he was going to marry. And Finn's love for his wife had never wavered, had never changed, and had never dimmed. It had grown stronger each day that went by.

Noah maintained eye contact with Sarah as he descended the lecture-room stairs until he was standing within a few feet of her. There was a myriad of emotions crossing her face, but she seemed more curious and a bit apprehensive than anything else. The last time they'd seen each other, they had just made love, and then she'd run away. He understood why. She was scared. He got it. He was a little scared, too. But together they could work through that.

"What are you doing here, Noah?" she asked. Her voice was guarded but not necessarily unfriendly. That was a step in the right direction.

"I wanted to take a class," he said with a smile.

Her brows rose. "Really?" she said; then her lip twitched the slightest bit. "Don't you have enough diplomas on your wall? I'd think a community college was a bit past you now."

"Hey, I'm not a snob. No college is beneath me," he told her. He wanted to reach for her, but he held back. "Let's get some dinner. I'm starving."

"I'm not hungry," she said. She shifted on her feet, as if she wasn't sure if she wanted to keep standing there or risk brushing past him. He wasn't sure he could let her pass without reaching for her.

"We haven't spoken in nearly a week, and we have a lot of work to do. I see no reason not to eat while working. Many people have made the art of working dinners a thing . . . last I heard, at least," he said with a wink. He was in a good mood, and he could see that was confusing her. Obviously she hadn't known how he'd respond to their last parting. He'd been upset. But he wasn't anymore.

She broke their heated gaze and ran her finger along the strap of her bag as her lips turned down in a frown. "I don't think this is working out for us, Noah. You and I both know the best thing I can do is step down so you can finish this project. Our personal problems shouldn't affect the outcome of such a needed facility," she told him.

He didn't take offense. He knew it was a great sacrifice for her to offer what she was offering. She cared enough about the veterans that she didn't want her personal issues to affect them. That only made him love her that much more. He didn't think this woman could do anything that would make him feel anything other than respect for her.

"I refuse to work with anyone else on this project. So if you do step away, then I guess a lot of people won't get to behold and utilize this beautiful campus. I guess you have to decide if you can work with me or not," he said.

Her head whipped back up, and there was fire in her eyes as she glared at him. He loved that fire. He'd much rather see that than sadness or defeat. Fire was good. Fire led to passion, and he knew Sarah was one of the most passionate women he'd ever met.

"You're being absolutely ridiculous, Noah. This project can go on without me. But we can't seem to get along enough days in a row to complete it. Your uncle is going to fire both of us if we don't make some sort of change," she warned.

"I'm really not worried about that because I know what you bring to the table, and I know we work better as a team than on our own or with other people."

Her eyes sparkled with tears that she quickly blinked away. He wondered if she'd had people discouraging her often in life. Was a lot of her bravado an act? That was a layer he'd definitely like to delve further into. Maybe she'd open the doors enough for him to understand more. Maybe it was just a matter of him opening up more so she could trust being vulnerable with him.

"I love this project enough to know when it isn't working," she said with a sigh. "How can we make it better?" Her voice was slightly pleading, and he wanted to pull her into his arms and hug her, to assure her everything would be okay. But he had to be very careful at the moment. He was trying to judge her body language to know exactly what she needed right now.

"I think I should be the one asking you how we can make it better. What can I do to make you want to stay?" he asked.

He moved closer, leaving her with little room to retreat. She looked behind him as if she wanted to run, but he was impressed when she stood her ground. Her shoulders stiffened the slightest bit, but she didn't flee.

"I want to tell you what I need is for you to leave me alone," she said with a sigh.

"Would you mean that?" he asked. He took a step closer. They were only about two feet apart now. He could feel the electricity between them. It was euphoria.

She sighed. "I don't like lying," she admitted.

"Then let go, Sarah. We don't have to plan an entire future; we can just get to know each other while we do this project. From the moment I met you, I haven't so much as looked at another woman. That means something."

She looked at him again with more vulnerability than he'd ever seen before in her expression. Maybe she was beginning to believe him. That would go a long way in them both accepting what was right in front of them.

"I'm not sure I can live in the heat of the moment," she told him.

He moved closer and ran his finger down her shoulder, then twined his fingers with hers. She didn't pull away from him.

"We've had some explosive moments together in the past year. We've had excitement and laughter, some thrills and scares. But we're drawn to each other. Why can't we just explore what we're feeling? I think this relationship deserves a real chance. And before you argue more with me, you should know that I've never spoken to someone the way I'm speaking with you. This is all new to me."

His last words seemed to knock down her defenses, because the stiffness in her shoulders drained away as quickly as it had appeared. She gave him a slight smile and squeezed his fingers.

"I don't understand how you're still around," she said.

"Because what you do to me is unlike anything I've ever felt before in my life. Don't you realize you're worth it?" he asked. Her eyes widened as if she'd never heard anything like that. He couldn't comprehend it. "You are a treasure, Sarah, an unbelievable treasure, and I'm so much better of a man to know you, no matter what happens at the end of the day."

She lifted her hand and ran it across his cheek. Then her thumb brushed his bottom lip, and he instantly hardened as he fought every instinct to not pull her tightly against him and take her mouth in a scorching kiss. But he was being vulnerable, being honest, and trying to give her time to come to the same conclusions he'd already come to.

It wasn't easy to wait to see what she had to say.

Silence greeted him for the next couple minutes. It felt like hours. Questions flashed through her eyes, but she didn't say anything. He waited . . . and waited.

Finally she smiled a bit, then stepped back.

He let her, waiting to see what she was going to say.

"I'll think about what you've said," she finally told him. She then grabbed her bag and walked around him. He desperately wanted to grab her, but instead he walked a couple steps behind.

"For how long?" he asked after another minute or so. They left the classroom and went down a hallway, where she stopped at her temporary office. She moved inside, and he followed. She scowled at him.

"I'm not sure," she said. He could feel the restlessness in her. He was feeling it, too. "But I think we should discuss it later. There's a lot I need to get done today."

"Nah," he said with a cocky smile. He shut the door behind him when he was fully inside. Then he clicked the lock. Her eyes widened, but he saw the arousal in her eyes. He wondered if she had a few teacher's fantasies of her own like he did.

"What are you doing?" she asked.

"I think you can figure that out, Professor," he told her as he began to slowly move forward. She took a few steps back until she hit the desk.

"This is a mistake," she said, but he saw the desire in her eyes. It would be a win for both of them.

"Then let's make it a good one," he told her. A shiver ran through her. She stopped talking as he pressed against her. "Do you want me to stop?" he asked, his lips less than an inch from hers.

There definitely wasn't a protest escaping her now. She was his—as much as he was hers. He had a feeling it was going to always be that way.

CHAPTER EIGHTEEN

Sarah stopped allowing herself to think and let it all go. It was always that way when she was in Noah's arms. The moment his lips touched hers, she was his. It was her mind after it was over that was her biggest enemy. She didn't want to let him in and then feel the pain of letting him go.

But what if she didn't have to let him go?

She was too afraid to think that way—too afraid of the pain it could cause.

Her doubts and fears were erased, though, as Noah's lips sipped on hers. He pressed against her, nothing between them. Her body heated, and she wrapped her arms around his neck and clung on tight as he kissed his way across her jaw to the gap in her shirt. The cool air was heated by his hot breath before his tongue swept across her skin.

He slowly, sexily undid the buttons on her blouse, exposing her flesh to his masterful touch. He took his time kissing and licking each new piece of skin that was exposed. She could barely do more than hold on as he melted her from the outside in.

When he reached the top of her lacy bra, a shiver traveled down her spine as her fingers tangled in his hair to hold him tightly against her.

"What do you want, Sarah?" he asked, his voice vibrating against her heated skin.

"You. I want you," she said without an ounce of hesitation.

She felt his lips curl against her skin before he nuzzled the lace of her bra out of his way. The front clasp came undone, and he swept his tongue across her hard nipple before latching on and sucking. She arched against him and moaned.

She barely felt movement as he walked her backward, and then she was falling forward as he sat and pulled her into his lap, never taking his mouth from her nipple. It tugged and strained as they fell, and she nearly orgasmed from the new sensation.

"Noah, please," she begged, not knowing what she was asking for.

He broke away, and she whimpered, not wanting him to stop for even a second. When she finally opened her eyes, he was holding her cheeks, looking at her so intensely she felt the burn of his gaze—felt it so deep it scared her more than anything else had.

"I will give you everything," he said. She tried to look away, but he wouldn't allow it. "I mean it, Sarah. My world is yours; all you need to do is accept it," he said. She couldn't say a word, didn't know what to say. "It's okay. I don't need a response. I just want you to know that."

And then he stopped talking as his mouth pressed into hers in another heated kiss that left her breathless and aching. He pressed up, and she felt how aroused he was. She wasn't sure who felt the intensity more, her or him, but she couldn't get close enough. She wanted the clothes between them gone.

He slid his tongue inside her mouth, and she pulled him closer as her breasts rubbed against his solid chest. There was too much space between them. She needed him buried inside her. She loved how skilled he was, loved their foreplay, but right now the only thing that could satisfy her was him buried deep inside her body.

He might think he could promise the world, but he didn't need to give her anything except exactly what he was giving her. If they could stay in this moment of bliss for all time, she wouldn't have a care or worry in the world, wouldn't have to think, wouldn't have to feel anything other than pure pleasure. She wanted to freeze this moment and hold on to it forever.

Noah was growing more impatient as his hands slid beneath her bottom, and he pulled her more tightly to him. She could have him inside her this very second if it wasn't for the damn clothes. But he liked to draw it out, liked to make her beg him to take her. She was so close—so very close to giving him exactly what he wanted.

One hand crept up the back of her shirt, and her flesh felt scorched as his fingers trailed their way up, kneading and touching every inch of her back. With his other hand, he pulled her shirt completely off, then gripped her breast and squeezed as his tongue circled her lips and dipped inside her mouth.

She loved the torture he was putting her through but finally came to her senses enough to give some back. She slid away a couple of inches on his lap and reached between them, easily finding his solid bulge and squeezing it as he'd been gripping her. This time it was Noah's turn to cry out as she kneaded his pulsing, hard flesh. She felt the tremble of his mouth against hers before she bit down on his bottom lip and then sucked it hard.

He moaned again before pulling back and looking at her with a hooded gaze full of heat and admiration, making her feel as if she was the only woman in the world for him. It was the most euphoric feeling she'd ever experienced. She wanted to keep putting that look into his eyes, wanted to please him as much as he was pleasing her.

"What you do to me . . . ," he said on a gasp before grabbing the back of her neck and pulling her forward again, kissing her hard enough to bruise them both. She was so lost in this man's arms.

They continued to kiss and touch as they undid one another's clothes. She wasn't sure who was doing what as buttons ripped and zippers came undone. They were so lost in each other she wasn't sure which way was up or down. It was the hottest experience she'd ever had, and that was saying a lot, since their lovemaking was always great.

She traced her fingers over the hard planes of his chest, fully satisfied at his beauty and hardness and the solid lines he worked so hard for and the slight sprinkling of hair that added to his manliness.

She broke away from his lips so she could kiss her way across his salty neck and suck on that corner of his shoulder that always made him squirm. Her fingers moved up and down his chest, his abs, and his sides, and she couldn't get enough of his heated skin.

She moved farther down, flicking her tongue across his hard nipple, making him tense as she nibbled his flesh. His fingers gripped her hair tightly, holding her close to his chest. She was just as turned on touching him as she was while he touched her. It was pure heaven.

The heat of him, the smell of him, the touch of him—all of it was intoxicating. She purred as she kissed and sucked her way across his chest and down the lined V of his abs. He shook beneath her warm mouth and wet tongue.

His pants were already undone, so she slid off of him and used her teeth to tug at the edges, making his legs tense. She looked up from her knees, her face inches from the bulge that was now barely covered. Keeping her eyes on his, she blew hot air against his covered arousal before leaning forward and gently biting him through the denim.

"Come here," he growled, his fingers tangling hard in her hair.

She shook her head and smiled as she licked her lips before bending forward and biting down, a little harder, enough to get his attention.

"Behave," she said, feeling sexy and powerful.

She tugged his pants away, and he broke free, his thick hardness springing up, the head beaded with pleasure, his flesh hot and begging for her touch. She wrapped her fingers around him, making him whimper as she flexed her fingers while moving them slowly up and down and letting her thumb brush softly over the head.

He was velvet and steel, hot and slick—perfect, utterly flawless.

He pulsed against her shaking fingers, making her quicken her movements as she squeezed a bit harder. His breathing grew more shallow, and his body was tense as she played with him, her mouth just above his flesh, her hot breath blowing across him.

He'd tortured her like this many times before, and she was greatly enjoying giving back to him. There was a bit of a backfire, though, because she was aching so badly for him it was making her squirm in her submissive position.

Though Sarah wanted to draw this out forever, she could no longer stand not tasting him. She leaned forward and took him into her mouth, sucking his hot flesh and moaning at the pure pleasure of his taste. She moved down, taking him deep as she moved her tongue in a circle. His thighs tensed beneath her chest as his fingers tightened in her hair, and a guttural cry of pleasure was ripped from him.

She stopped for a second, his head touching the back of her throat. She swallowed, and he jumped as he let out another moan. Then she moved back as she squeezed the root of him and sucked hard on his dripping head. She didn't give him a chance to recover before she did the entire process again—then did it over and over again until he was shaking beneath her touch.

She felt him tensing more, felt him nearing his peak. But with a growl and a tug, he ripped her away from his flesh. She tried taking him back into her mouth, but he wasn't allowing her to be in control anymore. When she opened her eyes and looked up at the heated gaze he was sending her way, she didn't mind one bit.

Her core pulsed, and she nearly came right there in front of him from nothing more than the promise of what he was about to do to her shining in his eyes.

Suddenly Noah was lifting her up and moving again, this time sitting her on the desk as he ripped away the rest of her clothes. His eyes were wild, and his body was tense, and she was more than ready for him. She opened her legs and lay there bare, ready and waiting and more than willing.

Noah reached between her thighs and ran his finger along her wet folds. One finger slid inside, and her bottom came up from the desk as a cry was wrenched from her. She wanted so much more than his hands inside her.

His hand pulled away, and then finally he was positioned where she needed him. But he didn't move. It felt like weights were on her eyes, but she managed to lift them halfway, and it was well worth it. He was standing over her, his solid flesh at her entrance, and his eyes were burning into hers. Her lips trembled as she tried to speak, but no words could escape.

"Now," he said. And with that he surged forward in a hard thrust that sent her sliding backward and had her screaming in pleasure.

He didn't give her time to recover before he slid backward and pushed forward again. He filled her so completely, so beautifully, that she couldn't do anything more than hold on as her pleasure built and her body turned to molten lava.

She somehow kept her eyes open as he moved faster and faster in and out of her heated, aching flesh. And then the tingles began. She went from beautiful pleasure to exploding lights and flashes of color. Her body gripped him tightly as she squeezed his flesh over and over again, her head thrown back, her body on fire.

Somewhere in the back of her consciousness, she felt him tense, felt the heat of his release shooting deep within her, felt him collapse on top of her. She barely had the strength to wrap her arms around his damp flesh and hold him tightly to her, not wanting him to pull from her body, not wanting to break this connection the two of them had. She was always greedy with Noah, always wanted more. She was afraid this time it was too late for her to turn back. He'd opened a new door within her, and she wasn't sure she'd be willing to try to close it again. She was barely recovering from the most beautiful orgasm she'd ever experienced, and the feel of his flesh pulsing inside her was waking her up again.

When he did finally pull back, she whimpered. But when her eyes opened, he was looking at her so intensely she wasn't sure what to do next. He cupped her cheek.

"Nothing in my life has ever come close to what just happened between the two of us. This is only the beginning, Sarah. You can try to hide from me again, but this will happen over and over again, because we're made for each other," he said.

Her throat closed with the emotion she was feeling, and she didn't know what she could possibly say to that, so she said nothing. He just gave her a knowing smile before he leaned down and gently kissed her.

Then he pressed against her, and she was thankful he wasn't expecting her to come up with something to say. Maybe he did know her more than she realized. Maybe this was meant to be.

She wasn't sure. All she was sure of was in this very moment right here and now, she didn't ever want to let him go.

CHAPTER NINETEEN

Sarah stood still while trying to comprehend what Noah was holding in his hands and saying. She was having a difficult time understanding his words. It had been three days since their out-of-this-world lovemaking in her office.

They'd spoken on the phone each day about work, but he hadn't brought up anything personal. Then he'd called about an hour earlier and told her to pack an overnight bag and to include sweats and a hoodie and swimwear; then he'd hung up before she could tell him no.

Now he was standing in her doorway.

"What are you doing, Noah?" she asked.

"We're going on a new adventure," he said.

"We're just going to pretend everything is normal?" she asked.

"Pretty much," he said with the smile that drew her in.

She could keep on fighting him but decided she didn't want to. It was that simple. What was the point? She was working with him, didn't want to stop at this point, and besides all that, she actually did miss him when he wasn't around. In other words, she was a mess.

"Where are we going?" she asked.

"You'll see."

She laughed, surprising them both. But then she grabbed her bag and purse and followed him out the door. They didn't speak as she climbed in his truck, and they drove for about an hour.

When they reached the water, she smiled. She followed him down to the docks and couldn't help but appreciate the beauty of the boat he moved over to. This was looking to be like a very good day.

It had been many years since Sarah had been on the ocean. There was something almost miraculous about the smell of salt in the air while wind whipped through your hair and you flew across the water. Getting away from the rest of the world for a few hours was something everyone should do at least once a month just to refresh the mind and soul.

It didn't take Noah long to get them both on the boat and to bring it out to sea. The surface was glassy and the wind mild. If Sarah could get her racing heart to calm down a little, she'd call this a pretty great day. But she couldn't help but look at Noah and think about what they'd been doing only a few days earlier.

Noah was being secretive about their next adventure, but she didn't mind. She had no doubt whatsoever that what they were about to do would inspire her. This entire adventure they were on was making her a better architect and taking her stress away.

Their ride took them about an hour, and then they were pulling up to a dock on one of the many Washington State islands. She had about a dozen questions for Noah, but they'd been silent all morning, and she was being stubborn and didn't want to be the one to speak first. She seemed to give in first all too often.

"Grab the green pack. We won't be back to the boat for a while, and I have some snacks," he said.

The sound of his voice startled her after silence for so long. She smiled at how nervous she was, then laughed when she stepped off the boat and found her legs a little wobbly.

"Guess I don't have sea legs," she said, her voice slightly scratchy. She wasn't normally a person who could remain silent for so long.

"You did amazing. I guess you don't get seasick," he said. "That's good, as I love a long day on the water. Throwing a pole in the water when you need to let your mind relax is a necessity."

"Maybe for you. I've never been a fan of fishing. It's boring," she told him.

He looked at her as if she was insane. "You've been fishing with the wrong people. I'll take you out, and I guarantee your mind will be changed," he said with confidence.

"I'll take your word for it," she said.

"Maybe we'll just have to make a little bet on it," he told her with a wink.

He definitely knew how to intrigue her. They were moving up the dock as they fell into an easy pace beside one another.

"What kind of bet?" she asked.

He laughed.

"Depends how confident you are," he told her.

"I'm incredibly confident," she assured him.

"Well, in that case, we have to come up with something good," he insisted.

"I can do anything I want to do, so it would be a pleasure to outfish you," she said.

He was definitely making her want to fish now, dang it. That's what he'd wanted to accomplish, but she never had been able to turn down a bet.

"Okay, hmm . . ." He looked as if he was really thinking. She smiled as a thought came to mind.

"Ever had rocky mountain oysters before?" she asked.

His grin fell away. "No, and I don't plan on it, either," he assured her.

"Loser has to eat them," she said, feeling quite proud of herself.

"Wait a minute," he said as he stopped moving.

"Nope. You said you'd beat me, so you shouldn't have a problem with the bet," she told him. Now she was the one goading him.

His eyes narrowed. "Fine," he said after several long moments. "It's the size of the fish, not the quantity."

"So when I catch the biggest fish, you'll be eating rocky mountain oysters," she told him. She was very proud of herself.

"You'll literally be eating your words," he said, smiling again. But she saw a bit of worry in his eyes.

They began walking again. She was already planning on her victory. Maybe she'd take a pic of him eating them and frame it for a Christmas present. It would be great. She was also wondering if the two of them actually did have a chance together. When she let her guard down with him, she really did enjoy her time in his company.

Thoughts like that were pretty scary, but life was about taking risks. If she always stayed in the safe zone, she wouldn't truly be living, and that wasn't a life she wanted to live. She just had to decide exactly how much risk she wanted to take.

They walked a trail on the island and passed through green forests and flowers that were blooming. The animals were chirping, and stress and artist's block were being replaced by magic and a myriad of possibilities. She could look forward to the future or keep living in the past. She was starting to believe the future was a much better place to be.

They walked through Frog Holler Forest and moved around the island for a couple of hours. One of Sarah's favorite sights was a tree that had a bicycle through the middle of it. She was fascinated by the sight of it.

"You see, there are strange things all over the world, but we live in the beautiful Pacific Northwest, where we can get inspired by everyday things. We can travel the world because it's amazing to do, but we don't have to," Noah told her.

"It's amazing how we live each day without taking time to look around," she said. She was incredibly grateful for her day with Noah. "We search and search for more and more and more, when sometimes the best things in life are right in front of us."

Her words stopped him in his tracks. The light was dimming, but she could clearly see his eyes, and he was obviously pleased by her words. She hadn't thought about them, just blurted. Maybe it was the relaxing day, maybe how kind he'd been, or maybe she was just so tired of fighting what she was feeling, but all of it added up to her saying what was on her mind.

"I think we run and run and run, and it's only when we slow down that we actually see that what we need has been there all along," he told her.

"Sometimes I'm not sure what you want," she admitted.

He cupped her cheek as he looked at her. His eyes were so intense she wanted to turn away, but there was no way she could do that right then. She was utterly mesmerized by this man. She had been from the very beginning.

"I don't always know," he admitted.

She smiled. "I can appreciate that."

They both stood there smiling at each other like a couple of teenagers. But she didn't mind. It was the best she'd felt in a long time.

"Our adventure for the day isn't over yet," he said.

"Oh, really?" she questioned.

"The best is yet to come," he promised.

"I can't wait."

Noah took her hand, and she clung tightly to his fingers as he led her along another path, then took her to the Palouse Winery. The sun set in the sky as they were seated on a patio in the corner, where a table was lit with candlelight.

And she was a goner.

"Will you stay the night on the island with me?" he asked.

There wasn't even a moment of hesitation.

"Yes."

And just like that the relationship she'd been fighting so hard changed again. But a moment could go from extraordinary to one of the worst of your life in a matter of seconds. It wasn't usual, but it could happen. Sarah and Noah had gone through many ups and downs over the course of a very short time period. Now that it had all happened, she wasn't sure she'd change any of it.

If everything was good all the time, then how would you truly understand it or appreciate it? Maybe there had to be trials along the way, and maybe that was where you truly found the character of a person or yourself.

They made it back to the hotel room, and Sarah began feeling sick. Noah put his arm around her, and her head started spinning—and not in a good way.

"Sarah?" he questioned. His voice sounded as if it were coming to her through a tunnel. She opened her mouth to speak but couldn't.

"Sarah!"

What was happening? Her body went limp.

"Noah . . ." She was able to breathe out his name on a sigh, and that took maximum effort.

The last thing she saw before blackness overtook her was total panic on Noah's face.

Chapter Twenty

Confusion filled Sarah as she drifted in and out of consciousness. At first she was only awake for seconds before blacking out again. Then she began staying conscious for longer periods, but she had no idea what was going on. Her entire body ached as if she'd just run a marathon.

The next time she was conscious, she tried focusing on what she could remember last. There'd been an amazing day on the island. A romantic dinner and a rush to a hotel room. Then all she could remember was dizziness and bewilderment.

And now she was here.

She opened her eyes and gazed up. The room was light, telling her it was daytime. She was alone and had to fight panic. She'd been with Noah when she'd passed out. There was no way he'd simply leave her. That meant he was somewhere nearby. But she wasn't even sure where she was. She opened her mouth to call out to him, but nothing came out.

What was wrong with her? Tears formed in her eyes as she tried talking herself down from the ledge she felt she was about to go over. She shut off the panic and concentrated on breathing in and out while trying to calm her racing heart.

She opened her mouth again, and this time sound escaped. It wasn't a word, but a squeak. The noise seemed like a booming shot in the quiet of the room. Her heart raced again.

There was noise in the doorway, and then the bed dipped and an arm wrapped around her, and just that quickly her panic eased. She took in another deep breath.

"I'm right here, Sarah. You're not alone," Noah said as his fingers rubbed along her stomach and side in a soothing motion.

It seemed to take maximum effort, but she managed to turn slightly to look at him. She had so many questions, but her throat hurt, and she wasn't sure she could carry on a conversation.

"What happened?" she finally managed to ask. Her voice was weak, but at least she was finally able to speak. Sarah would never be described as a quiet person, so it was probably a treat for Noah that she could barely talk above a whisper.

"You've been asleep for about sixteen hours, so I'm going to help you sit up to have a drink to see how you're feeling. You really need to have some food, too."

He kept his movements slow as he sat up, then gently placed his arms under her and helped her sit. The movement made her head slightly spin, but he just held her as she took more breaths, and soon the dizziness went away.

"What happened?" she asked again.

"You got a severe case of food poisoning. The doctor thinks you were allergic to something. You were in the hospital overnight and in and out of consciousness. Do you remember any of it?"

"No," she told him.

He smiled at her. "Then you insisted on leaving. He said as long as you take the meds, you were clear to go home but couldn't be alone."

She believed 100 percent she would've insisted on leaving the hospital. She hated them. She just didn't understand how she could've forgotten an entire day, especially when she'd been talking to people.

"I'm glad you took me away. I don't like hospitals," she said.

"I know. I remember the last time you were there," he said. He was rubbing his fingers through her hair, and the best medicine she needed right then was his touch.

"I don't get sick too often. Do they know what I might be allergic to?" she asked.

He shook his head, then grabbed the water next to him and handed it to her.

"You'll have to go and take tests as soon as you're feeling up to it," he told her. "Now take a drink. If you keep this down, you get some nice delicious bland soup."

"Ooh, sounds yummy," she told him, starting to feel better.

She sipped on the water and waited to see if she was going to feel sick. She felt seriously thirsty, so she took long pulls. He handed her some pills. "Take these, too."

She didn't argue with him but didn't like the shaking in her hands as she took the pills from him. Weakness wasn't something she accepted easily. She didn't like to rely on another person for her well-being, either. Trusting in other people was a scary thing. Besides her best friends, there weren't a lot of people she could honestly say she'd trust to take care of her.

"I hope this goes away quickly. We have way too much work to get done for me to be lying around," she told him. They were finally making great progress on their project, and she didn't want that interrupted.

"I think everything will be just fine if we take a few days off," Noah said with a chuckle.

"Are you using my sickness as an excuse to slack?" she asked. The water was really helping to perk her up. She was still tired, still achy, and definitely still sick, but she could at least smile again.

"Maybe I am. It's good to take time off," he said with a wink.

"Promise you aren't going to sneak off to work while leaving me passed out in this bed," she said.

Now that she'd committed to finishing this project, she didn't want to be left behind. She was beginning to trust Noah more each day, but there was still that insecure piece of her that worried.

"This project is all about the two of us. I promise: we started it together, and we'll definitely finish it that way."

His words made her smile—and relax. For a job she'd tried to quit multiple times, it was funny how anxious she was at the thought of being left out now. She was putting her heart and soul into this, and it would lead to so many other things in life as well. She could see the possibilities right before her eyes.

"Where are we?" she asked. She didn't recognize the bedroom. She looked around, and it didn't seem to fit him.

"We're at Crew's place in the guest cottage," he told her. "You've only seen the living room. It's a shame."

His words made her smile. She was finally in his bed again, but there was no chance of anything happening at this moment.

"I guess we missed out on that hotel room," she told him.

He looked a little surprised at her words. That was good. She needed to keep him on his toes. At least he could never say their relationship was boring. If anything, it was more like a roller-coaster ride. A *really* scary roller coaster.

She looked around the room, filled with light and soft colors. "This is beautiful. I can see why he bought the property. It seems like a lot to take care of for a single man, though."

"Yeah, I was surprised he bought it, but I'm glad, 'cause I don't know yet what I'm doing, and I don't mind sponging off him for a while," he told her.

"It's not sponging when you work as hard as you do and can afford to get your own place. It's taking time to be with your family and figure out what your next move is," she said.

"I'll have to tell Crew that when he gripes at me," Noah said with a chuckle.

"I love when you laugh," she said. She felt closer to him now than ever before. Being sick should be scaring her all over again. She seemed to get hurt a lot around this man. But she was just so tired of pulling away from him.

"You make me smile and laugh more than any other person I've ever been around," he said, his lips still turned up.

"Maybe I make you laugh *at* me," she said with her own smile. She chuckled a bit, then stopped instantly when it caused an ache to rush down her spine. His smile fell away as she winced.

"The pills will kick in soon, and you'll get more rest," he assured her.

"Apparently that's all my body seems to want to do," she told him with frustration. She didn't like to waste time by sleeping away entire days. There was so much life to live, and sleep took away from it all.

"Let's make sure we get some food inside you before you fall asleep again. The water is staying fine, so some soup and bread will be perfect," he told her as he shifted to climb from the bed.

She wanted to grab him and hold him to her. She didn't want to let him go. What in the world was wrong with her? She wasn't a clingy woman. She didn't say anything as he rose.

"I don't know how much I can eat. My stomach isn't feeling all that strong," she told him.

"Just give it a try. If it doesn't feel right, we'll do it again later," he told her.

Sarah lay back and tried to get comfortable, but it wasn't easy. The pills were kicking in and making her groggy, and she had her head turned to hear Noah. This clinginess had to be a response to her sickness, because if she turned into that girl who couldn't function without

Melody Anne

the guy, she was going to ask her friends to beat some sense into her. Maybe love wasn't as scary a notion as it had once been, but at the same time she needed to not have her world devastated if everything wasn't perfect.

Leaning against her pillows, she was comforted by the sound of Noah moving around in the kitchen, which had to be just around the corner from the bedroom. This cottage wasn't too big, which she liked. In the mood she was in, she wanted him nearby. She closed her eyes but opened them up again pretty quickly when she felt herself beginning to drift off. She needed to be awake for at least a little while.

It didn't take long before Noah returned, and the smell of the food drifting up to her woke her appetite up with a vengeance. She was hungrier than she'd realized. But she was also afraid of taking any of it in. He set the tray on his lap, and she looked at it a little suspiciously.

"I'll stay here with you. Just give it a try," he told her as he handed her the spoon and looked down at the chicken noodle soup.

"I can tell you had a good mom," she said with a smile.

His head tilted. "Why do you say that?"

"You're a good caretaker."

He smiled. "Yes. My mother was the best. Sometimes when I'm with you, I'm utterly heartbroken that she didn't get the chance to meet you. I have no doubt she would've loved you as much as you would've loved her." She was surprised when he slightly choked up. She was falling harder for him. Him showing her vulnerability made her want to pull him into her arms.

"I'm sorry you lost her. It hasn't been that long," she said.

She couldn't look at him, as she feared she'd break into tears, so she looked down at the soup instead and dipped her spoon. She took a small bite and chewed the noodles slowly.

When she felt no nausea, she dipped in for another bite.

"It's the worst thing I've ever gone through in my life. I can say with confidence it's the same for my brothers. We didn't have a father. He was a terrible man. But we had a mother that more than made up for it. I miss her every day, but some are worse than others because something happens, and I so want to call her or show up at her door and tell her about it. It's rough," he admitted.

"I didn't have good parents. I didn't have horrible parents, either. They were career driven, and they provided for me, but I was more of an incidental than a child. They'd give me gifts and tell me I was great when I brought home a good report card, but they weren't that loving, hugging, kiss-me-every-night type of parents," she said with a shrug as if she didn't care.

It was good to talk with him, because she was taking bites of soup without thinking about it. She picked up the bread and nibbled on it while she continued staring at the tray.

"I'm sorry, Sarah. Now I understand why you don't talk much about your family. I'm more blessed than I realize in the way I grew up. And I've lost my mother, but I've also gained an entire family who are just as wonderful as she was. I'm more than willing to share them with you."

She had to stop the bite she'd been about to take as her throat tightened. Some people might take his words as nothing more than just something people said, but she'd learned enough about Noah in the past year to know he didn't say what he didn't mean. For him to offer her his family was a beautiful gift she didn't know what to think about.

"Thank you for taking such good care of me," she said, deciding not to comment on the family statement.

"I love taking care of you. I love being by your side. I find it's where I'm happiest," he told her.

"You weren't at one time," she said. She didn't want to say it, but it popped out. His face fell.

"I screwed up. I thought I was worse in your life than out of it, and I ran. I won't do it again." Sincerity rang through his voice. Could she believe him?

The words made her heart skip a few beats. This downtime was making her so much more vulnerable than she'd ever allowed herself to be before. She wasn't sure how she felt about that, but she was also too tired to analyze it too much.

As if he felt the conversation was getting too intimate as well, he reached over and grabbed a slice of apple off her tray and bit into it. She took another bite. The pause gave her a chance to catch her breath and get her heart to calm.

Noah continued helping her eat the food on her tray, and she finished the entire bowl of soup and half a piece of bread and about a third of a banana. Not too bad when she hadn't eaten in over a day. She was feeling more than full. She set the spoon down, grateful her stomach wasn't stirring.

"What kind of pills am I taking?" She was surprised she hadn't asked before. She normally was so on top of everything pertaining to her life. That showed her how much she trusted this man.

He named something she didn't recognize the sound of. "They are an antibiotic," he added.

"Okay. I'm just so tired," she said. "Is that normal?"

"You're still healing, so it's more than normal. Your body needs rest to get better. You shouldn't fight it."

"I've never been good at taking orders," she said but softened the words with a smile. It was true that she wasn't, but at the same time she was really loving how much he was taking care of her.

"Well, since you gave me another of the biggest scares in my life when you passed out in my arms, then maybe you'll make an exception and listen to me a little," he said.

He got up and picked up the tray. She sunk down in the bed as she let the food settle. Her eyes were so dang heavy. But she also felt sticky and gross. She wondered if she had the energy to take a shower. That seemed like total heaven right now.

"I'm sorry I freaked you out," she told him. "I guess I've done that a lot in the time you've known me."

"Yeah, you have," he said. "But I have no regrets at all when it comes to you. I just wish I was able to protect you a little better."

He walked from the room, and she waited for him to come back before she responded to his words.

"You know it's not your job to take care of me," she told him.

"Maybe it's exactly what I want to do," he said.

He climbed back in the bed, then lay down and pulled her into his arms. She didn't even hesitate to curl up against his chest. She was so worn out, and it was exactly where she wanted to be.

Her eyes closed as she sighed in pleasure. The pillows were certainly much softer than his hard chest, but the smell of him and the security of being in his arms were pure heaven. She thought she could be happy to stay right there forever.

He rubbed on her back and ran his fingers through her hair, and she felt herself being pulled under fast. She desperately wanted a shower, but she wasn't sure she was willing to move from this spot.

"Were you the family caretaker?" she sleepily asked.

He laughed. "No. Not at all. That was Finn and Crew's job. Finn had to step up as the oldest when our father died. And Crew was always a natural protector. Hudson and Brandon were more of the class clowns. We all were completely different, but we have always loved each other immensely."

"How would your brothers describe you?" she asked.

"Probably slightly uptight and a workaholic," he admitted.

"Even now?"

He paused for a moment. "Maybe not. I'm finding more joy in life," he told her. "At least since I've met you."

She didn't want to change him. She didn't believe anyone should go into a relationship with the expectation of changing their partner. But she loved that she was making him smile, loved that she was helping him loosen up a little.

"You've made me take some pauses in life and smile a lot more," she admitted.

"Good. Now if we could just keep you out of harm's way, maybe we can smile a heck of a lot more."

She chuckled, feeling so at ease and completely happy.

"We can't prevent everything," she told him. "You just can't blame yourself for it. The wreck wasn't your fault, and this wasn't, either. But I do love very much that you care about how I'm feeling."

He didn't answer right away, and she felt herself being pulled closer and closer to sleep. She didn't want to stop talking to him, not when they weren't fighting and were actually communicating about something other than work, and she wasn't trying to walk away from him. But she wasn't going to last a heck of a lot longer.

He kissed the top of her head, and she felt incredibly peaceful. She waited, wanting to hear his voice. It was deep and sexy, and she could listen to him speak day and night.

"I can't change how I think and feel, but I'll try not to take the weight of the world on my shoulders. But don't ask me not to care or to not take care of you," he said.

She smiled against his chest.

"I wouldn't dream of asking that," she told him.

She felt his chuckle.

He kept rubbing her back, and this time as sleep began pulling her under, she stopped fighting it. She was right where she needed to be—in Noah's arms, hearing the steady beat of his heart and feeling his hands caressing her body. It was better than any medicine she could've been given.

The word *love* was on the tip of her tongue, but luckily she drifted off into darkness before she could say something she might regret later. She needed to analyze how she was feeling before she spoke. And maybe she was mushy because she was sick, and he was being so sweet. And maybe she was falling in love. She wasn't sure.

All she knew was she fell asleep smiling, feeling more content than she'd ever felt before.

Chapter
Twenty-One

Noah held on to Sarah for a long time, listening to her even breathing. He was slightly frightened at how unafraid he was. This was exactly where he knew he should be. With her in his arms, he felt he could keep her safe, felt as if he could conquer the world. She was his everything. He wasn't sure when that had happened, but he was sure he didn't want a life without her. He didn't want a single day without this woman. He couldn't imagine a lifetime of not seeing her.

And he couldn't keep himself from smiling, because he felt she was finally letting her guard down. She needed him as much as he needed her. There was no doubt in his mind that she was going to keep on fighting this, but he was hoping the fight would dwindle as time went on. Because once he grabbed hold of something, he didn't let it go. She was now his.

He drifted in and out of sleep as the sun began setting. He knew he should get some things done, but he couldn't talk himself into doing just that. He was far too happy to be right where he was. She was warm and soft, and he was where he belonged.

When Noah next woke, it was so dark he couldn't see anything in front of him. He'd always been a person to wake instantly. There was no hitting a snooze button or drifting in and out for a while. He was wide awake and instantly knew where he was. And the fact that Sarah was still in his arms made him smile. He could picture waking up this way every single day for the rest of his life.

She stirred against his chest and murmured something in her sleep as she clutched him a little more tightly. When her thigh rubbed against his, he had to clench his teeth together. Normally he'd flip her over and plunge deep inside her body. But since she was sick, that wasn't happening. And he felt like a pig at even having the thought when she'd been so miserable for days.

When she'd gone down in his arms, he'd felt panic as bad as when she'd been in the car accident. He'd always been protective of his mother and younger siblings. And the fact that the woman he was in love with kept getting injured in his presence wasn't helping his need to take care of her. He felt like less of a man because of it.

All he'd known when she went down was that he had to help her. He'd rushed her to the doctor, which had taken forever. And it hadn't even been a real hospital, as they'd been in the middle of nowhere. But they'd helped her, then told him lots of rest and relaxation. He was determined for her to do just that.

For too many years Noah had thought of no one other than his family and himself. There had even been a period he'd been pretty selfish, thinking of only himself, not even his family. Thankfully he'd grown out of that stage quickly. But one thing for sure was he'd never felt a need to take care of a woman. He'd always made sure the women he'd been with were pleasured, but he'd never felt a need to comfort them, to hold their hands, to place his hand on their backs as they walked somewhere.

He'd always enjoyed the curves of women, the softness of their skin, how they took care of themselves, and he'd loved putting a smile on their faces, but one was interchangeable with another. That was long gone now that he'd met Sarah. Now he felt more of a need to take care of her over taking care of himself.

If that didn't tell him he loved her, he wasn't sure what would. He was afraid to say those words out loud, but each day he was with her, he became more secure in his feelings and his mood. He wanted to be with her, and therefore he knew it was going to happen.

The reality was he'd been lost for a very, very long time. He was beginning to realize that he'd been searching for this one woman all of his life without realizing he'd been on a journey. That was a humbling thought.

She moved again, this time shifting her entire body. Her arm slipped down, and her fingers brushed over his painful arousal. No matter how much he told himself sex wasn't an option, wasn't going to happen, *couldn't* happen, his body wasn't listening.

He let out a groan as her fingers tightened for a second before relaxing. She snuggled in closer, and he wondered how much a man could take before having a heart attack. He tried scooting away. There was a thin line between pleasure and pain.

"No!" she grumbled as she followed him.

"Are you awake?" he whispered.

She didn't say anything as she tightened her hold on him. Her breathing evened out again as she relaxed. Was she talking in her sleep? He couldn't help but smile even while being in pain. She wanted him even in sleep. He was feeling pretty on top of the world.

He did need to get up, though. So he shifted again. This time she moaned. He kept moving, feeling pretty bad about it as she reached for him.

"Noah?" she asked sleepily.

"Sorry for waking you," he said as he sat on the edge of the bed.

"I can't see anything," she told him.

He reached over and turned on the lamp. She squinted at him, looking utterly adorable. Her hair was sticking out in all directions, her cheeks flushed, and her eyes brighter than he'd seen in days. She'd gotten some good rest finally.

"I didn't mean to wake you," he told her.

"It feels like I've been sleeping for a week straight," she said. "It's time for me to wake up." She slowly sat up. It was taking all of his restraint to stop himself from reaching over and grabbing her. He wanted her naked in his arms more than he wanted any other thing in this world. But patience was a virtue, or so he'd been told many, *many* times before. He'd never been one to display the virtue of patience.

"You haven't slept for quite a week, but at least forty-eight hours," he told her with a wink. He was still turned on, and his body was on fire, but he enjoyed their chats. He'd really liked the one they'd had before he'd fallen asleep. For every hour she'd been sleeping, he'd been awake and stressed, making sure she was okay. By the time he'd finally laid down, he'd conked out.

"I've really slept for almost two days straight?" she said, sounding horrified. She wiped a hand across her forehead and frowned. "I'm so disgusting right now."

"That's just not possible," he assured her. "You need to take another dose of medicine before we forget."

"No!" she said, then smiled gently. "Not yet. I need to be up for a little bit, and those pills seem to knock me out."

"If you're getting knocked out, it's because your body knows more than your mind what you need," he assured her.

"I understand when a person is sick, they need rest, but we also need baths and exercise," she told him. "I'm not sure if I'm so sore from being sick or from being on my back for two days straight."

There were much more pleasant ways he could picture her being on her back for forty-eight hours straight. That thought didn't help the problem he was currently having. He needed to get himself more under control.

Noah finally looked at the clock and was surprised to see it was two in the morning. He'd slept a solid six hours once he'd allowed himself to go to sleep. He'd drifted in and out for a good hour or two before that. He wasn't going to be able to go back to sleep, but he hoped she would. Then maybe by morning she'd feel up to getting out of bed for a while and stretching her unused muscles.

"I really want a shower," she told him as she ran a hand through her hair again.

"I'm not sure you should trust your legs enough for a shower right now," he said with a smile. She glared at him, and he laughed. "How about I get a bath ready for you? That will help with all the aches and pains. I'll even add bath salts."

Her frown instantly disappeared at the suggestion. She nodded her assent. At least she was growing more used to the idea of him helping her. She was probably one of the most stubborn, independent women he'd ever met in his life. It was just one more thing he loved about her.

But as he moved into the bathroom and started the hot water into the tub, he pictured her sitting in there in all her naked glory, soapy and slippery . . . whoa! That was a train of thought he absolutely, positively couldn't go down right now. He might be in a lot of pain over the next few days. He seriously might not survive it. But he'd take being in pain over her feeling anything bad, every single day for the rest of his life.

Once she was out of pain, though, he dang well was going to show her his best moves for possibly a week straight. She might be locked down in a bed for a long, *long* time. They had a lot of time out of the bed they needed to make up for.

When the bath was full, and the room smelled like a spa, he came back into the bedroom and found Sarah sitting up. Her eyes were still bright, but she already looked tired again. She was more worn out than she was willing to admit. He knew he could call her out on it, but he'd rather just be there for her and help carry her burdens.

She looked at him and let out a frustrated sigh as he moved toward her. "I'm seriously over this," she said. "Just sitting up feels like I just got done running a 5K. If I'm feeling this weak tomorrow, I might throw a major tantrum," she warned.

He chuckled again. She really amused him when she was grumpy. He was beginning to think there wasn't much she could do that he wouldn't find charming or amazing. Maybe that was the power of love. He wasn't sure.

"You're going to be back to a hundred percent before you know it. For now just enjoy being pampered," he told her. "I have a nice hot bath waiting for you that smells like peaches and cream."

"Ooh, that sounds like heaven," she said, smiling. "Even if I feel like a total invalid and am not liking it."

She shifted and attempted to stand, then plopped back down on the bed and looked up at him with tears in her eyes. His heart was breaking for her.

"It's going to be okay. I promise," he told her as he moved closer and knelt before her, placing his hands on her hips as he looked up. "I'm also sort of enjoying being your manservant."

At his words she smiled again. "My manservant?"

"I'm at your beck and call, my lady."

"Well, you are *literally* kneeling at my feet," she said as she wiggled her toes, which were pressed against the inside of his thighs. That didn't help his problem one bit. He let out a slight groan before he was able to stop it. Her smile fell as she licked her lip.

He had to turn away before he forgot she was sick. It would be easy to do.

Noah stood and scooped Sarah into his arms. She let out a sigh as she laid her head against his chest and wrapped her arms around him. At least she'd stopped fighting him.

"I could walk, but this is nice, too," she told him with a chuckle. "Maybe we should all have our own Noah to transport us this way."

"These arms are for you only," he said. He leaned down and brushed his lips across hers, and it helped settle his racing heart. This woman meant more to him than just sex. Yes, the sex was the best he'd ever experienced, but holding her was also amazing, and touching her lips with his was essential to his survival.

He set her down in the bathroom, then steadied her before letting go. "I'd be more than happy to help you get undressed since you're so weak right now," he said with a wink. He knew the words would fire her up, and he didn't want her in the tub too sleepy.

She glared at him. "I'm not that weak. And I'm plenty capable of getting myself undressed and bathing. You can go away now," she told him.

He grinned, leaned down, and gave her a hard kiss on the lips, then turned around and moved to the door. "I'm leaving it cracked open, and I'll check on you whether you like it or not," he warned.

She gave him another glare. "You know I have taken a bath or two in my lifetime." She looked so delicious leaning there against the bathtub with her flushed cheeks and heated eyes. It was taking some major willpower not to walk straight back to her and take her into his arms. He couldn't seem to keep his hands off her.

"But have you ever had help? That's a whole new experience," he said with a wink.

"Have you taken many baths with women?" she fired back with a glare. He felt almost giddy at the jealousy in her tone. If she was jealous, that was because she cared.

"Not once, but I'm always open to new experiences."

Her stiff shoulders relaxed. "I find it hard to believe you haven't, but I want to get in the tub before it cools off, so go away."

"Your wish is my command," he assured her as he gave her a bow. She tried to hide the smile, but he saw it. She enjoyed their sparring as much as he did.

He finally left. If he stood there much longer, he might find it impossible to leave. But as he moved out into the small living room, all he could picture was her slowly stripping away her pajamas, then sinking down into the bubbly tub. He closed his eyes and imagined nothing but water and soap covering her silky smooth skin. His arousal throbbed. He reached down and squeezed the hardness through his sweatpants. It didn't help the pressure to go away.

He moved to the kitchen and opened the liquor cupboard, grateful he had some smooth bourbon. He poured a double shot and downed it. Maybe it wasn't the breakfast of champions, but he needed the heat to burn down his chest. It helped a little—not much, but a little. There were some Pop-Tarts in the cupboard as well, and though he hadn't had one of those in years, it was surprisingly delicious.

About fifteen minutes went by before he *needed* to check on Sarah. He told himself it was only because she was sick, and he didn't want her falling asleep in the tub and drowning. But it was more of a calling that he just needed to be with her—or at least in the same room as her. He felt at peace when he was with her—that was, when she wasn't driving him absolutely crazy.

He moved to the door and didn't hear a thing. He wanted to pop it open, but he also wanted to respect her. So he called in instead. "Are you still awake?"

"Mmm, yep," she said with a content sigh. "This feels so good."

She'd made that same sort of sound before with him on top of her. He was very, *very* aware of that. The bourbon was doing nothing for him now. The two seconds of relief it had offered weren't nearly enough.

"Need some help?" he asked.

She chuckled. "I think I'm good," she replied. But there was no animosity in her tone.

"I'm gonna just check to see for myself," he told her. Then he slowly pushed the door open. She turned her head and looked at him, her eyes hooded, her mouth curved up in a content smile, her body barely covered by the depleting bubbles.

He might actually have a stroke. His heart was thundering and his body pulsing. He wondered if sex deprivation could cause a massive stroke or heart attack. At the moment that possibility seemed more than a little real.

"Thank you, Noah," she said before her eyes drifted closed.

He moved toward her, wondering how smart a decision that was in his current state.

"For what?" he asked. He couldn't see anything at the moment, as the bubbles were covering her, but he'd seen that delicious body before and knew exactly what the waterline was hiding.

"For caring so much and making sure I'm okay. I know this has been a pain for you, and I just want you to know how much I appreciate it."

"I like being your knight," he admitted. She was definitely sleepy, and he knew he should walk out of the bathroom and give her privacy, but she was like a siren calling to him. He couldn't seem to walk away.

"I'm surprised, but I like it, too," she said.

He shouldn't sit with her, but he just did it without a conscious thought of what he was doing. One second he was standing there looking down at her angelic face, and the next he was sitting on the edge of the tub, much, much closer to her soapy, flushed body.

"Well then, I guess you won't complain as I continue to watch out for you," he said. His voice came out almost reverently. What this woman did to him was shocking. But he wasn't afraid.

"I just might not," she said, her lips turned up in a content smile. She moved her legs, and her knee popped up above the bubbles, making his body stir once more. She was so unbelievably gorgeous lying there so vulnerable.

He didn't make a conscious effort to do so, but he reached out and ran his hand along the curve of her knee. Her skin was silky, tan, and beautiful. She was a perfect woman in every way he could've ever imagined.

Her eyes slowly opened, and their gazes connected in a heated look that had him pulsing. He'd wanted women before. He was a healthy man who loved sex. But he'd never needed a woman like he did her.

He wasn't sure how much time passed as they gazed at each other with his hand on her knee. He squeezed her warm flesh and told himself to behave. This wasn't the time for sex, even if she wanted it, which was probably not the case.

"You look a little dirty," she said, looking shy, which confused him. "Maybe you should clean up."

He was confused. "What?" He leaned closer to hear her.

"Do you want to join me?" Her cheeks flushed more than they already were, and his body went from hot to boiling.

Noah knew he wouldn't be capable of speech right then. He also knew he should tell her no; this was her turn. But he also knew she'd take that as rejection. She wasn't anywhere near a place she could have sex, but he certainly could suck it up and hold her, since that's what she wanted and needed. He still didn't trust his voice, though.

Slowly he stood and began peeling his clothes away. There was no chance he'd be able to hide his erection, but she might just have to suffer a little bit at the sight, 'cause he sure as heck was in a lot of pain. He had to keep telling himself, though, that even if she wanted sex, he couldn't do it. He had to wait until she wasn't sleepy, wasn't on meds, and was making fully conscious decisions before they made love again.

She watched him the entire time he stripped his clothes away. It didn't take him long, as he was wearing sweats and a T-shirt. When his pants came off, her eyes were drawn to the part of him that was hard and pulsing with moisture on the tip. She licked her lips, and he pulsed again. He was wondering again if he was going to be a man in his thirties who was otherwise healthy but would die of a stroke.

He didn't stand outside the tub long. He was hoping the hot water would ease some of the pressure. His heart was thundering as he sank into the tub behind her. She instantly leaned back against him as he wrapped her in his arms. She let out a sigh as her fingers lay over his.

He was hurting feeling her pressed against him and his hands caressing her smooth stomach, but he was also comforted. He really did love to be pressed against her in any way possible. Neither of them said anything for several moments, and he found himself beginning to relax. Of course sex was on his brain, but it was getting pushed back a little as he held her, and she fully sank against him, giving him her complete trust.

She sighed a couple times as he ran his hands along her stomach and arms, making sure to avoid her plump breasts and the junction of her thighs. He had willpower, but every person had a breaking point. He knew what his would be.

They stayed that way for long enough for the water to cool. He didn't want to let her go, didn't want to climb from the tub. He was too happy right where he was. She shifted as she began to cool and sought out his body for heat. She buried her head against his neck, and he felt he could stay in that place forever.

"I could fall asleep," she told him on a sigh, her lips moving against his skin. He chuckled as he shifted his fingers to rub her back. "I don't understand how I could sleep again after doing so much of it for two days."

"Don't fight the need for rest. The more you sleep, the sooner you'll feel better," he said. "Let's get you out of here."

It was almost painful to pull away, but he unwrapped his arms from around her, then climbed from the tub and wrapped a towel around his waist before reaching in and helping her stand.

"Now I'm cold," she said as her teeth chattered. He quickly wrapped her up in a towel and pulled her close as he rubbed her back, drying her off. She snuggled against him. He kissed her forehead, then gently lifted her into his arms.

"Noah transport at the ready," he told her.

He felt her lips turn up against his neck. He moved into the bedroom and laid her on the bed. She was stunning, with her hair cascading over the pillow and her flushed skin that was barely covered by the towel.

"Time for your medicine," he said, turning away.

"Okay, I won't fight it anymore," she said. Her eyes closed.

He got the medicine and helped her sit up to take it, then helped her lie back down. Not trusting himself to be naked beside her, he threw on a clean pair of sweats and then climbed in beside her. He was still aching, but the need to comfort her was driving him a lot more right now.

One thing Noah knew for certain was that he wasn't going to let Sarah run away from him again. He wouldn't ever wish her pain or misery, but he was enjoying being her caretaker while she was recovering. And in her vulnerability she was letting down her guard. He wasn't going to allow her to put it back up again. She was now his, and he wasn't going to ever let her go.

Noah felt like he was home for the first time in many years. He didn't want to roam anymore. He didn't want to be free. He wanted to be exactly where he was, with this woman at his side.

And he wanted it forever.

CHAPTER TWENTY-TWO

The rays were shining in through the window when Sarah next woke. Her body felt a hundred times better, but not yet perfect. She stretched and found herself reaching for Noah. She came up with cold sheets. Her eyes snapped open, and she looked about the room.

She smiled again, though, because there wasn't even a little part of her that was worried he'd gone somewhere. Something had shifted with the two of them the past few days, and she felt more confident in where they might be going. She wasn't sure of the answers, as they hadn't really discussed anything, but maybe she was ready to give it a real try.

Though she'd been in bed for days, she found herself snuggling under the blankets, not in a hurry to rise. She wasn't going to stay in bed all day as she had the day before, but a few more seconds to think while she was on her own weren't bad. She was grateful the achiness was beginning to dissipate.

It was so odd for her to let everything go and allow someone else to take care of her. But that's exactly what she'd done over the past few days. She'd heavily relied on Noah, and she wasn't even freaked out about it. The protection she'd built around herself for so long was crumbling a little more and a little more with each passing day.

Again that should make her worry, but right now she wasn't allowing those kinds of thoughts in. She was beginning to realize that if Noah put his mind to something, he didn't easily walk away from it. She wasn't sure why or how it had happened, but somewhere and sometime he'd decided he wanted to be with her, and they were doing okay together.

"Someone finally woke up."

Sarah turned to find Noah standing in the doorway with an amused look on his beautiful face. He was wearing a pair of snug jeans and a sweater that showcased his wide shoulders. She wouldn't mind looking at him all day long. He was better than any medicine a doctor could give her.

"I bet you're pretty hungry," he said.

Her stomach rumbled at the mention of hunger, and she laughed. "It appears so," she admitted.

"How are you feeling?" He hadn't moved from the doorway.

"I'm still a bit tender, but overall I'm much better," she said. She tried to move, to sit up, and found herself pathetically weak.

He came forward and propped some pillows up and helped her into a sitting position before straightening the blanket over her legs.

"Aren't you getting tired of taking care of me?" she asked.

He chuckled. "I never would've imagined how much I'd love taking care of someone—if that someone is you, of course," he said, looking serious. "So, no, I'm not getting tired of it at all."

His words filled her with warmth. "I truly do appreciate all you've been doing for me."

He rubbed his hand through her hair, then leaned down and placed a gentle kiss on her lips before moving back. "Thank you," he said.

"It's me that should be the one doing all the thanking," she said, feeling unusually shy all of a sudden.

"I know it isn't easy for you to let go of control and let someone in. I appreciate your trust in me," he told her.

She was growing emotional as the conversation continued. She just wasn't sure where to take it from there. Her stomach saved her when it gave a loud growl again, and Noah laughed.

"Let me grab you some food before you perish," he said as he walked from the room. She really should get up and go out to the table. But she wasn't 100 percent yet. Maybe food in her stomach would give her the energy to finally leave the bed. She didn't want to be in it again until she could do something a lot more fun than sleep.

It didn't take Noah long to come back with a tray balanced on one hand and a beautiful smile on those full lips of his. Now that she was feeling better, she was really wanting to get back to where the two of them had been a few days ago, before they'd been interrupted by her fainting spell. She was more than ready to be naked in his arms.

"That smells heavenly," she told him as he drew closer. He set the tray in her lap, and she was impressed. He'd made cream of broccoli soup, grilled cheese sandwiches, fruit, and cheese and crackers. It was enough food for four people, but she thought he had to be pretty hungry himself, since he'd been taking such good care of her.

"This is exactly what I want," she said. "Thank you again."

"No need to thank me. It was an easy meal," he said. He reached over and grabbed half a sandwich and took a big bite. A bit of cheese was on his lip, and she had the unbelievable urge to reach over and lick it off. How in the world could she be thinking so much about sex when she'd been so ill for days? Probably because that's what the man managed to do to her every single time she was in his presence.

"We need fresh air," he told her. He got up and moved over to the wide window and opened it. Immediately a breeze came in that rushed over her face and was just what she needed.

"I can't remember the last time I spent an entire day not stepping foot outside," she said as she nibbled on a cracker with cheese and looked out the window.

"I know the feeling. I prefer it outside day and night. In the summer it's hard to be indoors. Even in the winter I like to take hikes and enjoy the beauty we have all around us here in the Pacific Northwest."

"I've visited many places all over the world, and I always want to come back home. I feel sorry for people who live in the heart of cities. And though Seattle is a huge city, it's surrounded by trees and water, so if you have to be somewhere for work, I'd choose it any day over somewhere like LA, where you might go months without getting into the woods."

"There are forests not too far from LA, but yes, I do agree that it's easier to get to nature from Seattle than most cities."

"I'm not a big fan of city parks in the middle of the metropolis. I want real nature with water, trees, and animals. I guess I've gotten spoiled by it," she said.

The more they talked, the more she ate. He was helping her, for sure, but she was holding her own. It appeared she'd gotten her appetite back with a vengeance. She finished her soup and sandwich and was working on the chips, crackers, and fruit. There might be nothing left.

"Is the food giving you some energy back?" he asked when the tray was empty. "Do you need more?"

"No more," she said with a chuckle as she placed a hand over her very full stomach. "But yes, I feel better for sure. Definitely good enough to climb from this bed."

"I've enjoyed you all submissive and clingy the past few days," he told her. She knew he was saying it to get a reaction, but she certainly couldn't let that pass without some sort of comment.

"Mm-hmm, don't get used to it," she said with a mock glare.

"I wouldn't dream of it," he told her.

"I think I'll take a shower and then maybe attempt a small walk," she said. Right now she was feeling better, and everything in her wanted to push her limits, but she knew that would be foolish, and she knew Noah wouldn't let her do it, anyway.

"That's a great idea. I'll get this cleaned up. I know you're fine, and I promise not to look in on you unless you take too long, but for my sanity will you please leave the bathroom door cracked?"

If he'd demanded it of her, she would've argued, but he had been the one caring for her for days, and he was asking her nicely. She nodded, and he leaned down and gave her a slightly longer, hotter kiss than the one before. He pulled back, and she felt her head spinning. The man did things to her no one ever had.

He didn't say anything else, just grabbed the tray and left the room. Sarah was slow as she threw back the covers and shifted her legs over the side of the bed. She took her time placing her feet on the floor and held on to the bed as she stood.

"Are you okay in there? Don't be afraid to ask for help if you need it," Noah called from the kitchen.

"Thank you, Noah, but I'm fine," she assured him.

She stood up, and her legs were slightly shaky, but she was relieved when she took her first steps. She took her time getting to the bathroom and had to smile again when she found a fresh towel hanging up and a set of comfortable clothes sitting on the counter. He'd anticipated everything. He was spoiling her to the point she wasn't sure what she'd do without him when this was over.

She wanted to take a nice long hot shower, but the effort of washing her hair alone was zapping her energy. She couldn't even imagine what it would be like to be sick for ages on end. She was over it after a few days. She quickly washed her body, didn't worry about shaving her legs, then slowly climbed from the shower and took her time toweling off.

She was shaky and a bit weak, but she got dressed and managed to brush her hair. There was no way she was holding up a blow-dryer to dry it. She wanted to sit down—and not in the dang bed.

"Are you still good in there?" Noah called. It sounded like he was in the doorway to the bedroom.

"Yes, sir," she said.

He chuckled, but she heard his footsteps fade away. She wasn't going to admit it to him, but she liked that he was being protective and checking up on her. It made her feel secure. And if she did pass out, she wouldn't be left there for very long.

Sarah walked from the bedroom and found the living area spotlessly clean and cozy with a breeze blowing through it. Noah had all the windows open, and the scent of fresh mountain air was soothing to the soul. She thought about sitting outside, but there was a comfy-looking armchair in the corner of the room with a footstool in front. That looked more appealing than patio furniture at the moment.

"Can we take a short walk?" she asked. She wanted the chair but needed more movement.

"Yes," he said. He came to her side, and she didn't hesitate to put her arm through his. It was slow going, but they made it to the front door and moved outside. She took in the fresh air and felt tears sting her eyes. She couldn't stand not being in the sunshine for too long.

It took all her energy to move one foot in front of the other, so they didn't speak as they walked around the cottage and back. She was frustrated at how out of breath she was as they stepped back inside.

Noah assisted her to the chair, where they stood for a moment with her feeling the need to wrap her arms around him. "You're moving slow, but at least you're moving," he said with a gentle smile.

"That was my thought, too," she admitted.

Noah helped her ease down into the chair, then covered her lap with a blanket. She thanked him again. He moved over to a bookshelf and grabbed several books and came over to her, sitting down on the footstool next to her feet.

"We have thrillers, romances, and self-help books," he said as he flipped through them. "Which do you prefer?"

Sarah laughed. "You've thought of everything, haven't you? Are you secretly a caretaker?"

"Just for you," he told her as he handed over the books. She looked over each one and grabbed three.

"I'll check these out," she told him. She wanted the self-help book but didn't want to be obvious about it. He took the other ones back to the shelf.

Sarah opened the book and began scanning it. Normally she got so lost in a book the rest of the world completely faded. But not this time. This time, she kept glancing up and watching what Noah was doing. He moved about the cottage, fixing little things here and there, until he finally settled down on the couch with one of the thrillers she'd given back.

He was looking down, giving Sarah plenty of time to study him. She couldn't help but appreciate his beauty. She was also noticing how much she was enjoying this quiet, domestic moment. It was something she feared she might get very, *very* used to. She decided to read her book again until she got sleepy and closed her eyes.

They were heading somewhere. She'd just have to wait and see where exactly that was.

Chapter Twenty-Three

Noah wasn't sure how long he sat there watching Sarah doze in the chair. She was so damn beautiful, even being sick. There was nothing that could diminish her looks. With her guard down, her eyes shone, and her skin was flushed. She was everything he'd never known he wanted.

Yes, he still had minor panic moments when he realized he didn't think he could live without this woman. That must be what happened to a person. You were happily going along in life, perfectly content to be single, and then someone came along who took your breath away and became your second half. Maybe if the world realized what true love felt like, people would stop settling for mediocre. He'd been content with mediocre—that was, before Sarah had come along.

He had to get out of the cottage for a while, and he had a feeling Sarah would be out for at least a couple of hours. He was hoping his brother was home, because he could use some brotherly advice, though he probably wouldn't appreciate or like it once he got it.

Maybe by tomorrow Sarah would have more energy to move about. She wasn't the type of woman who could be kept down for too long. She'd start getting cranky soon if she didn't get movement. One of the things he loved so much about her was how active she was. The two of them together would never grow bored. That was for sure.

He truly had been enjoying taking care of her, though. He might have made that comment to get a rise out of her, but he did like her more vulnerable. He knew it would come few and far between while they were together. If there was something Sarah could do on her own, she would every single time. She was stubborn and independent—and he loved that about her, too.

Noah was a bit lost on what was happening to him. He'd never been a mushy guy, never had been more concerned about a woman than himself. He'd walked away so many times before, leaving them with a smile but never thinking of them again. And now here was a woman he wanted to drop to his knees for. It was strange, to say the least.

Noah stepped through Crew's house, at first thinking he wasn't home, but then he was relieved when he found him out on the back deck with a beer in his hand.

"Isn't it a bit early for that?" Noah asked as a greeting.

"It's five somewhere," Crew replied.

"What in the world has happened to my uptight brother?" Noah asked. "But of course, when in Rome . . ." He moved over to the outdoor fridge and grabbed a cold beer, then sat beside his brother. The first sip was heaven.

"Is Sarah feeling any better?" Crew asked. He'd been checking up on her, but Noah hadn't spoken to Crew since yesterday, and that had only been for a couple of minutes. He'd been tired himself, as he'd worried about her.

"Yeah, she managed to get a good amount of food in her, shower, take a short walk, and stay in the living room. She only lasted about an hour before she fell asleep in the chair, but I think the worst of it's over," he said. He hadn't gotten nearly as much sleep as her, and he was beginning to feel it.

Crew laughed. "I'm really enjoying seeing what this woman is doing to you. You're like a little puppy dog."

Noah glared at his brother. "I feel sorry for your patients," he said with a growl.

"I'm professional with my patients. You, on the other hand, I can give it to straight. You're a big boy and can take it—or at least you used to be, before you were so domesticated."

"I'm so happy you're amusing yourself," Noah told his brother. "And I thought I could come over here and have a real chat with you. Apparently not."

"When is the wedding?" Crew asked.

"Wedding? What wedding?" Noah asked.

Crew laughed again. His brother was in an unusually good mood on this sunny day. Noah was beginning to wonder if there was something going on in his brother's life he wasn't sharing with the rest of them.

"Don't pretend you don't know that's exactly where this is heading. First Finn fell, and now apparently you're following in big brother's footsteps."

"It's not like that," Noah said. But then he stopped. "I like her," he admitted.

"If you want to call it *like* for now so you don't panic, that's fine. That's how a lot of people get through the initial phases of love. But I'll say this with all kidding aside," Crew said before pausing. Noah waited. "Don't let her get away. It will be a lose-lose for both of you, because it's more than obvious how much you love one another, and I can tell you from my vast experience of counseling people that true love is a rare phenomenon."

Part of Noah wanted to counter his brother, tell him he was a fool. That was the old Noah, the defensive Noah. He'd never had a conversation like this with any of his siblings before, and it wasn't an easy thing to make yourself vulnerable. But the other part of him believed what his brother was saying. He knew he was falling in love with Sarah. He just didn't know what that meant exactly.

"Have you been domesticated?" Noah finally asked.

Crew laughed again. This carefree attitude from his brother was sort of freaking him out. Crew wasn't that guy. He was always the serious one, always the one telling the rest of the brothers to behave and grow up.

"I'm beginning to think it wouldn't be the worst thing in the world, but no, I haven't. Unfortunately in my line of work, I get to see everything that always goes wrong in relationships, and so it scares the hell out of me to get serious with someone."

Now it was Noah's turn to laugh. "But you're telling me I should marry Sarah?"

"I told you it's different with you and Sarah. It's real. That doesn't mean you'll never argue, and it doesn't mean it's all going to be fairy tales and pixie dust. It just means that you'll weather through every storm and grow stronger each time. You can give up on it, but I'm warning you you'll never find something like this again. When it's real, it's real forever. I think relationships like yours only fall apart because one or the other person allows it to. People forget the simple things: the kiss when their partner walks in the door, the thank-yous, the flowers and signs of appreciation. If you appreciate your spouse, you'll grow; if you stop appreciating them, you'll drift apart."

"I don't know how I feel about talking this deep with you," Noah said. He finished his beer and got up and grabbed another for both of them. He was restless and a bit uncomfortable, even though this was what he'd sought his brother out for in the first place.

"It's hard for us to hear things like this. But whether you want to take it all in right now or not, it's now in your head, and you'll have to process it over the next few days. I do this for a living, you know," Crew pointed out as he accepted the beer.

"Well, it's a lot of mushy talk," Noah grumbled.

"Maybe we should be secure enough in our masculinity that it doesn't worry us," Crew said.

That made Noah laugh. "I'm plenty secure in my manhood," he assured his brother.

"I've talked more with Finn since he's been with Brooke than any other time in our lives. He's a changed man—for the better, I might add. Maybe we truly do need our other half to be whole."

"Damn, Crew, you *really* have been thinking about this a lot," Noah said.

"Yeah. Losing Mom really rocked my world. I know it affected all of us, but it hit me harder than I ever expected it to. It's made me think about the future. It's made me sad that she'll never hold a single grandchild. It's made me realize maybe all of us should've grown up a little sooner."

"Mom would've loved Sarah," Noah said. "They would've gotten along so perfectly. She would've loved Brooke, too."

"Yeah, she would've loved any woman who loved her sons. None of us ever had to doubt how much Mom loved each and every one of us," Crew said.

"You'd think growing up with such a loving mother, we wouldn't be so hesitant about getting involved with women," Noah said.

Crew chuckled. "Well, we did have an awful father. That's going to make anyone hesitate a bit. I think part of it is all of us are a little afraid we might have some of his tendencies in us, and maybe we never want to put a woman through what he put our mother through."

Noah sat back as he processed those words. "I've never actually thought about that," he admitted. "But I think Mom more than made up for the DNA we're forced to share with that man. She gave us her blood, which is more powerful than his, and she raised us in a loving home. All we have to do is think of the lashing we'd get from her if we ever did treat a woman that poorly, and we're safe to never do it."

"I'd give just about anything to have a verbal lashing from her one more time," Crew said with a fond smile.

"Yeah, I'd give anything for a single day longer with her."

"So are you going to marry Sarah?" Crew said, changing subjects again. Noah knew it was partly because they were getting a bit too sentimental, and grown men weren't supposed to cry, and partly because his brother was like a dog with a bone and didn't easily drop it.

"I'm not willing to let her go," Noah said. That seemed all he was able to admit, at least at this particular moment.

"You're making my heart skip a few beats at your romantic words," Crew mocked.

"Hey! I'm trying here," Noah said with a frustrated sigh as he ran a hand through his unruly hair. "I have feelings for her that are stronger than *like* for sure, and there's so much I do love about her, but it is scary."

"And you might screw it up?" Crew said. His brother wasn't saying the words to be mean. He was simply reading between the lines.

"Yeah, I might screw it up. I've done it before where she's concerned."

They were both quiet for several moments as different thoughts went through Noah's head. He didn't think he'd be able to handle it if he messed up with her again.

"Well, then make a choice not to mess it up," Crew said.

"Just that easily?" Noah said.

"Just that simple," Crew stated.

"But I'll make mistakes," Noah said.

"Yes, you will, and so will she. But don't make them so big they aren't fixable. See that there's a problem, and put a stop to it right away. That's how this will last."

"I don't want to change who I am," Noah said. "But I don't want her to change, either. I just want to grow together."

"That's a pretty damn good place to be," Crew told him. "And with the help of our family, you have a lot of support. Sarah has a good support system, too. I think you guys will make it to the end of this road and be happier than you've ever been. Just stop playing games."

"You've changed a lot lately," Noah said. "I like it."

Crew laughed again. "I think I like it, too."

They changed the subject again and chatted about the veterans project and their siblings. Finn was now married, and it appeared that Noah was a goner. So the two of them wondered who'd be next. It wasn't a matter of *if* but a matter of *when*.

CHAPTER
TWENTY-FOUR

It was amazing how miraculous the human body was. No matter how sick a person got or how much they thought they were dying, the body was already healing itself, even when they were at their worst. Sarah almost didn't want to feel better on her fifth day with Noah. Because that meant she had no more excuses to stay in their cozy little world together.

And she very much liked their little world.

She loved that they were eating together, sleeping together, and spending the days and nights chatting and laughing and planning. They certainly had avoided the whole relationship topic, but she felt closer to him than she ever had before. She just wasn't sure exactly what that meant.

She'd leaned on him over the past five days more than she'd ever leaned on anyone, and she wasn't ready to stop doing it. But as she packed her bag and got ready to head back out into the real world, she couldn't help but feel sad and have so many unanswered questions she wanted to voice. She just wasn't sure how to go about doing that.

She should be more than relieved to get on with her life, to be able to get back to her daily routine. But what exactly was that routine?

What brought her joy? She knew being with Noah filled her with pleasure, but she wasn't sure what else did anymore. She had to figure it out. And it was probably much wiser to do that without Noah at her side. She couldn't seem to think straight when he was in the same room as her.

Maybe she'd get away from him and realize it was all just a matter of circumstance. Maybe she was only so clingy with him because she'd been sick and vulnerable. She didn't truly believe that, but she wasn't exactly sure what to believe.

She stepped into the living room with her bag and found Noah standing there. He wasn't smiling, but he wasn't exactly frowning. He looked pensive. Her face probably reflected the same exact look.

"It looks like you're all ready," he said. His tone was a little flat.

Damn, he was breathtaking. She didn't want to wake up each day without him being the first thing she saw. His face in the morning gave her pleasure. It was so strange for someone who'd been so independent for so long to rely on another so much for her own happiness.

"I guess I'm ready," she told him. The lack of excitement told her how unready she was.

"I'm not," he admitted, shocking her.

"What do you mean?" she said. She stood about ten feet from him, but everything within her wanted to close that distance between them and have him put his arms around her.

"I've liked our time together—a lot. I know, I know, you've been sick, and I didn't get pleasure out of that, but I've enjoyed very much us being together. I'm not ready for it to end."

"I don't know what that means," she said.

"I think we need to go on our next adventure," he said.

That perked her right up. "Really? What do you have in mind?"

He finally smiled—a real smile. She felt her lips pulling up as she grinned back at him.

"I think you trust me by now. Why don't we go by your place, pack a new bag, and I'll surprise you?"

The old Sarah would've instantly said no to this. The new Sarah was immediately intrigued. And there wasn't even a little part of her that wanted to say no.

"Okay," she said.

His grin grew even bigger, and he finally closed the space between them and pulled her into his arms. She'd slept in his bed for five nights in a row, and they hadn't once made love. Her body was on fire and filled with need, as she was sure his was, too.

Maybe now that she was better, and they were going off to some new place, they'd finally come together. His lips dropped to hers, and he gave her a kiss that had her head spinning and her core on fire. She'd thought she'd never want to see the cottage bed again, with how much time she'd been forced to spend in it, but after that kiss she was more than happy to have him escort her right to it.

But that was not what happened. Instead he let her go and bent down to pick up the bag she'd dropped during their kiss. "I was hoping you'd say that. My bag is already packed. Let's get to your place."

With that he turned on his heels, and she had little choice other than to follow him. She was slightly pouty as she walked to his truck and got in on the passenger side. He smacked her butt as she climbed in, then shut the door and whistled as he jogged around to his side of the vehicle.

She didn't speak to him on the way to her apartment. She was too hot and bothered and a little cranky that he was so easily resisting her. It had been forever since they'd last made love. And he'd been tending to her for days, half the time with her naked or barely clothed. She'd much prefer for him to lose control.

They got to her place, and she practically stomped up the stairs. She brought her bag in and tossed it in the corner before going to her bedroom and grabbing a new bag and throwing some clothes inside. He hadn't said how long this new adventure was going to take or what kind of clothes she'd need, so she brought a few different choices.

When she stepped back into the tiny living room and saw Noah taking up so much space, she realized how odd it was to have him there. It was much too small for such a large man, and with her gone so much, it smelled a bit stuffy. It wasn't much, but it had been home for her for a long time, and she appreciated the security of it.

The space was too small to have a lot of items, so she had minimal furnishings, and she despised trinkets of any kind. So besides her one bookcase loaded down with old books, there was nothing that wasn't essential to living.

"It smells in here," she said.

"Do you want to stay a bit and open some windows?" he asked. He wasn't confirming or denying the musty smell.

There was a flicker in his eyes that made her wonder if he had plans other than just letting the apartment air. She was tempted to say yes and see what happened. But she feared she'd be far too grumpy if nothing happened, and that would make the trip miserable.

Sarah was more than aware she was a twenty-first-century woman and could put the moves on him if she wanted to. But for some reason she wanted it to be him this time. Maybe it was because she'd been so weak and vulnerable this past week, and maybe because she wanted him to want her so much he couldn't resist. She wasn't sure what it was.

"No, I'd rather get going. If I sit for too long, I'm afraid I'll just go to sleep again. I'm feeling a hundred percent better now, but I don't trust my body a whole heck of a lot right now."

At her words his eyes examined her from head to toe, giving her tingles in all sorts of places. He could turn her on so easily with nothing more than a look. When he touched her, he turned her to putty in his hands.

"Your body is one hundred percent perfect," he assured her.

Her breath hitched, and she was ready for him to take her right there, wherever he wanted to take her. His eyes narrowed the slightest bit as he licked his lip, as if he could read her mind. Maybe he could. She never had been good at hiding her emotions. He looked as if he was trying to come to a decision, but then he turned away.

"Okay, we have some traveling to do, then," he finally said, his voice a bit terse. She wished she was brave enough right then to ask him what exactly was on his mind. Maybe he really just wanted to hit the road. And maybe she was underestimating his desire for her.

Sarah followed him from her apartment, and he made sure the door was locked before helping her down the stairs. She wanted to tell him she could do it on her own, but she was still slightly wobbly. Not much at all, but the last thing she wanted to happen right now was for her to trip and add another injury to her growing list of them.

She was both glad and sad about this next adventure. Because the more they did together, the more the project came along. They no longer had to deal with roadblocks or artist's fatigue. They were nearing the end of their journey—and it was much sooner than she was ready for. She didn't want this adventure to ever stop. But all good things eventually came to an end.

When Noah began driving in the direction of the airport, she could no longer keep her mouth shut. She'd thought their next location was in driving distance.

"Where are we going?" she asked.

He gave her a smile. He was more relaxed again now that they were moving.

"I'll tell you in the plane," he answered.

They pulled up to the private hangar where his plane was stored, and she couldn't help but smile. She really did enjoy riding in it. She'd miss doing that if she didn't ever get to again. It seemed that no matter what she did with Noah, though, it was a fun adventure. Maybe it was more about being with the man than what they were actually doing. Noah had definitely changed her mind about traveling.

They got inside the plane and lifted off. She was quiet as she watched the ground below them grow smaller and smaller.

"We're heading to one of the Andersons' famous vacation properties," Noah said. After silence for about fifteen minutes, his voice startled her coming through the earphones.

"Where is it?"

"It's just outside of Glacier National Park."

"Oh, I've never been there," she told him, instantly perking up. Her body was still dissatisfied, but at least this was going to be a fun day or two. Any property the Andersons owned was bound to be amazing.

"This place has a special meaning behind it," Noah said.

"I love a good story. Tell me," she insisted.

He chuckled, and she loved how the sound washed over her.

"Joseph and Katherine were on an anniversary trip and found the place in utter disrepair. It was going under. Katherine fell in love with it immediately, so without telling her, Joseph bought it and brought it back to its former glory and gave it to her at her next birthday party."

"The world thinks Joseph is a tycoon, but he's really nothing more than a sentimental husband and father and uncle," she said. One of the things she loved most about this project was getting such an intimate look at a man she'd admired from afar for a long time.

"I wish I would've known him while I was growing up. But my mother had valid reasons to keep us away. My father was such a bad man, and she wanted to stay away from his family. Maybe some of it was fear that they'd take us away, and some of it was shame, but I can't blame her. And I'm glad I get to know Joseph and Katherine now. I was suspicious at first, but I've come to realize what a great man he is."

"I love that in the end of her life, she gave you one last gift," Sarah said as she reached out and patted his arm. "Your mother sounds like she was an amazing woman."

"She was the best. I never wanted more than her and my brothers. I never thought I'd want more family. I was wrong. Because now that I have the Andersons, I can't imagine them not being in my life." He turned and gave her an intense look. "When I love someone, I love them for life."

A shiver ran down her spine. She wasn't sure what he was trying to tell her with those words. She still wasn't sure where all of this was going, but she was certain it was heading somewhere. She'd just have to try to have patience. That wasn't something she'd ever been known for.

"I want to open up more with you," he told her before she could reply to his last comment. She smiled at him.

"I think we're both doing that. I don't know when or how, but I think it just sort of happened."

Now it was his turn to smile. He reached over and grabbed her hand, squeezing her fingers tightly in his. They were opening up to one another. She hoped they'd both be strong enough not to shut down once more.

Before they could continue the conversation, they hit a patch of turbulence, forcing Noah to concentrate on flying. Sarah was okay with that. She was still slightly afraid, but not anywhere near where she'd been a while ago. She was going to give this a real chance. She was going to stop trying to hide from what she was feeling.

They chatted a little more as they neared Glacier. And then he began navigating the plane to the resort's private landing strip. Maybe they'd finish their conversation that night—and maybe they'd communicate in other ways. Either way it would be a win for her.

Chapter
Twenty-Five

Time was an odd thing. It was a certainty in life. And though there were periods in life it felt like time was moving faster or slower, in reality it was a constant that didn't change. There were twenty-four hours in a day and three hundred and sixty-five days in a year. There was the leap year, where one extra day was added, but other than that, time was always consistent.

So it was funny that people used sayings such as time was running out or time was getting longer or shorter. It didn't change. But it felt like it did. Life moved forward no matter how much a person tried to slow it down. And when your life was at a point where things felt uncertain, you had a whole new concept of the meaning of time.

Noah wanted to stop the clock. He wanted to slow time and freeze these moments he was having with Sarah. But he couldn't do that. The clock hands were going to keep on turning, and the seasons would keep on changing. All he could do was try to make the most of the time he had with her.

Was that going to be for mere minutes, or was it going to turn into forever? He wasn't sure he could answer the question. They were both in a new place together where they weren't fighting this thing between them, but at the same time, they hadn't decided where their journey was going to take them.

That all led him back to his quandary about time. How much time did he have left with the woman he was falling for more each day? Were they going to make it last? Or would they choose to walk away from one another? That question wouldn't be answered until the clock stopped. Maybe he'd choose to simply stop the clock. He could produce his own time.

Taking Sarah to this romantic resort was exactly the next step the two of them needed to take on this journey they were on. He didn't need any more inspiration to finish this project, but he wasn't going to tell Sarah that, because he didn't want their adventures to come to a close. He was liking them far too much. Each minute he spent with Sarah was another beautiful moment in his timeline of life.

"This place is beautiful," Sarah said as they drove along the trail to the main resort. The airport was about a mile from the building, and there were golf carts to transport them. Joseph had thought of everything when he'd brought this place back to its former glory. He'd made it better.

"There's a little bit of everything here for people seeking many different adventures. I've been wanting to visit since I heard about it," he told her.

"What are we looking for?" she asked.

"I want to see the layout. It's a good place to model the center after. There's a main lodge, cabins along the river, and so many activity areas, which I didn't even think about adding. There's fishing, rafting, horseback riding, and trails. If we have a resort-like setting, more veterans will want to come to the facility and get the help they so desperately deserve. Remember that session we had with Joseph a month back?" he asked.

"Yes, there were so many ideas thrown out, though; I can't seem to keep them all straight."

He laughed. "I know. When there's all of us in a room, it does get a little chaotic," he admitted.

"It is a little hard to get a word in edgewise when all the Andersons are grouped together," she said. His smile faded.

"I'm sorry, Sarah. I don't want you to ever feel that way. Your voice is appreciated and heard in this project."

She reached over and squeezed his arm. "I know. You've made me feel very involved. I was just making a joke."

He smiled. "Well, that's when the idea struck. I think we need to go back to Joseph and really pursue this."

"Let's see how it is first, but I'm thinking you're right. Just taking this trail is getting me excited," she told him.

They came out of the trail and then were both silent as they caught sight of the giant three-story lodge in front of them. It was beyond massive. Sarah gasped. Noah shouldn't have been surprised. Joseph never did anything on a small scale. It wasn't in his DNA.

A few people were wandering about, and there were animals roaming, but it looked like a very efficient and cozy operation, even with the massive size.

"Wow, now I'm thinking our main center isn't big enough," she said with a laugh.

Noah laughed, too, as he parked. "This is huge, but I think our center will rival it when it's all finished," he told her.

They stepped from the golf cart and both stood there gazing at the impressive building. "Was this here, or did he add it?" she asked.

"He built this one. The old lodge was old and run down and about half the size," he said. "I did my research on the place. He did make sure and leave the cabin they'd stayed in together—after having it redone, of course, but leaving the colors and style exactly the same. He's truly sentimental."

"Yes, he is. I think you are, too," she told him. Then she shocked him when she stepped up and wrapped her arms around his neck. He was frozen for a moment, but it didn't take him long to return the embrace. There was no better place he liked to be than in this woman's arms. He was ready to kiss her when they were interrupted.

"Looks like putting you in the birthday cabin was the right choice," a voice said.

Noah turned to find his brother Hudson standing there with a big grin on his face. He was coming down the huge lodge steps.

"Great timing as always," Noah said as he reluctantly pulled away from Sarah to shake his brother's hand. "Glad you could meet us here."

"Of course. I'm falling in love with this place," Hudson told him. A woman approached with a big smile. "This is Alice. She's run the place forever and will be keeping an eye on you to make sure you don't act up."

Alice laughed. "Ignore your brother. I'm a peach," Alice said. "It's so nice to meet you. I feel as if I know you all, since your uncle Joseph has gushed about his amazing nephews."

"This is Sarah, my partner on the project," Noah said. Sarah stepped forward and shook both Hudson's and Alice's hands. She'd met Hudson but had seen him less than the other brothers.

"It's a pleasure to meet you," Sarah said. She was in her element meeting new people. She certainly wasn't shy. Her confidence was something else he admired about her.

Introductions were such odd things. He'd never liked the formality of them. It was so much easier to just start talking to someone without all the hoopla. But pleasantries were a necessary evil.

"I like your girl," Hudson said quietly as Sarah and Alice spoke for a moment. "The birthday cabin was a good choice."

"I don't know what you're going on about with the cabin, but yeah, I like her a little bit, too," Noah said.

"It's the honeymoon cabin," Hudson said.

Sarah caught those words, and Noah was a little surprised when she flushed. She wasn't the type to get embarrassed too easily. He kind of liked it. She was a confident woman, but she also had an innocence about her that made him like her that much more.

"Quit being an ass," Noah said as he elbowed his brother.

Hudson didn't seem in the least offended. He elbowed Noah right back. "Okay, pry yourself away from your woman long enough to take a tour with me."

He wasn't going to bother telling his brother she technically wasn't his woman. Because he really did think of her that way, even if they hadn't made it official. They were adults, and they didn't need a high school ring to make something official. That thought led him to thinking about other sorts of rings, though, that would show the world she was his. That was a sobering thought. He'd never once considered buying a woman a ring. Now that the thought was in his head, he was afraid he wasn't going to get it out again. Damn. Maybe he should just accept what everyone else already saw.

"I better get you away from here before you put your damn foot in your mouth," Noah said. He then turned to Sarah. "I'll apologize for my brother. He's an ass. But I won't be gone too long."

She grinned. "Take your time. I'm going to check out the lodge."

"I'd love to show you the lodge after I show you your cabin," Alice told her.

"Thank you."

The two women took off, and Noah stood there for a minute watching Sarah walk away. He realized she was the first woman he'd ever been around who it pained him to see leave, even if it was only for a short time. He really was going to have to figure out what was coming next. He felt like that clock he'd been thinking about earlier was ticking a little bit faster.

"Let's go," Hudson said with a knowing chuckle.

Noah had the urge to slug his brother. What was wrong with his siblings lately? They were all giving him this look like he was a lost cause. Was that the same look he'd been giving Finn when he'd walked in the room announcing he was going to marry Brooke after knowing her for five minutes? Maybe.

He and Hudson strolled through the paths of the resort, and ideas were forming in his head as they watched different people doing a variety of activities. There were volleyball, basketball, and tennis courts. There were two swimming pools and hot tubs and secluded paths with picnic areas. Anything and everything a person could imagine existed on this five-hundred-acre parcel of land. He and Sarah should have come to this place in the beginning of their journey, because it was all he needed to complete the vision they'd set from the start.

But if they'd come here first, they wouldn't have had any of the other adventures the two of them had shared together, and that would be tragic. Every step of the way he'd gotten to know her a little more. And each time she'd opened up to him, he'd fallen a little more.

So he was glad this was the end of their treasure hunt instead of the beginning. He hoped she was just as inspired as he was. He and his brother chatted as they made a circle back to the lodge, where several firepits had been placed strategically to give guests private areas to gather with their friends and family.

"Are you inspired?" Hudson asked. "Because I'm ready to build more."

"Yeah, the wheels have been spinning from the moment I flew into this place," Noah told him. "This was the final piece of the puzzle I needed to know how to complete the project."

"Good. It's funny how long all of us have been drifting through life. It was horrible to lose Mom, but I'm so thankful she gave us Joseph and the rest of the Anderson family. I feel more settled now, and I feel like I'm finally ready to grow up."

Hudson's words shocked him. All of his brothers had been shocking him lately.

"What is happening to us?" Noah asked. He was utterly perplexed.

"I have no idea," Hudson said with a shrug and a laugh.

"I think maybe we've always had the foundation; we just needed to build the walls," Noah said with a shrug.

Hudson laughed again. "Hey! I'm the builder. Shouldn't that be my line?"

Noah was in a great mood. He was noticing he was in a good mood a lot more lately. He had no doubt that had a lot to do with a spunky woman he couldn't get off his mind.

"I might not put the pieces of wood together, but I sure as heck know how to bring a building together," Noah told him.

"You have an incredible talent," Hudson said.

He was so used to having a more joking relationship with his brothers that all of these deep talks were throwing him off a little. He couldn't say he didn't like it, though.

"Okay, we're getting a little too sentimental now. Let's have a drink and enjoy a good fire. Then I want to call it an early night."

"I bet you do," Hudson told him with a waggle of his eyebrows.

Noah wasn't even going to try to argue with that. He just went with his brother to find a drink. Then they returned to the fire and continued speaking about plans for the center as he waited for Sarah to join them. It took much longer than he wanted, but he sensed her coming near him before she said anything.

"I have so many ideas," Sarah said as she stepped up. He turned and immediately wrapped an arm around her back. He also noticed she looked a little worn. She wasn't at full strength yet, and he wasn't going to keep her out too late.

"We have food," Alice said as she set down a covered dish.

"I'm starving. It smells delicious," Hudson said.

"I think you're always hungry," Alice told him with a laugh.

"This place has good food. Of course I am," he said. The way Hudson was looking at the woman made Noah wonder if something was going on between the two of them. He was going to have to remember to ask his brother about it later.

They sat at the fire and had a nice meal. But there was now only one thing on Noah's mind, and he made some pretty quick goodbyes before he took Sarah's hand and led her away from Hudson and Alice.

It had been way too long since he'd been with Sarah. But saying that, even one day was too long, in his humble opinion. Judging by the sparkle in her eyes, she was feeling the exact same way. He sure as heck hoped so.

CHAPTER TWENTY-SIX

Alice had told Sarah how the cabin they were staying in was the one Joseph had brought his wife, Katherine, to that had made him fall in love with the place. She said it was impossible for a couple to use the cabin and not have a happily ever after. What scared Sarah more than using a honeymoon cottage was that she wasn't afraid of it.

She was beginning to see a future with Noah, and she wasn't sure he wanted the same. She knew he had feelings for her and knew there was magic between the two of them. She didn't know if it was strong enough to last forever.

Nerves filled her as they made their way to the cabin on a dimly lit trail. This place was filled with magic, taking down any and all of her guard. She just wanted to be with him, even if it was just for now.

They didn't speak as they moved together to the cabin. She had no doubt what was going to happen. She wanted it as much as him. She was feeling much better knowing it had been just as hard for him to wait as it had been for her. The looks he'd been sending her as they'd sat by the fire had left no doubt in her mind about how their night would end.

There was lust in his expression, but there was something more there, too. She wished she could trust fully what she was seeing. But there was still a piece of her that was afraid to trust the emotions. If she was a little braver, she'd try to have a talk with him. Maybe soon. But not tonight. She didn't want anything to ruin this night.

The cabin was unlocked, and they didn't need words as they stepped inside and shut the door. He immediately pulled her to him and captured her mouth in a kiss so sensual she melted against him.

Their clothes disappeared as he backed her up to the bed, only taking his lips off hers long enough to pull away both of their clothes. She knew his body as much as she knew her own now, but each time she touched him was just as exciting as the last.

He was so hard, so ready, she wondered how she could ever have doubted how hot their desire was for each other. He laid her down and stood there for a moment looking down at her. The look was so intense she wanted to hide. But her desire was too out of control to turn from him.

He joined her on the bed and ran his fingers over her heated flesh, skimming his fingers across her breasts and shaking stomach, over her thighs, and across her heat. He was barely touching her, and it was still almost too much. It didn't take much from him to send her over the edge of control.

She turned off all thoughts and focused only on what she felt. She needed him—only him. It was *his* touch, *his* body, *his* kisses that gave her exactly what she wanted. There would never be another she'd want.

He leaned over her, running his mouth across her skin, touching each new place until she was whimpering in the need for release. He knew exactly how to build her up higher and higher. His lips and fingers brought her to heights most people couldn't ever reach.

She held on, kissing him when he allowed it and touching him as much as he touched her, but there was no doubt he was in control. She was his to do with as he wanted. And she didn't even care about the loss of control.

"I can't get enough of you," he said as his tongue traced the curve of her neck.

"I want you inside me," she said as she wiggled beneath him.

"Always," he insisted.

"Yes," she said without a second thought.

But instead of burying himself inside her, he ran his mouth down her neck and over her breasts, taking time to lick and suck on her nipples. She squirmed beneath him, but he wasn't giving her what she wanted. She whimpered as his mouth moved down her stomach. She reached for him, tugging on his hair, but he wasn't budging from what he wanted.

Her hips arched as he ran his tongue over her hips. He found places on her body she hadn't even known were sensitive before him. This man knew how to bring her more pleasure than a person could ever expect to feel. And she wanted more. He made her greedy.

Her entire body ached as he swept his tongue across her thighs. Finally, he pushed her legs apart and ran his tongue across her heat. She cried out as he moved it up and down before circling that sensitive area that he knew so well.

He buried his fingers inside her as he sucked and nibbled. That was all it took to send her into an oblivion of pleasure. She shook beneath him as he swept his tongue across her flesh again and again.

She cried out his name as the last of her tremors took her to the highest peaks and then began to calm again. Then he slowly kissed his way back up her body as she lay there, unable to move. It took several moments for her to catch her breath.

She was still breathing heavily as he positioned himself above her, his thickness pressing into her hot core but not pushing inside yet. He didn't move, and she opened her eyes as much as she was able to.

When she saw the look on his face, she went up in flames again. No one had ever seen her the way this man had. It brought tears to her eyes. She wanted to freeze this moment and never let it go.

"Please," she whispered.

He leaned down and gently kissed her as he buried himself deep inside her. A tear escaped, but she didn't care. She loved him deeply, passionately, and forever. Nothing would change that.

His lips traced hers as he moved in and out of her, slowly at first, then with more urgency. She clutched him tightly as heat developed again. His mouth never left hers as they built their pleasure together.

Her next release came at the same time as his. They cried out as their bodies trembled together. And as he sank against her, she knew she was home. When he shifted, she whimpered her disapproval.

"There will be so much more, baby," he whispered as he pulled her tightly against him.

"Promise?" she said.

"Oh, that's a promise I'm more than happy to make."

She smiled as she closed her eyes again. She fell asleep in his arms, hoping this would be just one night of many.

CHAPTER TWENTY-SEVEN

Some mornings were good, and some not so good. Sarah could definitely classify this morning as a great morning. Her body ached everywhere—in a fantastic way—and she was hungry and sleepy, but the first thing she saw when her eyes opened was the sight of Noah sitting at a small table, sipping on a cup of coffee, staring at a newspaper. It made her smile. He didn't know she was awake yet, which gave her time to study him, and he was well worth studying.

They'd been up most of the night making love. She'd lost count of how many times he'd pulled her into his arms. But each time he did, she responded, more than happy for the pleasure she was about to receive. The more turned on he was, the more she wanted him. They had a passion most people only dreamed of having.

If they only had days left together, she could say she had no regrets. But if she had longer, she'd be okay with that, too. She was addicted to this man, and it was something she didn't want rehab for.

She lay there for several moments, not stirring. But he somehow sensed her eyes on him, because he turned and looked at her, a crinkle in the corners of his eyes, his lips turned up. For just the briefest of moments he looked so beautifully tender it brought tears to her eyes.

She thought about lying back and inviting him to join her again. They could remain in the bed together for a solid twenty-four hours, and she still didn't think it would be enough. This man intrigued her and turned her on. He made her laugh and cry and angered her sometimes. She'd take it all.

"Good morning, beautiful," he said, his voice scratchy and warm, making her insides stir.

"Good morning," she replied. "How are you feeling?"

He chuckled. "I should be the one asking you that."

"I'm feeling pretty amazing," she admitted. "A bit sore."

Her last words sent a surge of heat shooting into his eyes that made her insides heat up quick and hot. It was insane how much she wanted him all the time.

"I can make you more sore," he said. It was a promise she knew he could keep.

"Anytime," she told him with a wink.

"Maybe I should let you have your coffee first," he said as he poured her a cup and brought it over.

"Mmm, I like breakfast in bed," she said with a smile after sitting up and accepting the cup from him. "I like lots of things in bed," she added after her first sip. Coffee was fuel for the soul.

He chuckled again as he sat on the edge of the bed. He leaned down and kissed her while resting his hand on her thigh. She was melting all over again, ready to jump the man. She lifted her cup and took another sip before she caved and did just that.

"I'll bring you anything you want to bed," he told her as he sipped on his own cup of coffee with one hand while rubbing her thigh with the other.

She had to change the subject from sex talk. She should really shower first before they went another round. Of course maybe the two of them could just shower together. She wouldn't mind that at all.

"How did you sleep?" she asked, deciding to change the subject.

"Well, what little sleep I got was great," he told her. "Someone did a really good job of wearing me out."

For some reason his words made her blush. He chuckled again as he squeezed her thigh. The one thing she'd learned about Noah in the time she'd known him was he did nothing at half measure. He moved quickly in life, but she appreciated that. Right now he seemed to be slowing down a bit for her. She appreciated that as well.

This moment right here and now was what she'd describe as perfect. If she could, she'd make the rest of the world go away so she could just be there with him. Eventually she'd miss the people she loved, but in her perfect moment, it was a bubble, and that bubble wasn't allowed to be popped. So she decided to not have any negative thoughts.

But even though this moment was utter perfection, she knew the world had a habit of getting in the way of these sorts of moments. Humans were tricky beings. They'd hold on to grudges, fight when there was no need, and let pride stop them from being happy. She wasn't all that sure she'd be strong enough to rise above in the end. She sure hoped so.

Yes, it was true that she couldn't control everything. But she was in charge of her own destiny. She could decide to be happy, or she could wallow in fear. At this moment she chose happiness.

"I slept well when we actually slept, too," she told him.

"I want you again," he said as his fingers climbed up her thigh. That heat she'd been feeling turned immediately into an ache that needed to be sated. The shower could definitely wait.

"I'm right here," she said as she set her coffee cup on the nightstand.

He leaned down and kissed her hard as he set his own cup aside and lay down next to her. His hand slipped up and over her stomach, and he cupped her breast in his hand and pinched her nipple. She arched against him, instantly wanting more.

He leaned into her and ran his tongue over her lips as he continued kneading her breast. She wrapped a leg around him. She was ready just that quickly for him to be back inside her.

He gave her a scorching kiss that took her breath away before pulling back and looking at her. He looked hungry and confused at the same time. She could fully understand the feeling.

"I don't know how you do this to me, but I can't seem to get enough of you," he told her.

"I feel the same," she admitted.

He'd begun to lean into her again . . . when there was a knock on the door. Noah instantly looked irritated, which made her smile. She wasn't exactly happy about the interruption, but he looked ready to kill whoever had dared to come to their door.

"Just don't answer, and they'll leave," Noah said.

Another knock sounded. She chuckled quietly. "I don't think that's going to happen," she assured him.

"Shh," he said as he placed a finger over her lips.

She couldn't help but chuckle again, and it wasn't quiet. Noah glared at her as if it was her fault they were being interrupted.

"Come on, Noah. I'm not afraid to stand out here all day," Hudson called through the door. "I'll go and find a key."

"I don't think he's bluffing," Sarah warned.

"If you'd have been quiet, he'd have gone away," Noah told her.

She laughed again, not even trying to hide the sound this time. They'd been busted. And from what Sarah had learned so far about the Andersons, they didn't give up when they put their minds to something.

"Noah, I'm growing impatient," Hudson called again.

"Fine!" Noah snapped. He got up, moved to the door, and cracked it open. "Give me five minutes." Then he slammed the door in his brother's face. They both heard Hudson laughing on the other side of the wood.

He turned back and looked at Sarah, who was enjoying the show. She was being left needy and wanting, but the frustrated look on Noah's face made that well worth it. She might have a bit of an evil streak.

"Don't look so smug. I could nail a board across the door, and he'd never get in," Noah said.

She laughed again. She didn't normally laugh so much in the morning. She was enjoying it. "I wouldn't push him. He might come in through the ceiling."

Noah rolled his eyes. "I know. I'd better get out there. I can't believe we slept in until almost eleven."

"Considering we didn't sleep much more than a couple hours, you can't exactly call that sleeping in."

Noah quickly got dressed, gave her one more scorching look, then went to the cabin door and disappeared. Sarah was sad to see him go. She lay there for a few more minutes before climbing from bed.

She took her time taking a much-needed long hot shower, then finally was able to get dressed so she could get on with her day. There was a lot to explore in this wonderful place, and she wasn't sure how long they were going to stay, so she wanted to see as much as possible.

The first step outside the cabin was perfect. It was a warm day with a nice breeze blowing in from the mountains. No one was around, so she made her way up to the main lodge. She was ravenously hungry.

There were a few people milling around as Sarah made her way through the giant great room and headed toward the kitchen. Everyone knew that all the good stuff always happened in the dining area. Deals were made, people fell in love, and children were fed, all in the kitchen.

She was only a guest at this place, so she didn't want to step through the actual kitchen doors, but she was happy when she found Alice in the dining hall, speaking to an older couple. She approached and found a baby pug sitting on a woman's lap. The puppy looked at her suspiciously as she approached. She smiled. She'd always had a thing for pugs.

"We have brunch all ready to go," Alice told her as she moved closer.

"I don't want to interrupt. I was just going to say hi," Sarah said.

"Oh, please join us. We love coming to this lodge because we always meet such amazing people," the woman said. "My name is Eileen, and this is my husband, Ray."

"Thank you so much for the invitation. I'd love to join you," Sarah told them. She'd always enjoyed sitting with older couples, as they had the best stories to share. And she really wanted to get her hands on that puppy.

"This is Scooter," Eileen said. "I swore I'd never get a puppy again after we lost our Bella, but a friend of ours had puppies, and he was the runt of the litter, and when I visited, and he looked at me, I knew it was meant to be," she said with a chuckle.

"I knew her ban on dogs wouldn't last," Ray said as he reached over and squeezed his wife's thigh. She giggled like a teenager as she looked at her husband with adoring eyes. Sarah found her cheeks blushing a bit at feeling like an intruder in the intimate moment.

"He's a beautiful puppy, and he seems pretty protective of you already," Sarah said with a chuckle as she reached slowly toward the dog. His ears went back a bit, but he slowly leaned forward and sniffed her hand. After a moment he decided she wasn't an enemy and gave her a soft kiss that made her smile.

After a moment the dog was scooting toward her, and Sarah looked at Eileen with hopeful eyes. The woman laughed.

"Would you like to hold him?" she asked.

"Very much," Sarah said. "I've always had a soft spot for animals, but I live in an apartment and can't have any."

"Oh, that's just tragic," Eileen said as she handed over the pug, who stretched up on his small legs and sniffed Sarah's chin. She was grinning from ear to ear.

"Eileen and Ray spend about a month a year with us, and I'm sure the guests are going to love little Scooter," Alice said. "They sure adored Bella. We all miss her."

Eileen's smile fell away as her eyes teared up. "It's just tragic to me that our dogs only live for ten to fifteen years. I think they should grow old with us. But I wouldn't trade a single moment I've had with any of my beloved pets."

"I couldn't agree more," Alice said.

Right then Scooter jumped up and licked Sarah on the chin, which made her giggle. She was instantly in love with the animal.

"Thank you for sharing your puppy with me. I needed a fix," she said as she scratched Scooter behind the ears.

"Of course, my dear," Eileen said. "Anyone who loves one of our animals is instantly okay in our books."

"Yes, most of the time we like our pets more than our children," Ray said with a chuckle.

"Animals are loyal, that's for sure. They love us no matter what we do or say," Sarah said. She wished the same could be said about humans. But kids got mad at you, and people tended to go away. An animal never would.

"Maybe you should get a puppy of your own. I know some apartments allow them," Alice said.

"Is it that obvious how much I need a dog?" Sarah said with a sad laugh.

"Yeah, it's pretty apparent," Alice told her.

Sarah's heart clenched. She was so confused about where her life was heading. But sitting there holding the puppy was calming her. She'd woken up in such a good mood, but no matter how much she wanted to hold on to that, she was very much aware that her future was completely undecided.

"Maybe I'll take your advice to heart," Sarah told her.

Before Alice could say anything more, they looked up to find Noah and Hudson coming toward them. Noah looked at the puppy on her lap and smiled. He easily moved toward her and knelt down.

"Did you find a new friend?" he asked.

"Yes, I'm thinking I need one of my own," she said. She only looked at him for a moment before her attention went right back to the dog, who was now snuggled in her lap, looking perfectly at ease.

"We had dogs growing up, but I haven't had one since I lived at home," he said as he reached out and petted the pup, who reveled in the attention.

"I've never owned one of my own. I've always just enjoyed my friends' pets. I have spent some time at the Humane Society, though. When I need a fix, I do some volunteer work."

He looked at her as if he was thinking about something, then shook his head and focused on the dog again.

"I hate to take him away, but we're going to go on a walk now," Eileen said. Sarah reluctantly handed over the pup, and Eileen and Ray slowly walked off.

Alice went in the back and got food for everyone, and they all had a quiet brunch together. Sarah wasn't sure what tomorrow was going to bring, but for some reason she was feeling sad all of a sudden. After her amazing morning she didn't like it at all.

They finished up, and Noah reached over and squeezed Sarah's hand. "Are you ready to stimulate your brain?"

"Of course," she told him with a forced smile. "What's on the agenda for the day?"

"We're going to walk the grounds and jot down notes. Whatever inspires us we'll take back to the drawing board," he told her as he stood.

She joined him, then turned to Alice. "Thank you so much for a wonderful meal. I'm really enjoying this place," she told her.

"I truly hope you'll come back over and over again. Our best customers have been coming for years. Your next time here is on the house."

"I will definitely take you up on that," Sarah told the kind woman.

She and Noah walked outside, where their golf cart was waiting. "Wouldn't it be better to walk and take notes?" she asked as he led her to it.

"This property is too extensive. This will be better," he said as he helped her inside, though there weren't any doors. She still liked the gesture.

A notepad and pen were already waiting for her, which she was glad for, since she hadn't thought about bringing them. The two of them began driving, and after a bit she was glad for the wheels. As much as she needed exercise, this property was really large, and she didn't think she had the energy yet to walk that far.

For some reason Noah was really quiet all of a sudden, and it was making her uncomfortable. She wasn't sure what was going on. They'd made love all night and then had been so happy just a couple of hours before. She was trying to get herself to ask him what was going on, but she couldn't seem to get the words past the lump in her throat. What had happened in the hour they'd been apart?

He drove the two of them up a steep path and then stopped. "I like the view from here. Let's get out for a minute and stretch our legs," he said. His voice was so cold. She wasn't liking it.

"Sure," she said. He didn't come around and help her, and she didn't want to tell him it bothered her.

They stood side by side, overlooking a cliff, and finally she couldn't take the silence any longer. This moment right now was why she'd so wanted to freeze other moments. How could two people go from utter happiness to total awkwardness in such a short amount of time?

"Is everything okay, Noah?" she finally asked. She couldn't stand it any longer.

He didn't answer her question, but as he looked over the cliff, he did speak.

"Hudson said Joseph fell down this trail over here. He was knocked out for a little while, and when he came to, he found Katherine kneeling over him with panic in her eyes. He told her she was his everything, and he'd never depart this world knowing he was leaving her behind."

He seemed perplexed by this story. She was even more confused.

"The way they feel about each other is unusual in my experience. It's special. I think everyone hopes for a love that strong," she told him.

"Yeah, I never believed a love like theirs was possible," Noah said. "But I see it every time they're together. I almost feel like an intruder when the two of them look into each other's eyes."

"I've seen that myself. It's so beautiful," Sarah said. Then she took a deep breath. "What has you so pensive?"

He was quiet for several moments. "I don't know," he finally answered. She was afraid he did know. She was afraid he'd gotten freaked out by their own intimacy. That was why she'd been afraid to let her guard down. She had a feeling it wasn't going to end well for her.

"This is moving a bit too fast for you, isn't it?" she finally pushed.

He looked at her as if he had a lot to say, but no words came from his mouth. He looked away and gazed back out at the beautiful view before them, but he was still silent. Sarah decided not to push any further.

"We have more to see," he finally said.

She felt heartbroken, but she didn't push him anymore. She'd asked, and he'd given her an answer by not answering. It seemed that maybe her bubble had been popped—long before she was ready for it to be.

Chapter Twenty-Eight

The rest of her day with Noah was quiet as they looked over the grounds and took notes. Nothing else personal was said, and without Noah having to tell her, she knew they wouldn't be staying another night. Something had happened in the hour after he'd left the cabin that had changed their circumstances.

She really wanted to know what that was, but she wasn't going to push. She'd begun to hope the two of them would have a future together, but somewhere deep inside she'd known it was too good to be true.

But even knowing that, she'd learned something invaluable in her time with Noah; she'd never settle again. She wouldn't stay with someone because it was comfortable or easy or because of a fear of being alone. She wanted extraordinary for the rest of her life, or she wanted nothing at all. Noah had given her a gift. And even though her heart was shattering into a million pieces right now, she was also thankful, because he'd made her see there was so much more to life than simply existing. She wanted to soar from this day forward.

She hated saying goodbye to Hudson and Alice, who seemed confused by their early departure. They'd both assumed the two of them would stay for at least one more day. She'd pasted on a smile and hugged them both before Noah drove them away, back to the private runway.

They didn't talk, just as they hadn't most of that day. She was more exhausted than she was willing to admit, but she was so sad it would be impossible for her to sleep. What she truly wanted was to lie down alone in the dark and cry for an hour or two. She didn't even know why she needed to cry; she just knew she needed the release.

She didn't mind having bad moments in life. Without the bad a person truly couldn't appreciate the good. And though she and Noah had shared both good and bad moments, she wouldn't give any of it up, because she'd grown so much as a person in her time with him. She was just wondering how he was planning on ending their time together. Was he going to tell her goodbye, or was he going to disappear? She guessed she'd soon find out. A person should always listen to their gut, and everything in her told her he was pulling away from her.

It didn't take them long to arrive back at the plane, and she loaded her bag while he did his preflight checklist and made sure everything was safe. She was normally excited to get up in the air, but today she was wondering if this was the last time she'd be this intimate with him. Even though it felt like a goodbye, she vowed to enjoy her last moments of being that close with him.

She wondered if it was better to know if something was ending or not. There was a bittersweetness to it, but then a person had a chance to say goodbye, even if it was silent. Maybe that was better than not knowing.

They were up in the air before Noah spoke again. The sky was clear, with no turbulence. It was looking to be a pretty uneventful ride, at least physically.

"I think we have everything we need," he said. His voice sounded void of emotion. She didn't like it.

"Yeah, I have a feeling this is the last of our treasure hunting," she said, forcing a laugh she didn't feel. She didn't want him to know how sad she was. She didn't want him sticking around if he didn't want to be there.

"I've really enjoyed our adventures together, Sarah," he said. He reached over and squeezed her leg before removing his hand. There was such finality in his voice. She couldn't take it anymore.

"Please tell me whatever it is you need to say."

He was silent for long enough that she thought he wasn't going to answer. The tears she'd been fighting for hours were so close she prayed they wouldn't fall. She could hold them back until she was alone. She refused to be one of those people who begged another to love them.

When he did finally speak, she heard the regret in his tone. "I got a call about five minutes after I left the cabin this morning."

"From the tone of your voice, I'm guessing this wasn't a good call," she said, trying to make her voice sound normal. She could hear the tears but hoped he couldn't.

"It's about a previous job," he said with a frustrated sigh.

Now she was really confused. She didn't know what to think. She didn't say anything, just waited for him to keep talking.

"I'll be gone for at least three months," he finally said.

That was when her heart sank. He was leaving her. He was telling her, without saying the words, that their time had come to an end. By the time he came back, too much time would've passed, when they were finally getting to a point they could actually begin to look at their time together as a real relationship. It was too soon for them to be apart for three months. They were too fragile at this point to be separated that long.

She'd tried believing this whole time this was no more than a fling, but somewhere along the way she'd fallen for this man. She hadn't wanted to, but he'd slipped in. Now she wasn't sure what to say to his words. She didn't want him to know how upset she was. She wished he'd waited to tell her this, even though she'd pushed to hear it. But now she was trapped in the plane with him with nowhere to go. She wasn't sure how much longer the flight was supposed to last, but at this moment if there was a parachute, she'd be willing to jump.

"I'm sure you're excited to go on a new adventure," she said. Her voice was so fake she could barely stand it.

"I normally would be," he told her with another sigh.

"What's keeping you from being excited?" she asked. She was trying to keep it together, trying to keep the conversation going.

"I find I don't want to leave you," he told her.

That made her heart skip a beat, though she told herself not to go there. He was conflicted. That didn't sound like a man in love; it sounded like a man who didn't know what he wanted.

"And if you leave, that's the end of whatever this is," she said. It wasn't a threat; it was a statement. It just seemed logical. They were too fragile to handle the separation maturely.

He sighed. For a man who never seemed to be at a loss for words, he was sure having difficulties finding them now. She wasn't sure what she'd say if he vowed undying love for her right now. From his tone, that wasn't going to happen, though.

"Honestly, part of me wants to ask you to wait for me." He stopped, and she didn't interrupt. "And the other part knows that's unfair. I've already put you through enough without asking you to wait to find out if we have a future together." She was glad to hear regret in his tone, but it wasn't enough to make her ask him to stay or to tell him she'd wait. It seemed that it just was never enough with the two of them. He'd give her a little, and then he'd run a lot. That wasn't a healthy sign of a lasting romance.

"Look, Noah, I'm not going to lie and tell you there's nothing between us, but if you want to go, that should be your answer. I'm not going to regret what we've shared, but if it was meant to be, there'd be zero hesitation on your part. The fact that you're torn tells us both you need to go."

This time she reached over and squeezed his leg. She wanted to let him know she wasn't angry or upset. She was being realistic. It appeared their time had come and gone. Neither of them was to blame for it. At the end of the day, it just wasn't meant to be.

She felt them begin to descend, and she'd never been more grateful in her life. She wasn't sure how much longer she'd be able to hold on to her barely there control. In a small way she wanted to draw out their last moment together, but the realist in her knew this needed to end quickly. The Band-Aid had to come off. He was silent as he navigated the plane into the airport that would pull them away from each other for good.

She knew she'd see him again. They'd be at the grand opening for the center at the same time, and he was an Anderson, and his brother was married to one of her best friends. They'd never be completely free of each other, but hopefully the next time they came together, she'd be in a much better place.

He landed smoothly and taxied to the hangar. There were no more words that needed to be spoken. There were a million things she could say, but at the same time she wouldn't change their last night together or even their last week. It had been magical and perfect, and she'd dream about it for a very long time to come. She couldn't even imagine anyone coming close to Noah Anderson in her eyes. He might've ruined all future relationships for her.

They parked the plane, and he turned and looked at her. Sadness filled her because she knew this was their goodbye. She needed it to be quick. Before she could stop them, a few tears slipped.

"Sarah . . . ," he said, but he stopped when she held a hand up and covered his lips.

"It's okay, Noah. It really is," she said. More tears fell.

"I'm sorry," he said. She was in so much pain, and there was no stopping it now that she'd let it in. She had to get away as soon as possible. But she needed to say goodbye. The next time they met, it would be as nothing more than acquaintances. She hoped she had plenty of time to prepare for that.

He reached over and kissed her. There was no doubt in her mind it was a goodbye kiss. It broke her heart into a million pieces, but she reached up and laid her hand over his heart for one last moment as she kissed him back. She was in love with this man, and she didn't regret a thing, even while losing him.

But it had to end, so she pulled back. She cupped his cheek and looked in his eyes. "Thank you, Noah. This has been wonderful," she said. She ran her thumb across his bottom lip; then she unbuckled her seat belt and opened the door and slipped from the plane. She had to look back at him one last time. "Goodbye, Noah."

At those words, she turned and walked away. She had to force herself not to turn around again, and she kept her composure until she'd circled the building. She was going to fall apart, but she had to get home first. She concentrated on taking one breath in and one breath out.

She'd just said goodbye to the love of her life. She could see now why people were so afraid to fall in love. When it ended, you truly lost a piece of your soul. Maybe in the end it wasn't worth it. She might not ever know. Because there was no way she'd ever make herself vulnerable enough to find out if there could be a happily ever after.

If he truly loved her, he wouldn't leave her, and he wouldn't let her walk away. The fact that he was allowing both things to happen told her his love was only fleeting. Maybe she'd been testing him without realizing she was. Maybe she just wasn't strong enough. She couldn't answer anything right now. She could barely move forward.

It wouldn't last. She'd been through hell before, and she'd climbed her way out. She'd do it again this time. But for tonight she was going to cry, and she was going to mourn her loss. And that was okay, too. Sometimes a strong person needed to fall, just so they had the opportunity to lift themselves up again.

CHAPTER TWENTY-NINE

Noah was a fool. He was a complete and utter moron. He'd watched Sarah walk away, knowing how much pain she was in, and then he'd gone in the opposite direction of her. He could tell himself all day long that was work, and that was what had to be done, but he was still a fool. Each one of his brothers had no problem repeatedly telling him that same thing.

Still he'd left.

And he'd lasted less than a month.

He'd been miserable—utterly, hopelessly miserable. The need to travel the world and create works of art had forever been ruined for him. He didn't want to do it anymore unless Sarah was at his side. He might've screwed that up so badly, though, that he'd never get the chance. Or maybe he'd damned them both to an eternity of misery. He wasn't sure.

He pulled his truck down the road and drove toward the local bar he'd asked his brothers to meet him at. They'd agreed, telling him it was about time he'd gotten his ass back to town. He was wondering if tough love was what he wanted to deal with right now. In the mood he was in, it might not be such a great idea. But he'd missed his siblings almost as much as he'd missed Sarah. He'd grown far too domesticated in his time creating the veterans center.

And he didn't care. He was no longer afraid of settling down. He just prayed he could convince Sarah he'd never break her heart again. He'd done it one too many times. But hopefully she'd remember the good more than she remembered the heartbreak. He needed his siblings' advice before he went to her, though.

It was a Friday afternoon, and the bar was surprisingly crowded for that time of day. Maybe everyone had decided to take an early weekend. Maybe it was filled with foolish idiots like him. He wasn't sure.

He walked inside and found his brothers in the back, with Finn sitting there hoarding a large basket of food. Noah plopped down next to him and grabbed some of his brother's fries. There was nothing like comfort food when you were feeling like the scum of the earth.

"I'll get more food. It looks like Noah's in a mood. I guess the lecture we all planned on giving him isn't necessary," Hudson said with a chuckle.

"Lecture?" Noah said as he downed some more fries.

"Yeah, the one that tells you what an idiot you are," Hudson said before he stood. "But you obviously already know that."

Noah glared at his brother, but he couldn't argue with the man. He was a complete moron. "Get some cheese sticks," he called out.

The waitress came right then with a bucket full of beers, and Noah gave her a thankful smile as he grabbed one and popped the top off.

"With service like this, I see why it's our favorite bar," Noah said. He took a large sip, then let out a sigh. This right here was what he'd needed for the past month. Well, this and one feisty brunette in his arms. He hoped he'd get both.

"Crew, make sure to order extra. When your brother is a fool, it calls for a lot of beer and bar food," Finn said with a laugh.

"You love being the secure married one, don't you?" Noah said with a glare.

"I sure as hell do. It wasn't long ago that I looked just as miserable as you do now. I didn't always make the smartest decisions when I was chasing Brooke," Finn said with a shrug. "But luckily I wised up and won her love."

"We'll never know how that happened," Crew said with a roll of his eyes. "She's far too good for you."

"Don't tell her that. I don't think she's figured it out," Finn said, then downed the rest of his bottle of beer and grabbed a new one.

"Yeah, love does tend to blind us all," Crew said.

"Are you in love?" Noah asked his brother.

Crew shook his head. "I don't need to be in love to know that. I see it every day in my line of work."

"You see the bad of love. You don't often see the good," Finn pointed out.

"All love has its ups and downs. But I'm starting to see past the fronts so many people put on," Crew said.

"You all annoy me. Love is for weaklings," Brandon said as he leaned back in his chair. Noah had the urge to kick the legs and see his little brother fall on his ass. As if Brandon could tell what he was thinking, all four legs hit the floor, and he glared at him. It was too bad. He should've been quicker.

"I called you guys here for a reason," Noah said as he reached into his coat.

There was total silence when he pulled out a black box. There was no doubt at all what was inside the velvet case. A man didn't have that expression while holding the small square thing without it having meaning behind it.

Noah didn't say anything. He just waited to hear what would come from his brothers' mouths. He had no doubt he was making the right decision. He just wasn't sure if she'd take him back. They hadn't spoken since he'd left. He'd kept track of her, though, and knew she was sad. It broke his heart.

"You screwed up pretty badly. If you want her to take that, you're going to have to do some serious groveling," Finn said after a stunned minute of silence.

"Yeah, she's been sort of a mess since you left town," Brandon confirmed.

"Brooke and Chloe might've even hired a hit man to shoot your sorry ass," Hudson told him.

Noah looked to Crew and waited for his remark. Crew smiled.

"I think you'll get the girl," Crew said, shocking them all.

"What in the world has happened to you?" Brandon asked. "I don't know if you're really Crew, or if aliens have taken over your body."

"People change," Crew said with a shrug.

"So what exactly are you going to do?" Finn asked. "It can't be lame."

"I've never done a lame thing in my life," Noah said, offended by the thought that he was capable of that.

"Well, then maybe you should stop hanging out with us and go get the girl," Crew said.

His other brothers smiled at that statement. "I'm actually scared," he admitted.

"That's because you have something to lose," Finn told him. "But she does love you, so don't give up, even if you have to grovel. It will be well worth it."

"I never thought I'd agree with that statement, but I do," Noah said.

"I can come and videotape it for you," Brandon offered.

Noah stood. "No, thank you. I don't want an audience for this," he said with a laugh. He felt lighter than he had in a while. He was glad he'd come to see his brothers before posing the most important question of his life to the woman he refused to live a single moment without from here until eternity.

He left the bar, his brothers calling out their final pieces of advice as he walked from the crowded joint. It was most definitely time to get the girl. He was more than ready—had been ready from the first time he'd laid eyes on her. It had just taken him far too long to realize that. At least he'd never be a fool again.

CHAPTER THIRTY

Though Sarah had told herself she wasn't going to be one of those women who cried for weeks or months over a man, she'd failed miserably. From the moment she'd walked away from that plane nearly a month ago, she'd been utterly miserable. She thought about him day and night. There were so many times she'd picked up her phone wanting to call him, wanting to hear the sound of his voice.

But he'd left her . . . again. They'd parted on a good note, and she wanted it to remain that way. That didn't take away her pain, but at least it kept her pride intact. The project was over. She stood alone, gazing out at the veterans center property. It was beautiful. The first building was almost complete, and there were markers where everything else was going to be built. They'd soon have an opening ceremony, and Hudson would be busy constructing all the other buildings while the rest of the Andersons did their jobs as well.

It had all come together, and she'd been a valuable part of that. Her name would go down in history as the coarchitect on this project, and she'd never have trouble finding work again. But for now she couldn't even think of working. She'd been paid well for this project, and that gave her a month or two to figure out what would come next. But she was having a very hard time letting go of this one. Once she did, she'd have to fully let go of Noah, too. That was much easier said than done.

She had found herself at this site far too often. Maybe it was because she'd spent time with Noah there, and maybe it was because it was so peaceful. She wasn't sure why she kept coming back. Besides modifications that would have to be done once in a while, her part of the project was over. It was time to let it go. But so far she hadn't been able to do that.

She sat on the steps of the main lodge, facing west. It was her favorite place to watch a sunset. It brought peace to her heart when nothing else seemed to do that. She heard tires moving up the gravel road and thought about hiding. She wasn't in the mood to visit anyone. But since her car was the only vehicle out there besides the one heading her way, it would be more than obvious she was hiding if she tried to get away at this point.

So instead she looked toward the road as headlights turned the corner. When she saw the truck pulling up next to her car, her heart stalled. Noah wasn't in town. That couldn't be him. Was she so desperate for a glimpse of the man she was now hallucinating? The headlights went out, and she waited, not even realizing she was holding her breath.

The driver's door opened, and a tall man stepped to the ground. She felt her eyes sting with tears as she saw Noah. He looked right at her. The sun was low in the sky, but there was enough light to see him, though she couldn't tell what his expression was.

He moved toward her. She wanted to run and hide. It was too soon to see him. She wasn't ready yet. He was supposed to be out of town. She was supposed to have had more time to gather herself.

He moved with purpose, and soon he was at the bottom of the steps, only about ten feet away. The sun sank a little lower in the sky.

"Hello, Sarah," he said. He whispered her name almost reverently, and she wasn't sure if she'd be able to talk. She swallowed the lump in her throat and tried to keep her expression blank. She didn't want him to know how much she was hurting.

"When did you get back into town?" she asked. There was a slight scratch to her voice, but she was managing to keep herself pretty under control, considering how badly she was torn up inside.

"Today," he told her. "I couldn't be away any longer. I screwed up bad."

Though she didn't want to feel it, a glimmer of hope seeped into her heart. She was being foolish. This man had hurt her more than once. She'd be a fool to let it happen again.

"You do tend to screw up a lot," she said. She couldn't force a smile.

He climbed the steps, then knelt down in front of her. The sight of him there was too much, and she couldn't hold back her tears any longer. She hated him a little for that.

"I don't want to do this, Noah. Please go," she said. "We've already said our goodbyes."

He reached out and took her hand. She didn't try to pull it away. It wouldn't do any good. As soon as she was sure her knees would hold her, she'd stand up and be the one to leave. She wasn't going to be able to stand around there very long.

"I've messed up a lot in my life, but never more so than when I let you leave that airport. I shouldn't have accepted the job. I was miserable from the moment you walked away. I don't know when it happened, but I fell hopelessly in love with you this past year. I fought it like a wild stallion fighting not to be tamed, but I finally realized that was foolish. We all search for our other half whether we know it or not, and what I failed to realize soon enough was that I've always been looking for you. I'm sorry I've ever made you cry. I'm sorry I made you feel like you didn't matter. You're my world, Sarah. I know it will be hard for you to trust me, but if you give me this one last chance, I promise to do all in my power to not ever hurt you again."

Tears streamed down her face as he looked her deep in the eyes, apologizing. She could see he meant the words.

"I think you're just lonely," she told him. "But if I said I forgive you and jumped back into your bed, you'd get scared again and run away. And I can only be left so many times before I can't bear the pain anymore," she truthfully told him.

He pulled a box from his coat and opened it. A beautiful sparkling diamond shone in the setting sun. She glanced at it, then back at him.

"This isn't for a night, Sarah. This is forever," he told her. "I don't want to spend a single day without you. I knew this long ago; I just didn't know how to get out of my own way," he said. "Marry me. Make me an honest man, and let me love you like you deserve to be loved for the rest of your life."

His eyes grew suspiciously bright, and he didn't even try to look away from her. She was shocked by how much vulnerability he was showing. She could try to fight this, could list a million reasons why it might not work, but sometimes a person just had to take a leap of faith. She was miserable without him.

"I love you, Noah," she said. "You hurt me more than any other person ever has, but you've also brought me more joy than anyone else."

He smiled at her as he pulled the ring from the box and held out his hand for hers. He was telling her the choice was hers. She shook as she gave him her hand, but he didn't place the ring on it. He was waiting for her to say the word.

"Yes, Noah," she whispered. She could barely get those two words past the lump in her throat.

He beamed before he slipped the diamond on her left hand. It was a perfect fit.

He stood and pulled her into his arms, and finally his lips pressed against hers. The second she was in his arms, she knew she was right where she'd belonged all along. There was no use fighting this. They were supposed to be together. They'd both made mistakes along the way, but none of that mattered. In the end all that counted was now they'd get their happily ever after.

"Let's go home," he said.

"Yes, home," she agreed.

He picked her up and carried her to his truck. They'd get her car another time. Or maybe send someone for it, because she didn't want to be apart from him for a single second for at least the next thirty days. They'd been apart long enough. But none of that mattered anymore. Now they had an eternity to make up for it all.

EPILOGUE

Brandon was a middle brother out of five obnoxious boys. That had made him work that much harder his entire life to stand out. He didn't want to be forgotten in the shuffle, and he had a lot to live up to with four outstanding brothers.

But he felt he'd made his path in life, and he was happy where he was—most of the time. Watching two of his brothers fall in love had left him longing for something he'd never wanted before. He wasn't amused by the feeling. But he couldn't seem to shake it, either.

Currently he was at his brother Noah's place, celebrating his engagement. Brandon was happy for Noah and Sarah. It hadn't appeared as if the two of them were going to be able to work things out there for a while, but apparently it was true love, and true love always prevailed.

Brandon took a sip of his beer as he scanned the room, then locked eyes on the spirited woman who turned right at the moment his eyes were drifting to her appetizing cleavage. When his gaze met hers, she appeared less than amused. She said something to Brooke, who chuckled, then glanced over at him with sympathy.

He was officially confused.

That was until Chloe began marching straight toward him, fire in her eyes. She didn't stop until she was clearly within his personal bubble. Her hands were on her hips, and her eyes lit up as she glared at him.

"How are you doing, Chloe?" he asked with a smirk before taking a slow pull from his bottle.

He always had carried a thing for petite blondes. And Chloe was full of fire and energy, and he wouldn't mind being the one to show her some new adventures and maybe work on taming her a little. He had no doubt that if she could read his mind, he'd be dead within seconds.

She poked him hard in the chest, startling him. For such a small thing the jab had stung a little. He wasn't admitting that even under the threat of death. His brothers would never let him live that one down.

"Let's get one thing clear, Brandon Anderson," she said in a low throaty voice that did funny things to his body. "Don't be getting any ideas just because my two best friends have fallen under some crazy spell and have gotten all gooey. I'm not like them, and I won't be following in their footsteps and having some fling with an Anderson."

Brandon stared at her for a second, replaying her words. He realized she was dead serious. He knew it might be detrimental to laugh at the moment, so he kept his smile held back, though it wasn't easy to do.

"Crazy spell?" he questioned.

"I don't know what in the hell is going on in this town, but people seem to be falling into lust or love or whatever emotion they are feeling far too easily. So don't you be over there giving me that Anderson eye and checking me out."

She was now tapping her foot, and he was more turned on than ever.

"Are you trying to warn me off?" he asked, unable to keep his lips from turning up a little. That made her eyes narrow even more.

"I'm stating a fact. There is nothing in this universe that will cast a spell on me. I'm not interested." She seemed to have realized how close she was to him, and she took a step back. He moved forward. If she could invade his space, that gave him the right to invade hers.

"Now, darling, I think you're being unreasonable," he said with as much charm as he could muster.

"My name is Chloe," she said with a huff.

"Come on, darling; *Chloe* is adorable, but I like pet names."

"You're a real pain in the ass, Brandon," she said. "I'm finished with this conversation." She turned but was stopped in her tracks by a massive wall of chest.

"You're just the two I've been looking for," Joseph Anderson said in his typical booming voice that had Chloe jumping a little. She was obviously on edge.

"Why are you looking for us, Mr. Anderson?" Chloe asked.

"Now Chloe, I've insisted you call me Joseph," he said with a shake of his finger.

"I'm sorry, sir," she said. She sure was humble with Joseph. Brandon wouldn't mind a little bit of that humility directed toward him.

Joseph's brows rose at the word *sir*, but he didn't correct her again. Her cheeks still flushed a nice shade of pink, though.

"Noah and Sarah have finished the drawings for the rest of the outbuildings for the property, and Hudson is building as quickly as he can, but we've gotten the green light on the main building," Joseph said with a huge grin.

"That's wonderful," Chloe said with a big smile. "Why aren't you announcing it to the rest of the room?"

Brandon wasn't sure what was going on here, so he just waited.

"Because now it's time for the two of you to work together," Joseph said as he eyed both her and Brandon.

"I don't understand," Chloe said. She didn't look as if she wanted to argue with Joseph, but Brandon had to admit he wasn't sure what Joseph was talking about, either.

"I want these soldiers to have the best of everything, including a top-notch building with a state-of-the-art kitchen. I wouldn't have it designed by anyone other than you," Joseph said, as if to do anything else would be foolish. "And since Brandon is our electrician, you'll have to work closely together to get it right."

Chloe looked as if she'd just been awarded a million-dollar lottery ticket and then had the thing shredded right in front of her. She opened her mouth to speak, then shut it again, then opened it . . . all without words coming out.

Brandon couldn't have been more pleased. Maybe it was time for him to speak now.

"I'm honored to be working on this project," he told Joseph. "And I agree with you that there's no one better than Chloe to make sure it's finished to perfection."

"I only pick the best, boy," Joseph said as he slapped Brandon hard enough on the shoulder to knock him off his feet. Luckily they'd been planted firmly, as he was very aware of Joseph's congratulatory pats.

"Good. Good." Joseph went into detail about his excitement for the center to open. But Noah was only half hearing him now. His full focus was on Chloe, and this was one project he wanted to stretch out as long as he could.

Because at the end of the day, he was going to see if he could make some sparks happen with the feisty blonde. He had a feeling they'd set the entire kitchen on fire by the time they were finished.

ABOUT THE AUTHOR

Photo © John Evanston

Melody Anne is the *New York Times* bestselling author of several popular series: Billionaire Bachelors, Surrender, Baby for the Billionaire, Unexpected Heroes, Billionaire Aviators, and Becoming Elena. She's also written a young adult series and solo titles, including a thriller. Armed with a bachelor's degree in business, Anne loves to write about powerful businessmen and the corporate world. She's sold over seven million books to date and can be found on the world's most distinguished bestseller lists. Beyond that, she loves getting to do what makes her happy—living in a fantasy world. When not writing, Anne spends time with family, friends, and her many pets. A country girl at heart, she loves her small, strong community and is involved in many projects.

Keep up with the latest news and subscribe to her newsletter at www.melodyanne.com. You can also join her on her official Facebook page, melodyanneauthor, or on Twitter @authmelodyanne and Instagram at MelodyAnneRomance.